One Step Forward

One Step Forward

ROSIE HARRIS

This edition published 2003
by BCA
by arrangement with William Heinemann
The Random House Group Ltd

CN 115230

Typeset by Deltatype Limited, Birkenhead, Merseyside

Printed and bound in the United Kingdom by
Mackays of Chatham Ltd, Chatham, Kent

To Fiona and Stephen Kendall-Lane

Acknowledgements

My sincere thanks to my agent, Caroline Sheldon, also, to Kate Parkin, Kirsty Fowkes, Georgina Hawtrey-Woore, Justine Taylor, Lizzy Kingston, Sara Walsh, and everyone else in the Heinemann/Arrow team who have all played such a supportive role.

Chapter One

Eight-year-old Katie Roberts struggled to her feet and wiped away the tears streaming from her big grey eyes with the back of her hand. She would remember September 1926, and starting school in Tiger Bay, for the rest of her life.

Her long fair hair was caked with mud and there was a cut on one cheek of her heart-shaped face. Her white pinny was stained with grass and mud, her blue cotton dress was torn and there were angry red patches on her arms where the other three children had seized hold of her and forced her face down onto the ground.

Around her mouth were cuts and grazes where one of the boys had forced a handful of grass, flower heads and mud between her lips.

'Don't cry, you're all right now!'

Although her lip was bleeding she tried to smile as she looked gratefully at Aled Phillips, the gangly older boy who had rescued her from her tormentors.

Inwardly she was shaking with fear. Ever since she and her mother had come to live in Tiger Bay a month ago her whole life had changed and most of the time she felt lost and forlorn.

She thought back with deep longing to the time when her entire universe had been her home in Catherine Street, where she and her mam and dad had lived with her nana, Sian Roberts.

In those halcyon days, life had revolved around Katie's needs, her likes and dislikes. Nana Roberts had always been petting her, asking her what she wanted to do, or what she would like to eat. She had cared for her, cuddled her, taken her out to the park or to the shops, read stories to her and sung her to sleep at night for as long as Katie could remember.

There had never been any loud voices or harsh words when she'd lived in Catherine Street, not until the day the police had come and taken her father away.

That was when everything had started to change.

They claimed that Lewis Roberts had been stealing but Nana Roberts declared that was nonsense. Why should he steal when he had everything he wanted?

Sometimes Katie found it hard to remember exactly what he looked like. At other times she could see him clearly, as if he was standing right beside her; a handsome, stocky-built man with grey eyes and a square chin, a glass of beer in one hand and a cigarette in the other.

When she'd been very small he used to carry

her on his wide shoulders all the way from Catherine Street to Roath Park. She remembered how she used to cling onto his shock of black hair, scared she was going to fall off because he walked so fast.

She hadn't seen him since the two policemen came hammering on the front door, but Nana Roberts told her he'd been sent to prison and wouldn't be coming home again for ages and ages.

Her mam had cried for days, bringing out huge blotchy red lumps on her face. She kept saying she really hated him for the disgrace he'd brought down on their heads, and that she would never be able to show her face outside again.

Nana Roberts had tut-tutted a lot as if she was going over and over everything in her head. Sometimes her lined face had looked so sad that Katie had cried as well. Not harsh, ugly, choking sobs like her mam made, but snuffly mewing sounds just to show how much she cared.

She'd expected Nana Roberts to pick her up and cuddle her and feed her sweets to make everything better, but she'd simply ignored her. Then, a few weeks after her dada had been taken away, Nana Roberts had gone upstairs and shut herself in her bedroom.

Hours later, when her mother told her to go and tell nana to come down and have a cup of tea she'd found her sprawled on the bed, her face a funny grey colour. She'd tried to waken her, but even though she'd shaken her arm and tugged at her black skirt, Nana Roberts had gone on sleeping.

Katie knew something was wrong so she'd gone back downstairs and tried to tell her mam, but Rachael had been too immersed in her own grief to take any notice. It was almost dark before Katie managed to get her mam to go upstairs to see what was wrong with Nana Roberts. And by then it was too late.

Her mam started screaming, rushed down the stairs and banged on the front door of the house next door, gabbling so hysterically that Stan Parsons couldn't make head or tail of what she was saying. He'd called out to his wife, Mona, and the pair of them went upstairs to Nana Roberts's bedroom to find out for themselves what had happened.

Katie watched in terrified silence as Mona held the hand mirror to Nana Roberts's mouth and then shook her head sadly when nothing happened. Not a single blur appeared on the shining surface, only a reflection of Nana Roberts's small round face with her eyes tight shut and her grey hair drawn back into a tight bun on top of her head.

Stan Parsons went for an ambulance, but when it arrived the men didn't even bother to carry Nana Roberts downstairs and put her into it.

'She's dead, mun! Looks like a heart attack.

Been gone for hours, I'd say. Left it a bit late, like, to send for us, didn't you?'

Katie's mam had looked bewildered. 'I . . . I didn't know there was anything wrong,' she whispered.

'Not been having a barney, the two of you, then?'

Her mam had shaken her head. 'No, nothing like that. She did have something of an upset a couple of weeks back, mind.'

'Oh yes?' The ambulance man looked at her questioningly.

'Bit of bad news, like, about her son,' Rachael said evasively. 'Upset her a lot, there's no doubt about that.'

'Better send for your doctor,' the ambulance man advised. 'No point in us taking the old lady to hospital when she's been dead for hours now, is there?'

That was when everything seemed to get really bad. There were people coming and going to the house for several days after that, Katie remembered.

The doctor had come right away with his black bag, and a stethoscope dangling around his neck like a necklace. He hurried upstairs with her mam and they'd shut the door, so she could only sit on the stairs and wait and wonder what was going on.

A little while later Father Patrick came, rosary beads in hand and an elaborate stole draped over his black vestments. She and her mam followed him upstairs and they'd all spent a long time in Nana Roberts's room saying prayers, mostly *Our Father* and *Hail Mary* over and over again.

The next day, two men in black brought a shiny wooden box and stood it on the big table in the best room. Her mam said it was a coffin and that they were going to put Nana Roberts in it so that she could go on sleeping peacefully for as long as she liked.

Later in the week, a horse wearing black feathers on its head and pulling a long carriage with glass sides stopped outside the house. Her mam said it was the hearse and that it had come to take Nana Roberts, and all the flowers that friends and neighbours had brought along, to the church for Nana Roberts's funeral.

Katie didn't like that part at all. Even though it was a warm summer day she'd had to wear a black dress, shiny black shoes and long white socks, and her long fair hair had been tied back with a black ribbon.

Her mam had been wearing black as well. With her shining fair hair and slim figure she'd looked lovely, even though her face had been sad and there were tears in her eyes. They'd sat in the front pew in church, which was full of Nana's friends and people who lived nearby. Father Patrick said special prayers and lots of things about Nana Roberts that she didn't understand.

Then they'd all gone along to the cemetery

and Father Patrick had said more prayers as the men who were carrying her nana's coffin lowered it down into a big hole.

Her mam had thrown some earth down onto the coffin and she'd been told to do the same. She had shaken her head and hidden behind her mam. She didn't want to throw dirt down onto it because she knew Nana Roberts wouldn't have liked that one little bit! She felt angry that her mam had done it, even though Father Patrick had done the same.

Nana Roberts always liked things to be spick and span. She hated dust, cobwebs and dirt of any kind. She liked everywhere to be scrubbed spotless and polished until you could see your face in it. She always put old newspapers down on the floors when it was raining so that no dirt was walked indoors.

Katie hadn't wanted to come away and leave Nana Roberts there. She'd be so lonely all on her own, she reasoned. Anyway, how were they going to manage without her? She was always in charge of everything at home. She was the one who laid down the law and made all the rules. It was Nana Roberts, not her mam, who did all the cooking and the baking. It was Nana Roberts she turned to when she wanted something, so she knew she was going to miss her something terrible.

They'd left all the lovely flowers and wreaths behind in the cemetery. Her mam said that after the men had filled in the grave they'd pile them all on top of it. Her mam promised they'd both come back the next day and make sure they were arranged properly.

Katie had thought that meant things would go back to normal after they'd made sure the flowers were all in the right place. She knew the house would seem empty without Nana Roberts bustling around with her duster and polish, but she thought that perhaps her mam would do all those sort of things instead.

It hadn't been like that at all. Next morning her mam had said they had to start packing. At first she'd been quite excited because she thought they were going on holiday. She remembered when Nana Roberts had taken her to Swansea and they'd stayed in a boarding house for a whole week. It had been wonderful! She'd been able to play on the sand, building sandcastles with her bucket and spade, and she had gone paddling in the sea until the water came right up over her knees.

It wasn't going to be like that at all this time. She couldn't believe it when her mam said they were packing because they were leaving Catherine Street and never coming back.

'Where are we going, then?'

'I'm not sure yet, cariad. We have to find somewhere cheaper to live. This was Nana Roberts's house, see, and now the landlord wants us out.'

'Why?'

'Someone else is coming to live here.'

Katie felt bewildered. 'Why don't we want to live here anymore?' she asked.

Her mam hugged her. 'We do, cariad, but we can't afford the rent. Your poor mam hasn't any money. Nana Roberts was the one who paid all the bills, even before your dada went to prison. Now we've got no money coming in at all, not even money to buy food. That's why we'll have to move out of this lovely house and find a cheap room somewhere. I'm going to have to get a job, cariad.'

As she piled all her clothes, dolls and toys into one of Nana Roberts's big suitcases, Katie pursed her little rosebud mouth and frowned. It didn't make any sense at all to her. Why did they have to move? If her mam was going to go out to work then why couldn't they pay rent like Nana Roberts had done and stay where they were?

She tried to ask her mam about this, but Rachael was too worried to listen, let alone give her an answer.

'You go and pack your dolls. I'll explain everything to you later, I've far too much to do now,' she said rather crossly. 'There's a man coming here later on this morning to tell me how much he will give me for Nana Roberts's furniture and I want to make sure everything is ready for him.'

'I've already done that!' Katie told her. She sat on the windowsill and watched as her mother emptied out all Nana Roberts's clothes from the big mahogany chest of drawers and from the cupboards and drawers in the matching dressing table.

'Can I look at Nana's jewels?' she asked plaintively.

'Yes, if you want to. Make sure you don't drop any of them on the floor, though, or put them down anywhere and forget them. I'm taking those to the pawnbroker later on to see what he will give me for them.'

Katie picked up the handsome walnut box with its elaborate gold leaf decoration that had been Nana Roberts's pride and joy, and scrambled up onto the bed with it. Carefully she turned the little gold key. As she opened back the lid, displaying the assortment of rings, brooches and necklaces inside, she looked at her mam accusingly. 'Are you going to sell all of Nana Roberts's jewels?' she frowned.

Rachael pushed her straggling blonde hair back behind her ears and her hazel eyes were clouded with unhappiness as she nodded. 'Yes, cariad,' she sighed. 'We'll need every penny to get by on for the next few weeks until I find some work, so I'm afraid they'll have to go.'

'Every single one of them?' Katie persisted.

Rachael nodded, then hesitated. 'Well, perhaps you could keep just one piece. You decide which one you like the best.'

'They're all lovely!'

'I know that, but we need the money. No

more arguing. If you can't decide which piece you want then I shall sell them all.'

While her mother polished the furniture to make sure it was looking its very best, Katie spread out all the pieces of jewellery and looked at each one of them very carefully, trying to make up her mind which one she liked the most.

She was still sitting on the windowsill doing this when the man who was to buy the furniture arrived. She felt the tears in her eyes as she saw the horse and cart with two men on it stop outside. A rough looking man in brown cord trousers, brown tweed jacket and wearing a greasy brown cap, jumped down and walked to their door.

He knocked so loudly that Rachael almost jumped out of her skin. Then she smoothed back her untidy hair, straightened her apron and went to open the door.

Jake Adcock was a burly man with small sharp eyes and a heavy moustache, which he kept stroking as if it helped him to think. He pawed over the furniture, sniffing and stroking his moustache, and pushing his cap back on his head as if he couldn't make up his mind whether to buy the pieces or not.

Rachael followed him from room to room, nervously rolling the edge of her apron between her fingers. She kept opening her mouth to speak, then closing it again and chewing on her lower lip as if afraid she might say something to upset him or put him off the deal.

'Look yer, missus, it's a load of terribly old stuff you got here,' Jake Adcock told her. 'Worn out most of it! Not sure if I want to take it off your hands or not.'

'It's been very well looked after,' Rachael told him timidly. 'And it was top quality when my mother-in-law bought it.'

He pushed his cap back and scratched his head. 'That was a long time ago though, wasn't it, missus?'

Rachael nodded but didn't answer.

'Tell yer what, I'll give you twenty pounds for the lot, and I won't charge yer anything for taking it all away. How's that?'

Rachael looked shocked. Her thin down-turned mouth quivered and she looked so worried that Katie jumped down off the win-dowsill and went over and clung to her arm.

Rachael looked down at her and then hugged her close.

'I was expecting a lot more than that,' she told Jake Adcock in a strained voice. 'It's all me and my little girl will have to live on until I can find work.'

Jake Adcock pulled at the ends of his droopy moustache. 'I'm being generous, missus, but if yer want to try someone else then it's up to you.'

Rachael felt undecided about what to do. She knew he was cheating her. She was sure that if

Lewis had been there he would have managed to get twice that amount for his mother's belongings.

Katie sidled away and went back to the windowsill. She didn't like this man one little bit and she certainly didn't like the horrible things he was saying about Nana Roberts's furniture.

Jake Adcock's eyes followed her as she began picking up the rings and brooches she'd been looking at and putting them back into the jewellery box.

"Course, if you've got anything else yer want to sell, missus, then I might be able to do yer a better deal.'

Rachael shook her head. 'That is everything she left. Except her clothes.'

'I suppose I could give yer a few bob for those,' he said reluctantly, 'though if they're anything like the furniture they'll only be good for the rag and bone man. Isn't there any jewellery? Rings, and bits and bobs of that sort?'

Katie tried to push the rings and brooches she was sorting through under her skirt out of sight, but he'd already seen them and his eyes were glistening greedily.

'There's a few pieces, but I didn't think you'd be interested in things of that sort. I ... was going to keep them, or perhaps sell them later on.'

Jake Adcock shrugged. 'It's up to you, missus, but if it's now yer wanting money then I'd do yer a better deal than old Manny the pawnbroker, mind. Right twisting old tyke he is and no mistake. Shall I take a look and see what you've got to offer?'

Rachael shivered. She felt so completely out of control. She needed money now, enough to pay for a room for the two of them and keep them in food for at least a couple of weeks until she could find herself a job.

'Yes, I suppose you could look at them,' she agreed cautiously. She took a deep breath and looked Adcock straight in the eye. 'They're good pieces, all of them, mind. I won't be selling unless you make me a decent offer.'

Adcock placed his hand on his wide barrel chest. 'Cross my heart, missus, I'll be as generous as a man can be.'

'Katie, bring that box of nana's things over here,' Rachael told her.

'Yes, Mam.' Katie hesitated for a moment then scrabbled all the pieces she'd been looking at together and pushed them into the box higgledy-piggledy. She didn't stop to lay each one in its own little velvet nest because she didn't want them to look nice, she didn't want this horrible man to take them away.

Jake Adcock's eyes gleamed avariciously as he sorted through the contents of the jewellery box, but when he looked up his face was dour and he was pulling at the ends of his moustache as if he wasn't sure what to do.

'Another fiver for the clothes and bedding and another fiver for this lot, how about that?'

'No!' cried Katie. 'They're worth tons more than that! They're worth a fortune! My nana called them her Crown Jewels.'

Jake Adcock scowled at Katie, frightening her so much that she felt tears stinging her eyes.

'Mrs Roberts always did say they were all valuable pieces,' Rachael agreed.

'Duw anwyl! Yer a hard woman to deal with,' Jake Adcock muttered. 'Tell you what, missus. Seeing as how I'm kind-hearted and can see you're in a spot of trouble, I'll make my offer up to fifty pounds. That's my final offer, mind. Fifty pounds and that includes everything in the house!' He gave a deep belly laugh. 'No wonder they call me generous Jake. Fool to myself, I am.'

'Very well then.' Rachael made her voice casual.

Fifty pounds! It seemed like a fortune and far more than she had expected. With fifty pounds she'd not only be able to pay a month's rent in advance on a cheap furnished room, but she'd have enough left over to feed them for three or four weeks as well. By then she would have found a job and they'd have no worries.

Katie watched wide-eyed as the man called out to the lad he'd left outside holding the horse and the two of them began moving the furniture out and piling it on the cart.

He left the jewellery box until last and he

tucked this under his arm after he'd counted out a pile of dirty notes and handed them to Rachael.

'Right, that's it then. Good luck to yer, missus.' He doffed his cap and made for the door before Rachael could even count her money.

Katie looked around the bare rooms. Every step she took echoed and she wondered where they would be sleeping that night now that all the beds and blankets had gone. There wasn't even a kettle left on the hob or a cup in the kitchen cupboards. Jake Adcock had stripped the house bare.

'Come on, Katie,' Rachael held out Katie's coat for her to put on. 'We'd best be going.'

'Yes, Mam.' Katie fastened up her coat then stooped down and opened up one of the suitcases.

'Come on, girl, what do you think you are doing? If we go now, before the rent man comes, that will be one less thing to pay out for and he'll never find us once we've left Catherine Street.'

'I want to put these in my suitcase, Mam,' she giggled, as she fished a ring and two brooches out of her knicker leg, 'they're scratching my botty.'

'Katie! Where did those come from, they're out of Nana Roberts's jewellery box!' Rachael exclaimed in shocked tones.

'You said I could keep whichever one I liked best. And I liked all of these.'

Rachael regarded her severely for a minute then she burst out laughing.

'Fair-dos', I suppose,' she said as she shrugged on her coat and pulled her blue cloche hat well down on her ears. 'What Jake Adcock didn't see and doesn't know about he'll never miss, will he!'

Chapter Two

Finding a room that they could afford turned out to be very difficult for Rachael and Katie.

'Why couldn't we have stayed with Mr and Mrs Parsons?' Katie snivelled, as once again a door was slammed in their faces.

She was tired and hungry, and it was starting to rain. Her shoes were pinching her toes and the suitcase she had to carry made her arms ache.

'They wouldn't want us, cariad. They don't talk to us since your dada was taken off to prison.'

'They came to Nana Roberts's funeral.'

Rachael sighed. 'I know that, cariad, but that was because they were fond of your nana and wanted to show their respect to someone who'd lived in Catherine Street for over thirty years.'

Katie's big grey eyes clouded with tears. She didn't understand this. If they still loved her nana then why did they hate her and her mam and not want to have anything to do with them? It wasn't her mam's fault that her dada had gone to prison.

'Well, we've tried everywhere we can afford in Splott and Grangetown so it looks as though there's nothing else for it but Tiger Bay,' Rachael said wearily.

She picked up the two suitcases she was carrying and nodded towards the one that Katie had dropped by her feet. 'Come on, pick that up then and we'll get a tram down Corporation Road to the Pier Head before we're soaked to the skin.'

'Where do we go now, Mam?' Katie asked despondently as the tram reached the Pier Head and they stood in the roadway with their suitcases on the pavement by their feet.

'I don't know, cariad,' Rachael told her jadedly, 'but we must try and find somewhere before it gets dark otherwise we'll be spending the night on the street huddled in a doorway.'

'Mam, we can't do that!' Katie exclaimed in horror. Katie looked at the people hurrying by who were of every colour and every nationality.

'Come on, Mam.' She picked up her suitcase and dragged at Rachael's arm with her free hand as she felt terror churning inside her. 'Let's hurry up and find somewhere.'

The sudden jerk startled Rachael, causing her to drop one of her suitcases. It landed heavily on the ground and the locks burst open, spilling everything inside it out onto the wet pavement.

'Now look what you've made me do,' she snapped crossly.

'I'm sorry, Mam! I didn't mean to make you drop it,' Katie snuffled plaintively as she got down on her knees and gathered together the clothes and shoes that had fallen out, and tried to ram them back into the suitcase.

'Now then, what's going on here?'

Katie and Rachael both looked up startled as a man's deep voice boomed out over their heads. Katie looked at the big black boots only inches from her face. Her heart pounded nervously as her eyes moved up and she saw the dark navy-blue uniform and the shining silver buttons of a policeman.

'Are you two running away from home?' he asked as he tapped his trouser-leg with his baton.

'No, we are looking for somewhere to stay though,' Rachael said, as she stood up and faced him. 'Can you help?'

The policeman tapped the baton against his leg several times before he answered. 'Just the two of you, is it?'

'That's right. Me and my little girl.'

'What sort of place are you looking for?'

'Something cheap and clean and respectable, of course. One room would do.'

'Hmm!' He looked from one to the other of them speculatively. 'Where've you come from?'

Rachael hesitated. 'Cathays. Catherine Street, Cathays.'

Katie looked up into his broad red face and remembered the other two policemen who had come to the house and taken her dada away with them. This policeman looked much kinder.

She gave him a smile. She felt sure he was going to help them.

'We were living with my nana in her house but she's died and now we have nowhere to live,' she told the policeman.

He looked at her gravely. 'I see. And where is your daddy?'

'He ... he's away at the moment,' Rachael said quickly.

'My dada's been taken to prison,' Katie told him. 'I'm not supposed to tell anyone where he is, but since you're a policeman I expect you know already.'

The constable tapped his leg several more times with his baton. 'What did you say your name was?' he asked Rachael.

'My name is Katie Roberts,' Katie piped up before Rachael had a chance to answer.

'I see!' His stern gaze went from her, back to Rachael. 'So why are you looking for somewhere to live in this area, Mrs Roberts? There must surely be better parts of Cardiff where you can find accommodation than down here in Tiger Bay. Why didn't you stay in Cathays? Nice tidy place to live, that is.'

'None of our friends or neighbours in Cathays want to know us, now that my husband is in jail,' Rachael told him bitterly. 'I've tried all over the place in Splott and Grangetown, but no one wants a woman with a kiddie in tow, see. I thought people mightn't be quite so picky down here.'

The policeman nodded understandingly. Taking out his notebook he wrote down an address. 'Here, try this place,' he said, handing the scrap of paper to Rachael. 'It's not a palace, mind, but you'll find it is reasonably clean and the folks that live there have never been in any trouble with the law.'

'Thank you.' Rachael gave him a wan smile. 'Can I say you sent me?' she asked.

He frowned and tapped his leg with his baton again. 'You can, but it might be better if you said a friend told you ... that's if they ask,' he said at last.

'Very well ... and thanks again,' she murmured, as she continued collecting up the miscellany of articles strewn on the pavement.

He waited until Rachael and Katie had put everything back in the suitcase and shut the lid down before he moved away.

'Where is this place, then?' Rachael called after him. 'How do I get to it?'

He turned sharply and gave her brief instructions before walking away briskly, leaving them to make their own way.

'Louisa Street is fairly near, so let's give it a try,' Rachael pronounced, picking up two of the cases and indicating with a movement of her head that Katie was to take the other one.

'Now remember,' she warned Katie, 'not a word about your dada being in prison. You understand?'

'What shall I say, then?'

22

'Nothing! Or simply that he is away.'

Rachael walked in silence, saving her breath to give herself the energy to carry the cases. Katie grizzled and moaned as the case she was carrying banged against her legs, but Rachael took no notice. She knew that if she stopped and put down her own load she would never be able to gather the momentum to pick them up again.

The terraced houses in Louisa Street opened straight onto the pavement. As they reached the door of No. 10, Rachael put down one of her cases and studied the scrap of paper to find the name of the woman living there.

Alys Morgan was a big buxom woman in her late fifties with small hard black eyes like currants in her puffy white face. A cigarette with an inch of grey ash on it dangled from one corner of her thin-lipped mouth.

She answered the door wearing down-at-heel slippers, a flowered print overall hiding her drab grey dress, and with her streaked hair imprisoned in metal curlers that stood out above her brow like a tiara.

'Yer wanting something?' Her beady eyes took in the cases. 'A room is it?' She held out a grimy hand. 'Five bob a week and money up front. Take it or leave it.'

'I'd like to see it first,' Rachael told her, spiritedly.

Alys Morgan folded her brawny arms over her massive chest. 'Darw! Choosy sort are you?

Leave your stuff there then; the kid can look after it. It's the back room at the top of the stairs. Go on up and have a look at it. I'm not taking you up, my bloody varicose veins are killing me!'

She drew heavily on her cigarette as she waited for Rachael to return and Katie watched fascinated as the tip of grey ash shivered and collapsed into a powdery mess down the front of Alys Morgan's wraparound overall.

'Don't your mam smoke, then?' She coughed as she brushed the ash away with her hand.

Katie shook her head, her eyes widening as Alys Morgan sucked deeply on the cigarette and a red glow showed at the end.

Rachael stared round the back bedroom in distaste. The walls were covered in a drab, striped wallpaper that was so faded it was difficult to discern what the original colours had been.

A three-quarter-size bed was pushed tight against one wall to make room for a bentwood chair. The only other furniture was a chest of drawers that had a cracked piece of mirror hung on the wall over it. A chipped washbowl and cracked jug stood on top of the chest. They were a muddy green colour with faded red cabbage roses painted on them.

There was no space for a wardrobe but a row of metal hooks had been hammered into the wall down one side of the room.

Rachael pulled back the washed-out pink

candlewick counterpane that covered the bed. Beneath it was a dingy grey blanket and, surprisingly, clean white sheets and pillowcases.

It certainly wasn't ideal, she thought miserably, but she didn't really have any choice. At least the bed was clean she consoled herself, as she went back downstairs.

'I'll take it,' she told Alys Morgan.

'Five bob then, missus. Like I told you, rent has to be paid in advance.'

'And I want to know a bit more about what I'm getting for my money before I hand it over,' Rachael told her as she searched inside her handbag for her purse.

'What d'yer mean by that?' Alys Morgan frowned.

'Well, do I have use of the kitchen? Where's the lavatory? Is there a lock on my bedroom door and do I get a key?'

Alys Morgan's lips curled. 'I don't wait on you, if that's what you're wondering. You can boil a kettle or heat a pan of food up in the kitchen on the landing. It's alongside the lavvy and you share both with the others who have rooms upstairs. You'll be expected to scrub it out once a week like the others do. As for a key, there's no locks on any of the rooms and no one has a key to the front door except me. I lock that when I go to bed, otherwise it's always on the latch.'

'So anyone can walk in and out at any time of

the day and there's nothing to stop them taking things from my room?'

Alys Morgan's dark eyes hardened into angry bullets. 'They can try! They have to get past me first. My kitchen door is always open, see, so I can spot who comes in and who goes out. All my lodgers are honest and respectable and they'd be out on their ear if I caught any of them messing about in a room that wasn't theirs.'

Rachael sighed, then counted out the necessary coins into the other woman's outstretched hand. It certainly wasn't ideal, certainly not what she had been hoping for, but it was the first time she'd even got as far as seeing a room. At least this woman hadn't slammed the door in her face and told her that she didn't want any brats in the place.

Alys Morgan checked the money Rachael had given her then dropped it into the capacious pocket in her floral overall.

'Better take yer cases on up to your room then, hadn't yer,' she stated. 'Someone might go sorting through them and take some of your precious belongings if you leave them lying about on the doorstep,' she added acidly.

Chapter Three

Settling into the cramped bedroom and having to share the primitive conditions provided at No. 10 Louisa Street was an unsettling experience for both Katie and Rachael. Not only were both of them missing their friends, but the accommodation certainly wasn't what they were used to having. Rachael felt thoroughly miserable as she remembered her lovely bedroom back in Catherine Street with its blue floral curtains and matching counterpane. Katie's room had been pretty, too, with its pink and white curtains and matching eiderdown.

The kitchen on the landing, which she was told she would be sharing with the families living in the other two upstairs bedrooms, had once been the bathroom, and so it was right next to the lavatory. Rachael took a quick peek in there first. She noticed that the scrubbed wooden seat had a gaping crack in it at one side, and that the stained linoleum was littered with bits that had dropped there from the squares of newspaper that hung from a piece of string tied to a nail halfway up the wall.

In the adjoining room the washbasin acted as a sink, and someone had left a pile of dirty dishes soaking in it. The bath was covered over with a plank of scrubbed wood to provide a makeshift worktop. Standing on it was a gas ring and alongside that was a badly dented tin kettle and two battered aluminium saucepans.

On the wall above the bath were three shelves, one each for the occupants of the bedrooms. Two of them were crammed with an assortment of cups, plates, dishes, jars, and packets of food. The third shelf held only oddments of china and Rachael assumed this must be for her use.

Desperate for a drink, Rachael lit the gas ring and placed the tin kettle on it to boil. As she took down cups for herself and Katie, and rinsed them clean under the washbasin tap, she realised that she had no tea or any milk. The feeling of frustration and despair brought tears to her eyes.

'Katie, run back downstairs and ask Mrs Morgan if she can spare me some tea. Hurry up, cariad, I'm dying for a drink, and I expect you are, too,' she urged, when she saw Katie hesitate.

As the child made off, Rachel leaned over the banister and called down, 'and a spot of milk if she can manage it!'

'By the sound of it all you've got is hot water so yer'd better come on down here and have a cuppa,' Alys Morgan yelled back.

Rachael took a peek at herself in the cracked flyblown mirror over the chest of drawers and shuddered. She prided herself on being slim and trim, but now she looked terrible. Her hair, that she usually wore caught back at the nape of her neck with a broad slide, hung in untidy strands. Her face looked grey and her hazel eyes were lacklustre with exhaustion.

The blue cotton dress she'd put on clean that morning was creased, and it was grubby down the front from lifting the suitcases after they'd been standing on the wet pavement.

All she wanted to do, she thought irritably, was to sit quietly for ten minutes, close her eyes, rest her aching feet and drink a cup of tea. After that she'd start the depressing task of unpacking their cases and trying to find somewhere in the room to put their belongings.

She suspected that behind Alys Morgan's invitation was curiosity and the hope of prising information out of her about her background.

The moment the thought entered her mind Rachael felt a frisson of alarm. Hastily, she smoothed her hair, pushed her feet back into her shoes, scrambled over the cases piled between the chest and the door and rushed down the stairs. Katie was already down there and she was such a chatterbox that she'd be telling Alys Morgan far more than Rachel wanted her to know, just like she'd done with the policeman.

Alys Morgan's kitchen came as a shock. The room was stiflingly hot and smoky. It was obvious from the way it was arranged that Mrs

Morgan not only lived, cooked, and ate her meals there, but that she slept there as well.

Every wall was covered with shelves and in turn they were crammed with everything from pots and pans, cups, saucers, plates of every size, glasses, ornaments, and curios of every description, from a cuckoo clock and some gigantic sea shells to china houses and figurines.

Rachael breathed a sigh of relief as she saw Katie was standing just inside the door, open mouthed and enthralled, and realised that so far she hadn't said a word out of place. She was gazing around her in awe, mesmerised by the assortment of things on display. With any luck, Rachael thought, Katie was so bemused that she wouldn't say a word about their affairs to Alys Morgan.

'Sit yerself down then,' Alys told her, nodding at a padded rocking chair that was on the other side of the fire grate and which was identical to the one she was sitting in.

Her chair creaked protestingly under her bulk as she reached out for the aluminium teapot standing on the hob and poured out a stream of rich dark tea into a flowered china cup. 'Help yerself to milk and sugar then, they're all on the table,' she said, as she replenished her own cup.

'Now what about the little one? This tea's too strong for her, mind, but she's welcome to some milk,' she said, pulling a white enamel jug closer to her and lifting up the piece of beaded net that protected it from the countless flies buzzing around the room.

'You'd like a bakestone, too, wouldn't you, cariad?' she invited, as she half-filled a cup with milk.

Katie smiled and nodded, but she couldn't stop her eyes wandering back to all the things on display.

'It's like a shop in here,' she gasped in disbelief. 'Are all these things yours?'

Alys Morgan smiled proudly. 'They certainly are, cariad! Every single one of them has been given to me by grateful tenants. They've all said this place was like a second home to them and they'll never forget it. You're going to love living here, mind, once you've unpacked all those cases and got yourselves sorted out.'

Katie pulled a face. 'I don't like our room very much. It's an awful lot smaller than my bedroom was at home and my mam says we both have to sleep in the same bed!'

'Well, there's lovely that will be for you. Be able to snuggle up all cosy like, won't you!' Alys Morgan smiled at Katie, but immediately turned to Rachael. 'So it's not what you're used to, eh? Things a bit hard for you at the moment, are they?'

'A little,' Rachael murmured stiffly. She didn't want to discuss her affairs with Alys Morgan or with anyone else, but she didn't want to antagonise her either.

'No husband around at present, then?' Alys probed.

'He's away at the moment. He'll be home again soon,' Rachael told her.

'Oh? Working away, like, is he?' Alys Morgan persisted.

Rachael bit her lip and shot a warning glance at Katie, who she could see was on the point of speaking out. 'Something like that,' she said quickly.

'Never around when you want them, are they,' Alys Morgan said cryptically. 'Mind, this old General Strike seems to be changing all our lives.'

Her beady eyes gleamed and, guessing her curiosity was insatiable, Rachael hastily swallowed down her tea and made to leave.

'Come on, sit back and have another cup, and give the little one a chance to eat another of my bakestones. Lovely they are. Only made them this morning. Try one for yourself. Or would you rather have a fag?'

She rummaged in the deep pocket of her overall, pulled out a packet of Woodbines and held it out, but Rachael shook her head.

'Thanks, but I don't.'

'Never? Oh I like a ciggie with me cuppa. I find one perks me up no end and you look as though you need something to cheer you up,' she added critically. 'Sure you won't have a drag?'

'No. Thank you all the same.'

Alys Morgan tipped a cigarette out of the packet and lit it with a spill that she thrust between the bars of the grate into the glowing heart of the fire.

'Now then,' she inhaled a lungful of smoke and coughed noisily as she turned back to Katie, 'you haven't even told me yer name yet, cariad!'

'It's Katie. Katie Roberts and I was born in May 1918 and I'm eight years old and I really would like another bakestone, please, Mrs Morgan.'

'There's a clever girl, one who knows her own mind. Like that, I do, a child who can speak up for herself. So, what school have you been going to then?'

'St Catherine's. It was at the end of the road where we lived and I used to go all on my own.' Still talking, she helped herself to another bakestone from the plate Alys Morgan held out. 'Mam or my nana would stand on the doorstep and watch me walk down the road and they'd stay there until I was in the school playground. When it was time to come home again, one of them would be out on the doorstep waiting for me.'

'There's nice for you. You all lived with your nana did you?'

Katie nodded, her eyes filling with tears, and for a moment she couldn't even speak. She wanted so much to be back at her old home in Catherine Street. She'd loved Nana Roberts an awful lot, especially the way she used to cuddle her and fuss over her. She couldn't believe that her nana was dead and gone forever and would never buy her any more pretty clothes or sweets.

'Her nana died only a week ago,' Rachael said in a low warning voice.

'Darw! There's sad for the two of you and on your own an' all.'

She turned back to Katie. 'In September you'll be going to a new school now you've moved here, then,' she said, as if trying to jolly her up.

'School?' Rachael looked shocked. So much had happened so quickly that she'd forgotten all about that. A feeling of panic welled up inside her. What sort of area was this for Katie to have to go to school in? The school in Cathays had been well run and the teachers kindly disposed towards the children. There had never been problems of any sort since the day she'd started there. Katie was bound to miss the teachers who'd always been so kind and helpful, as well as all her little friends.

'You'll find sending her to school in Tiger Bay will be a lot different than it was in Cathays,' Alys Morgan commented, as if reading her mind.

'I'm sure Katie will soon settle in. She's very bright and loves reading and writing.'

'Mawr! That might please the teacher, but it will only put up the backs of the rest in her class,' Alys Morgan commented dryly.

'We're not even sure which school she'll be going to yet,' Rachael pointed out quickly.

'You'll not have much choice! All the little ones from around here have to go to the Infants' School in Bute Terrace. Very mixed, I can tell you. Absolutely all sorts go there. Rough some of them are, too. What will her dada have to say about that?'

Rachael flushed. 'He ... he leaves all those sorts of things to me,' she said awkwardly.

'Not much option if he's away, I suppose,' Alys commented with a keen glint in her eye. 'So is your dada a sailor then, my lovely?' she asked, looking straight at Katie.

'No, no he's not a sailor,' Rachael said quickly.

'Sorry! There's daft I am, jumping to conclusions. I thought when you said he was away, that was what you meant!'

'No, he doesn't go to sea,' Rachael repeated lamely.

'Well, that's a relief. Cruel the sea is, see! My old man went down with his boat five years ago, in the spring of 1921. Drowned like all the rest on board.'

'I'm sorry to hear that. Very sad for you.'

Alys Morgan shrugged her massive shoulders. 'Most of the menfolk around here either go to sea or work down at the docks. That's why I thought he must be a sailor.'

Rachael stood up and reached out a hand to

35

pull Katie to her feet, anxious to forestall any further questions.

'You've been very kind to us, Mrs Morgan, and that cup of tea has put new life into me,' she said hurriedly. 'We'll go now and unpack our cases and get settled in before bedtime. I'll need to nip out for one or two things for our breakfast so I'll do that first.'

She still felt hurt and humiliated by the situation she found herself in and she didn't want to discuss her personal business any further. Her nerves were raw and every question Alys Morgan directed at her felt like picking at a scab until it was bleeding.

'You can leave Katie here with me if you like, you'll get around quicker on your own,' Alys Morgan suggested craftily. 'She can have another of my bakestones and then we can have a nice little chat and she can look at all my treasures.' She turned to Katie with a smile. 'You'd like that now, wouldn't you, cariad?'

'No, I'll take Katie with me,' Rachael said quickly. 'I think she's had quite enough excitement for one day and anyway I'll need her to help me carry the shopping back,' she added firmly.

Chapter Four

Throughout the hot August evening the house in Louisa Street seemed to be full of strange noises as the occupants of the other rooms arrived home and cooked meals in the kitchen that was alongside their room.

As she unpacked the things she thought they would be needing right away, and put them into the chest of drawers or hung them from the hooks on the wall, Rachael could hear snatches of conversation coming from the other rooms. Once, she thought she heard the voice of a young boy and it made her wonder how many people there were altogether in the house. As well as the three bedrooms there were two rooms downstairs, as well as the kitchen where Alys Morgan appeared to live. These would be occupied by tenants as well, Rachael was sure of that, and she wondered where they did their cooking.

Worn out by all that had happened that day, Katie had fallen asleep almost as soon as they'd arrived back with the shopping. Her appetite had been satisfied by all the bakestones she'd eaten. Rachael decided to make herself a cheese sandwich and left Katie to sleep.

When she finally crept into bed alongside Katie she felt so exhausted that she expected to be asleep in minutes. However, the moment her head touched the pillow, her heart started racing and images of all that had happened to them that day reeled through her mind, almost as if she was sitting in the pictures.

The bed was lumpy and the pillow hard, and as she lay there in the sweltering darkness she was sure she could hear mice gnawing and the scratching sound of cockroaches as they roamed the walls.

What had happened to them that they had been reduced to this sort of existence, she thought bitterly. From a very respectable home in the best part of Cathays to a lodging house in Tiger Bay.

In the past she had often resented the way that Lewis's mother had ruled the roost in Catherine Street, but now, looking back, she could see what an easy life she'd had.

It had been Sian Roberts who'd shouldered all the responsibilities for running the house. She'd simply helped with the cleaning, the shopping and occasionally with the cooking, and looked after Katie.

Sian had even paid the rent and the grocery bills from the pension left by her dead husband, insisting that Lewis kept his wages to spend on his family. Rachael sighed. There had been no worries about money at all, not until Lewis was sent to prison and Sian had her heart attack.

That had been so sudden. There'd been no warning at all. She'd been in her sixties, of course, but she was a bundle of energy and never had a day's illness, not even rheumatism or any other aches and pains like those most elderly people complained about.

It must have been the shock and shame because of what had happened to Lewis, Rachael thought morosely. She still found it hard to accept that he'd turned out to be a thief. She'd fallen for his suave good looks and his smooth charm and had been so much in love with him that she still couldn't believe he had done such a thing.

She'd been shocked when they'd given him a nine-year sentence. 'That means it will be 1935 and Katie will be seventeen,' she'd gasped.

'He'll be out in less if he behaves himself,' the solicitor told her confidently.

Even so, it meant she would have to provide for herself and Katie for a long time to come. There'd not be a penny piece coming from him. Which meant that all she had in the world was the money Jake Adcock had paid for Sian Roberts's furniture and belongings.

Fifty pounds had seemed like a small fortune at the time, but she'd already made a small hole in it and she'd make an even bigger one tomorrow. There were so many things they needed. She hadn't given a thought to hanging onto any of the household items like cutlery and crockery. She hadn't even got a pudding basin!

Not that she'd have much chance of making puddings on a gas ring, she reminded herself sadly.

She didn't like Alys Morgan very much, she reflected. Nosey old woman! She didn't want her luring Katie into her room and prising information out of her. She'd have to have a serious talk to Katie in the morning and warn her that she mustn't talk about their affairs to other people.

There was also the question of making arrangements for Katie to go to school. Because it was the summer holidays she'd forgotten all about that when she'd been looking for somewhere to live. The school Katie had attended in Cathays had been a Catholic one, because Sian Roberts had been a strict practising Catholic and had insisted that was where she must go.

Well, Rachael thought stubbornly, she hadn't been brought up a Catholic; she'd only converted to the religion when she'd married Lewis. Now, though, she'd keep herself and Katie well away from them. They asked too many questions about your life. The priest expected you to confess to everything you said or did. Much as she'd liked Father Patrick, she'd hated that part of the religion.

Once Katie was attending the Infants' School in Bute Terrace she'd find herself some work. She'd open up a Post Office Savings book and put what was left of the fifty pounds in there. It would be a comfort to know it was there if she ever fell on really hard times and needed it. With luck, once she had a job she'd be able to manage for them to live on whatever money she earned. She was still planning a new life for herself and Katie when she finally drifted off to sleep.

When she was wakened next morning by loud noises from the adjacent rooms, Rachael sat bolt upright in bed, thinking for one minute that she was still back in Catherine Street and that the place was being burgled. Then the happenings of the past few days came rushing back into her mind as she looked around the dingy, crowded bedroom in dismay.

Her sudden movements wakened Katie who stretched and yawned and, like her mother, wondered for a moment where she was.

'What time is it, Mam?'

Rachael shook her head. 'I've no idea. We should have kept the clock. I'll have to buy one when we go out this morning. I'd better get one that has an alarm,' she added, 'otherwise you won't be up in time for school in the mornings.'

'Do I really have to go to a new school?'

'I'm afraid so, cariad. We're miles and miles from Catherine Street.'

'We could catch a tram every morning and I could take my dinner with me and you could come and pick me up at night,' Katie suggested.

Rachael shook her head firmly. 'It's out of the question, I'm afraid. You have to go to the

41

nearest one, because while you are in school I will be working.'

Katie looked puzzled. 'Where are you going to work?'

'I don't know yet. Finding a job is something else I've got to do. Come on,' she pushed back the bedclothes and stepped out onto the linoleum. 'Let's get dressed and then we'll go and buy that clock and all the other things we need.'

The morning's shopping made a larger hole in Rachael's money than she had expected. She not only bought a clock, but some cutlery and china. She stocked up with basic items of food like tea, sugar, bread, margarine, and other things to keep them going. She also bought a small frying pan and a saucepan because she didn't relish using the grimy ones that were in the shared kitchen.

As she and Katie unpacked the shopping, Rachael wondered where she was going to keep everything. The single shelf that was theirs in the kitchen wouldn't provide very much storage space, and she wondered if it was safe to leave things in there since she didn't know any of the other tenants. Alys Morgan hadn't even told her their names. That was probably her own fault, she reflected, because she had cut Alys Morgan off short when she'd felt she was prying.

Later today she'd make a point of asking her. She might even be able to tell me where I can find work, Rachael thought hopefully. Fortunately the summer holidays were almost over and Katie would be at school from now until Christmas. Even so, it wasn't going to be easy fitting in her time at work to coincide with school hours.

While they'd been out shopping she'd explained to Katie why she didn't want her telling Alys Morgan, or anyone else, about what had happened.

'You shouldn't have told the policeman that your dada was in prison,' she said gently.

'He'd know anyway,' Katie said sulkily.

'No, he probably wouldn't. He patrols a different part of Cardiff. He certainly wasn't one of the policemen who came to our house in Catherine Street,' Rachael told her firmly. 'Anyway,' she added, 'you are not to talk about it at all. Understand?'

Katie gave an exaggerated sigh. 'If you say so. I don't see why it has to be a secret, though,' she pouted.

'Well, you would if you stopped to think back to what happened to all your friends in Cathays when they heard that your dada had gone to prison,' Rachael told her sharply.

'That wasn't their fault! It was their mams and dadas who said they weren't to play with me anymore, or have anything to do with me,' Katie said sullenly. She didn't want to be reminded of the snubs and jeers of the last few weeks in Catherine Street before Nana Roberts had died and everything in her life had started to go wrong.

'Yes, I know, cariad. That is what I am trying to explain to you. If you tell people that your dada is in prison then they won't want to have anything to do with you. Mrs Morgan might even ask us to leave her house,' she added, as an extra warning.

'I wouldn't care if she did,' Katie retorted. 'I hate it here. It's dirty and smelly and I hate sharing a bed with you.' Tears welled up in her grey eyes and spilled down her cheeks. 'I want to go back to Catherine Street, and go to my old school. I don't care whether anyone talks to me or not. They probably won't talk to me at the new school because I won't know any of them,' she added logically.

Rachael sighed. 'I know it's hard, my lovely, but it's the way things are and we've got to make the best of it.'

'Why couldn't we have stayed in Nana Roberts's house?' Katie persisted.

'I've already explained. We couldn't afford to do so. We hadn't the money to pay the rent.'

'We've got to pay rent to Mrs Morgan and if you are going to go out to work to do that then we could have stayed where we were, and you could have gone out to work and paid the rent there.'

'It's not as simple as that, Katie. The amount of rent I'd have to pay to keep our home in Catherine Street would be five times as much as I have to pay for our room here in Louisa Street, because that was a whole house, remember?'

Katie finally accepted the situation but she'd not been happy, and even when Rachael had bought her an ice-cream cornet and let her eat it as they walked along she was still ill-humoured.

Rachael decided not to pursue the matter. Katie was a bright child and, because up to now she had spent most of her time with grown-ups when she was not at school, she was quite sensible for her age. Rachael was sure that once she'd had time to think about what had been said then she'd see the sense of it all.

Like Katie, she wished with all her heart that they could turn the clock back and find themselves once again in Catherine Street whether the neighbours ignored them or not. Lewis being accused of stealing and sent to prison was a nine-day wonder, and would probably soon be forgotten by most people.

She knew she had to try and put it to the back of her own mind. What still upset her was the fact that when she'd gone to the prison to tell Lewis that his mother had died he blamed her!

He'd been so bitter, insisting that it was all her fault because she had refused to tell the police that at the time of the robbery he had been at the pictures with her, watching Charlie Chaplin in *The Gold Rush*. If she'd done that, he pointed out, then he would have been in the clear and his mam would still be alive and well, and they would all still be living happily in Catherine Street.

He'd been scornful when she'd said she

couldn't lie like that, in case they'd asked her what the film was about and she'd never seen it.

When she asked him if he had any money put away, that he could let her have for her and Katie to live on, he had laughed at her and said he had never saved a penny in his life. He reminded her that his mother had had a regular income and paid all the bills, so he'd spent what he earned on things for her and Katie, or gambled it on the horses.

In the short time he had been in prison he seemed to have shut himself off from reality. He'd merely shrugged when she told him that she couldn't afford to go on living in Catherine Street.

'It's no good asking me for money, you'll have to move somewhere cheaper and get yourself a job,' he'd told her, almost as if she was a stranger.

She'd come away feeling depressed and wondering if there was any point in visiting him again.

Chapter Five

When she'd lived in Catherine Street, Katie had looked forward to going to school each day. Nana Roberts had always inspected her to make sure she had on clean socks, a clean pinny over a clean dress and that the ribbon that tied back her hair was in a firm neat bow, before kissing her goodbye.

Sometimes it had been Nana Roberts who'd stood on the doorstep watching her run down the street until she reached the school gates at the end of the road. At other times it had been her mam who stood there to make sure she arrived at school safely.

Once inside the school gates she had sought out her friends and they'd played or talked until the bell went. In the classroom they sat down in rows and the day began. She'd enjoyed learning new things each day and being taught to read and write.

Now, or so it seemed to Katie, all that had changed. School was no longer a joy, but something that had to be endured.

She would never forget her first day at the Infants' School in Bute Terrace. Her mam had made sure she was wearing a nice dress and a clean pinafore, the same as she used to do when they lived in Cathays. She'd walked with her, holding her hand as they approached the school yard and went in to find the head teacher.

Mr Isiah Samuels was a thin, gaunt-faced man who was almost bald and who wore gold-rimmed glasses that made his eyes look like shiny green marbles. Most of the time he seemed to be looking over the top of them.

He kept them waiting in the corridor until all the children had taken their places in class and the registers had been called. When that had been done and the registers brought to his study by a child from each class, he called them in.

He was sitting behind a high desk, dressed somberly in a grey suit and a stiffly starched white shirt with a high collar. He asked Katie her name and, after he'd written it down in one of the registers, he barked out endless questions to her mam about what school she'd attended in Cathays and what class she'd been in.

Katie had felt quite frightened when he told her mam that she needn't stay any longer. Her mam had given her a quick hug and then Katie was left there on her own. Standing in front of his high desk, she fidgeted from one foot to the other, unsure what she was supposed to do. When she really thought he'd forgotten all about her he suddenly looked up, staring over the top of his gold-rimmed glasses as if he wondered what she was still doing standing there.

'Right, Katie Roberts,' he barked. 'Go along to the classroom that is opposite here and tell Miss Wells, who is the teacher in there, that you are a new girl and that I have added your name to her class register. Can you manage that?'

Katie nodded and moved quickly towards the door. Once across the hall, her knees felt wobbly as she gingerly opened the classroom door. She peeped inside and saw thirty pairs of eyes staring at her. She felt so nervous that, for a moment, she couldn't even see the teacher. In a daze she walked towards the high desk and, in a tight little voice, repeated what Mr Samuels had told her to say.

Eunice Wells was in her forties, a dumpy little woman with mousy brown hair, dull skin and pale blue eyes. She was in the middle of a lesson and her frown made clear her displeasure at being interrupted.

'Go and sit down and pay attention. I'll speak to you at the end of lesson,' she told Katie briskly.

Katie looked around for somewhere to sit, but she was so nervous that she couldn't see if there was a spare seat anywhere.

'Sit on the end of the front bench,' Miss Wells told her irritably. 'Move up the rest of you!' she ordered sharply.

Trembling, Katie sat down where she was told. For a moment she was so frightened that she didn't notice who was sitting next to her, but when she did, she drew in her breath in shocked surprise. The boy next to her was completely black. His skin was black, his hair was thick, black and curly, his hands were black and even his lips had a blackish tinge to them. The only thing about him that was white was his teeth, and they shone out like lumps of white china when he turned and grinned at her.

Furtively, she looked around at the other children sitting close by. There were several more who had tight, black, curly hair and their skin was as black as the boy she was sitting alongside. Several other children in the class were coloured but their skin seemed to be more brown than black, almost as if they had been lying out in the sun a lot. Another boy she noticed had straight black hair, and his eyes looked like slanting slits and his skin was a strange yellow colour.

She felt uneasy. So far, except for a girl with long hair that was so much fairer than her own that it looked almost white, she hadn't seen any other white children in the class. Even that girl, with her vivid blue eyes and pink shiny cheeks, looked different in some way.

She couldn't keep her mind on what Miss Wells was saying for wondering what all the other children sitting behind her in the class looked like.

At playtime, she stood shyly on her own, wondering if any of them would talk to her. At first they seemed to ignore her. Then a little knot of girls started pointing towards her and giggling behind their hands.

When she saw they'd moved into a huddle with a group of boys, and they were all looking across at her, she knew she could expect trouble.

A second later she was surrounded.

'We've got something for you,' one of the boys grinned. He was sturdy, older than her, wearing grey shorts and a red jumper that had the elbow torn out of it, and he was obviously the ringleader.

'Go on, Zeph, give it to her,' one of others shouted.

The girls giggled expectantly.

Before Katie knew what was happening another boy had grabbed hold of her arms and pulled them behind her back, making her scream out in pain. As she did so, Zeph tried to ram a handful of mud and weeds into her mouth.

She struggled to free herself from the boy's clutches but, even though she succeeded in pushing him away, others grabbed at her arm, forcing her face down onto the ground.

She knew she was at their mercy and, as her face hit the ground and she felt a stone cut into her lip, she stopped struggling, knowing she was only making things worse for herself.

When one of the boys slammed his boot down on her back she couldn't hold back her scream of pain or the tears that came into her eyes.

Suddenly, when she felt she could stand it no longer, they all seemed to melt away and she found herself being pulled unsteadily to her feet by a gangly boy who looked older than she was.

'Don't cry, you're all right now!' he told her.

Before she could answer, the bell sounded and playtime was over.

Wiping away the blood that was trickling down her face from a cut on her cheek, Katie trailed after the rest of her classmates as they made their way back to their desks.

'So what have you been up to, Katie Roberts?' Miss Wells asked, regarding her with displeasure.

As Katie opened her mouth to explain there was whispering and giggling from the rest of the class.

'By the look of things you've been brawling. Now we don't stand for that kind of behaviour here. If it happens again you'll be sent to Mr Samuels for the cane!'

Tears flooded Katie's eyes as she heard the others sniggering.

Miss Wells rapped sharply on her desk with the long round wooden ruler that she used to point out things on the maps which hung all around the walls.

'That will do! Silence! Hands on your heads all of you, this minute. Now sit like that for five minutes and I don't want to hear a sound. You will make up the time; the whole class will be kept in after school tonight.'

After that there was no time for talking or teasing as they all had to recite the multiplication tables that Miss Wells chalked up on the blackboard.

When the midday break came, Katie once again found herself the butt of teasing and bullying. Questions were fired at her relentlessly and, whatever she said, they poked fun at her answers.

'Where d'yer live then?'

'Louisa Street.'

'Lousy Street! Bet you've got nits,' one of the boys laughed and, pulling the ribbon from her hair, threw it on the ground and stamped on it as if pretending to find some and kill them.

'Where did yer live before Lousy Street then?'

'Catherine Street in Cathays.'

'So why did you leave there? Were you kicked out because your dad didn't pay the rent?'

Katie shook her head as she faced her tormentors. So many of them were a different colour to her and looked so strange and foreign that she was afraid of them and what they might do to her. Tears filled her eyes and brought a lump to her throat. She missed her dad and Nana Roberts, and kept remembering how happy they'd all been in their lovely home in Cathays.

'What's yer dad do then?'

'He's away.'

'Away? What does that mean?'

Katie shrugged and didn't answer. She'd remembered her mother's warning and now she understood why she'd been told not to tell anyone that her dad was in prison.

'Bet he's run away because you look so stupid,' someone sniggered.

'Only babies have lace on their clothes and ribbons in their hair when they come to school,' one of the girls jeered.

Hands reached out and pulled at the lace trim on the bodice of Katie's dress. As she fought them away there was a sound of cloth tearing as the lace trimming was pulled off.

To hide her tears, Katie bent down and picked up her hair ribbon, which was now grubby and soiled from being trampled on. Immediately, one of the girls snatched it from her hand, holding it tantalisingly in front of her, just out of her reach. Then a black boy grabbed it and began waving it in the air like a flag.

'Give it back and leave the kid alone or I'll knock your heads together.'

The command took both Katie and her tormentors by surprise. She looked around quickly and to her surprise saw it was the boy who had defended her earlier in the day.

'None of yer business what we do, Aled Phillips, you're not in our class,' one of the boys piped up cheekily.

'If you don't stop I'll report you to Mr

Samuels for bullying, and then you'll have the cane,' he responded calmly.

'Sneak!'

'Shut up, he can report us, he's a prefect.'

'Only for his own class.'

'But he's older than us, Mr Samuels will believe him.'

Reluctantly, they shuffled away from Katie.

'You all right now?' Aled asked her as she dried her eyes with the back of her hand.

Katie nodded. 'Thanks,' she whispered.

Aled grinned, his dark brown eyes confident. 'Don't take any notice of them. They won't bother you again, I'll make sure of that.' He smiled at her shyly. 'They are jealous of you, see, because you're wearing such a pretty dress.'

'My mam will be ever so cross when she sees the state I'm in.'

'No she won't,' Aled told her reassuringly. 'She'll understand. You tell her it's only because you're a new girl. Tomorrow everything will settle down and you'll be able to make friends with them.'

'I don't think I want to,' Katie snuffled. 'They're all horrid and cruel at this school ... except you.'

Aled smiled. 'I used to get teased just the same once.'

'Why?' Katie looked at him in surprise. 'Was it because your dad was away?'

'It was because I haven't got a dad at all. He

died before I was born. I live with my mum and gran, see.'

'I used to live with my nana . . .'

'There's the bell, you'll have to tell me about it some other time,' Aled told her. 'Tie your hair back and show them you don't care what they say or do. Go on!' He gave her a friendly push. 'Hurry up or you'll be late and then Miss Wells will tell you off.'

Chapter Six

Christmas 1926 was the bleakest Katie Roberts had ever known. In the past when Nana Roberts was alive it had been something she'd looked forward to for weeks and weeks.

Every day when she'd come home from school there had been lots of wonderful, exciting smells wafting from the kitchen. One day it would be the Christmas cake baking. Another day it would be the rich Christmas pudding mix, waiting for her to give it a final stir and make a wish before Nana Roberts divided it into two or three basins, and covered each of them with buttered greaseproof paper and a floured cloth. That done, she would simmer them one at a time in her biggest saucepan for hours and hours.

As Christmas drew nearer, she and her mam would go shopping in town for presents for Nana Roberts and for her dada, and back at home she would hide them away. In the weeks before Christmas, all kinds of strangely shaped parcels were tucked away in wardrobes or piled on top of high cupboards where she couldn't reach them.

She and her mam would sit for hours making

long trails of paper chains. Her dada would spend a whole weekend putting them up, as well as the very special ones that belonged to Nana Roberts. These were kept from one year to the next, stored away in a big box that stood on top of the mahogany wardrobe in her nana's bedroom.

On the last day at her old school, before they broke up for Christmas, there was a party. Everyone had to take their own mug and plate and, after the sandwiches and cakes that their mams had sent along were eaten, they would sing carols. Each of them was given a present, usually a book, before they went home.

And that was only the start of Christmas!

On Christmas morning her stocking, bulging with little packages and with an apple, an orange, and bright new shiny pennies tucked down in the toe, was always there at the bottom of her bed.

Nana Roberts always insisted that all of them, even her dada, went to the special sung Mass on Christmas Day.

The vegetables were all prepared the night before and the huge chicken was stuffed ready to go into the oven, so that it could be roasting while they were in church. The Christmas pudding was placed in a big saucepan on the side hob to warm through.

After they'd eaten a huge Christmas dinner they would all sit around the fire in the best parlour and open their big presents. She always had far more than anyone else, Katie remembered. Not only were there all the ones she'd written to ask Santa Claus to bring her, but several surprise presents as well.

Then her mam and dada would play games with her while Nana had a snooze until it was time for tea.

Christmas Day tea was always very special. There would be jelly and custard as well as mince pies and Christmas cake. They would all wear paper hats and pull Christmas crackers.

After tea, while nana and her mam cleared up, her dada would play some more games with her until it was time for her to go to bed.

Thinking about her dada brought a lump to Katie's throat. She hadn't seen him once since the policemen had come to their house in Catherine Street and taken him away. He hadn't even come to Nana Roberts's funeral.

Her mam didn't seem to want to talk about him, except to keep warning her not to tell anyone that he was in prison. She wouldn't even explain why the policemen had taken him away or why he had been sent to prison.

All she would say was, 'He won't be home again until you are a big, grown-up girl, so forget about him.' Katie kept wondering how she was expected to forget about him when she loved him such a lot and missed him so much.

Every night when she went to bed she lay there in the darkness thinking about him before she went to sleep. Sometimes he seemed so real that she could feel him holding her hand or kissing her goodnight.

Every night in her prayers, she asked God to keep him safe and bring him home soon. If she had to wait until she was grown up then she was so afraid that he may have forgotten her or that he mightn't even recognise her.

Her dada had always been the centre of things at Christmas and they'd had such fun together. This year, she thought unhappily, it seemed she'd be lucky if she got a single present or a real Christmas dinner.

Her mam kept repeating that they had to be careful how they spent their money, because she still hadn't managed to find a job and they'd spent most of the money that Jake Adcock had paid her for nana's furniture.

It was only one of the problems that haunted Katie. The worst one of all was Bute Terrace Infants' School, even though she had now been at the school for almost four months.

The faces of the children in her class would be grinning down at her as she lay on the ground. Black ones, white ones, Chinese, Indian, Scandinavian, Italian and Spanish, and she was so afraid of what they would do next that she would wake up screaming and shaking.

Whenever that happened her mam would cradle her in her arms, cuddle her tight and tell her it was all right, but it didn't stop the terrible dreams from coming back time and time again.

After that first terrible day she had refused to

wear any dress that had lace on it, or looked the least bit pretty. Fortunately, the weather had turned colder so she was able to wear a thick jumper, pleated skirt and knee-high socks like most of the rest of the girls did. She'd hoped that if she no longer looked different then she would be accepted, but it didn't work.

One of the reasons was that she never played with any of them after school. She couldn't ask them to come home with her because there was no space in their one room, and her mam wouldn't let her go to their houses unless they were white.

Katie couldn't understand why her mother worried about such things. Half the time she didn't even notice what colour or nationality the other children were that she mixed with at school, but her mam didn't like her playing with them and said she must never go to their homes.

In Katie's eyes this didn't make sense, as most of the people living at No. 10 Louisa Street were foreigners. In one of the other rooms upstairs there was a Chinese man and his wife, Mr and Mrs Singh, who rarely spoke to Katie, even when they passed on the stairs or met in the kitchen.

In the other room there were the Belazzios, an Italian family. The woman, Bella, was fat, and had huge dark eyes and olive skin. She always looked as if she was pouting, as though some-one had displeased her and made her cross.

Her husband, Gianni, who was a waiter at a restaurant on Bute Road, was fat, too, but he was always smiling and jolly, and he was always singing at the top of his voice, even early in the morning. They had a baby, Orlando, who was only just starting to walk. Katie often heard it crying in the night so perhaps that was why Mrs Belazzio always looked so unhappy.

Downstairs, in the big front room of the house, there were the Smithsons. Lee Smithson worked as a stevedor on the docks and often came home with bulky parcels from the ships he'd unloaded. When that happened there would be tantalising smells of exotic foods wafting up the stairs that made Katie's mouth water.

They had one boy, Bruno, who attended the same school as she did. He was in a lower class but his mam, Ella Smithson, had said she could walk along with them to school, but her mam wouldn't let her.

'You and Mrs Smithson could take it in turns,' Katie pointed out, but Rachael wasn't interested in cooperating.

'I don't want to start anything like that,' she told Katie rather sharply. 'If I let you walk to school with them then the next thing we know I'll be expected to collect Bruno or, worse still, take him in the morning. If he isn't ready when we want to leave then it will mean you'll be late for school, and then you'll be in trouble with Miss Wells.'

Magda Sorenson lived in the other room downstairs. Katie thought she was beautiful and couldn't understand why her mam didn't want to be friends with her. Magda was Swedish, statuesque with flowing blonde hair, a lovely oval face and a warm smile. She spent a lot of her time during the day sitting in Alys Morgan's room, drinking tea and gossiping.

She had lots of friends of her own. Katie had seen them popping in during the evening, one after the other. They didn't seem to stay very long and when she peeped down over the banister she'd noticed that they were mostly men who came to call.

Katie thought Magda, with her vivid blue eyes and long fair hair, was lovely, but not nearly as beautiful as one of the girls in her class called Juanita.

Katie ached to look like Juanita. Her skin was the colour of rich chocolate, she had huge dark eyes and when she smiled her teeth were sparkling white and perfectly even. Best of all, though, was Juanita's hair. It was so dark it was almost black and it was in tiny, tiny plaits all over her head. Katie had tried counting them, but Juanita always seemed to move her head before she was finished. She wished she knew her better so that she could ask her exactly how many plaits there were.

Rachael had been furious when she'd begged to have her hair done like that.

'Please, Mam. Little plaits all over my head, it

would look lovely. And then, if we ever sit next to each other in class we'd look like twins.'

'Twins!' Rachael snapped. 'Do you know what you're saying Katie? Juanita's father is an African!'

Katie looked puzzled. 'What does that matter?'

Rachael sighed. 'I'd rather we didn't talk about it any more,' she said firmly. It wasn't only the colour of the girl's skin she minded, she'd become used to seeing people whose skin was black, brown, yellow or something in between since they'd moved to Tiger Bay. It was the kind of food such foreigners ate and their different behaviour that bothered her. She didn't want Katie mixing with any of them.

'Do as I say and stop talking to her, do you understand?' she snapped.

'I'll have to talk to her if I sit next to her in school,' Katie protested.

'You can always swap seats and sit next to someone else,' Rachael suggested. How could she explain to Katie that she didn't like her sitting next to a coloured girl? She knew Juanita's mother was white but her father was a full-blooded African. Like Juanita, his skin was almost black, his black hair was coarse and wiry and covered his broad head in tight curls. Juanita was so pretty because she hadn't inherited her father's thick lips and broad nose, but had her mother's more finely-chiselled features.

'Mam! I think Juanita is lovely,' Katie told her defiantly. 'I wish I could dress like her, too. She wears bright scarlet skirts with yellow jumpers and brilliant green ribbons all at the same time, and it looks lovely. And she wears bright pinks and blues . . .'

'That will do,' Rachael snapped, and then felt guilty as she saw the tears glistening in Katie's eyes because she'd spoken so harshly.

She felt devastated. She'd made a terrible mistake coming to Tiger Bay to live and now there was nothing she could do about it. Most of the money she'd received from the sale of the furniture was gone. She'd even had to sell the few pieces of old Mrs Roberts's jewellery that Katie had hidden from Jake Adcock. The only way she could move to a better neighbourhood was to find a job and earn enough money to do so. The moment Christmas was over she'd start looking again, and this time she'd be prepared to take anything she was offered.

It wasn't simply being surrounded by abject poverty that upset her – there had been barefoot children in Cathays – it was the mix of people of so many different races that she didn't like. Their ways were so different to hers. She might live in Tiger Bay, but she didn't wish to become involved with any of them and she was determined to protect Katie from their influence.

From the very first moment they'd moved there she had refused to let Katie play out after school. Even when Katie said that most of her class met up by the side of the canal, or swung from the lampposts in the nearby streets, she wouldn't let her join them.

Many of them teased Katie unmercifully about this, and it gave them something else to taunt her about when she was at school.

As Christmas approached, they all boasted about the wonderful time they would be having and all the presents they were hoping to get. Katie kept quiet and refused to answer them or respond to their taunts, even when Ffion Jenkins and Megan Edwards pushed her into a corner of the playground and bombarded her with questions.

'Is your dad going to be at home for Christmas?' Ffion Jenkins asked her.

Katie remained silent, unsure what to say.

'Why can't he come home for Christmas? You've never even told us where he is?' Ffion persisted, her dark eyes curious.

'Go on then, tell us,' Megan Edwards prompted. 'I bet you haven't really got a dad at all, that's why you don't talk about him.'

'Of course I have a dada,' Katie defended hotly. 'He . . . he's away on important business.'

'So important that he can't even come home for Christmas?' Megan giggled, her dark eyes widening in surprise.

'It can't be very important business or you and your mam wouldn't be living in one room in Louisa Street,' Ffion pointed out pertly.

Katie tried desperately to think of some

believable reason why they were living there. She had once told both girls about the lovely home she used to have in Cathays, but that had only made them more curious about why she and her mam had left there and come to live in Tiger Bay.

'I'm not allowed to talk about what work my dada does, but he will be coming home after Christmas and bringing me loads of presents,' she told them.

From the looks they exchanged she was sure neither of them believed her.

Rachael knew Katie was unhappy, but there was not a lot she could do to make things better. Their money was worryingly low, and although she had tried everywhere she'd not managed to find any work.

The rent for their one squalid room had to be set aside, despite whatever else they went without. If she didn't pay that, then they would find themselves out on the street.

In desperation, Rachael sorted out some of their clothes to sell, to try and raise some money for extra food at Christmas. It broke her heart to do this because Nana Roberts had spent hours making some of the pretty dresses for Katie.

She said nothing to Katie and told herself that it was silly to keep them because Katie had grown so much that they probably wouldn't fit her any more. Even so, as she packed them up and caught a tram to the open market at The Hayes, hoping she'd get a better price for them there, she felt as guilty as if she was stealing them.

With the money she managed to get for them she bought some apples and oranges and a box of dates because she knew Katie loved them. She was tempted by the scraggy chickens that were for sale, remembering the big plump ones they'd always had for Christmas dinner in the past, but knew that even if she could afford one she would find it difficult to cook it.

Instead, she bought sausages because she knew Katie would enjoy them, and some corned beef to have cold for their tea on Christmas Day. As a special treat she also bought a small iced cake with a robin on it and a decorative red and silver band around it.

At the very last minute she counted out the coins in her purse and decided to walk back to Louisa Street, instead of catching the tram, so that she would be able to spend the few pennies on coloured crepe paper to make some decorations to brighten up their room.

The atmosphere at No. 10 Louisa Street on Christmas Day was strange. The Italians had started celebrating in earnest the evening before. Friends crowded into their room, laughing, squabbling and singing. Baby Orlando's crying added to the noise and it was long after midnight before their revelry died down and others in the house could settle to sleep.

Even so, Katie was awake at first light. She

knew how little money her mam had to spend on luxuries, so she was afraid to feel for a stocking at the foot of her bed in case she was disappointed.

There was one, though!

Excitedly, her hands went over its bulky shape trying to guess what the contents might be. In the tip of the toe she could feel coins. She also identified an apple and an orange, but after that she had no idea what mysteries there were.

In the cold light of early morning she pulled them out, her excitement mounting as she unwrapped each one. As well as the box of dates, which took up the entire length of the leg of her stocking, there was a comic, a box of paints, a dainty flowered handkerchief, a pair of woollen gloves, and some thick warm socks. At the very tip she found the apple, an orange and some shiny new pennies.

After breakfast, Katie wanted to go to Mass like they used to do, but Rachael, who had a head cold, said she didn't feel well enough to do that.

'Sit and read your comic until it is time for our Christmas dinner,' Rachael told her, 'and this afternoon I'll sit and play games with you.'

Halfway through the morning, Gianni Belazzio knocked on their door and with a beaming smile he requested that they should join him and Bella for a glass of wine to celebrate Christmas.

Politely, but very firmly, Rachael refused.

Chapter Seven

Rachael found that refusing to have a Christmas drink with the Belazzios had repercussions. The Italians regarded it as a slight and commented about it to all the other families living at No. 10 Louisa Street when they joined them for a drink to celebrate Christmas.

'Snotty cow! Who does she think she is!' Alys Morgan declared, as she downed her third glass of red wine and held out her glass for a refill.

'She never will get to know us if she carries on like this,' Ella Smithson stated. 'I wanted her to take it in turns with me to take her kiddie and my Bruno to school, but she wasn't having any.'

Mr and Mrs Singh simply nodded their heads, but said nothing.

'Maybe she is shy and feels she does not know us all very well,' Magda offered charitably.

None of them could understand what it was that kept Rachael from accepting their hospitality, but they resented her attitude.

While the rest of the occupants enjoyed themselves, drinking wine and eating mince pies, Rachael served up a meal of sausages and mash for herself and Katie, and instead of a portion of rich Christmas pudding they shared the apple and orange that had been in Katie's stocking.

For Katie it was the most miserable Christmas she'd ever known. Her mam promised to take her up to the city centre during the holiday so that they could see all the shop windows which were still bright with Christmas decorations, but she kept putting if off because of the weather.

'It's far too bad for us to walk the whole length of Bute Road and until I can find a job I can't afford to waste money on tram fares for something like that. Every penny matters and buying food comes first.'

Because the weather was so cold they felt hungry, and because they were hungry they felt the cold. Day after day there was rain or sleet and the grey skies and keen winds carried a threat of snow.

Katie read the comic that had been in her stocking over and over, did all the puzzles in it and even painted some of the black and white pictures with the paints from her new paint box.

There was so little else to do. When her mam was in a good mood they sang songs and hymns and carols together, but most of the time her mam sat hunched in a chair, her head in her hands, brooding.

'You don't have to wait until I go back to school if you want to go out and get a job,' Katie told her. 'I don't mind staying here on my own.'

'No, cariad, I don't want to do that,' Rachael

assured her. 'I'll start looking as soon as you go back to school.'

Their room was icy and they had no way of heating it. A great deal of the time Katie stayed huddled up in bed because it seemed the warmest place to be.

Lying there with the blankets pulled up to her chin, she would drift off into dreams about what her life used to be like. Or else she would fantasise about the sort of fun and adventures she and Juanita could have if only they were best friends and her mam would let them play together.

She also went over in her mind all the teasing and tormenting she had to put up with at school. Even so, she was looking forward to going back to school because it would be warmer there than it was cooped up in an icy cold room all day at home.

She spent a great deal of time thinking about how the rest of the class would act when she went back to school again and how she would deal with them.

1927 is a brand new year, she told herself, so her New Year's resolution would be that, whatever happened, she would stand up to them.

All her plans came to nothing. The new school term proved to be a tremendous surprise. On her first day back she was ready to face up to whatever teasing came her way, but found that no one bothered her at all. Megan Edwards and

Ffion Jenkins, who had taunted her the most, seemed pleased to see her.

For the first couple of days Katie was cautious about talking to them, wondering what they were plotting. Then she realised there were other new kids for them to tease and chivvy, and that she was now accepted as one of the class.

Once Katie was back at school, Rachael knew she hadn't any excuse not to do something about finding a job. The trouble was she had no idea where else to look as she had tried shops in the city centre, hoping to find work as a counter assistant or in the storerooms.

Now she tried to find work as a waitress, kitchen hand or shop cleaner, but she had no success at all.

Every time she was turned down she suspected it was because of her shabby appearance, and since she didn't have the money to buy anything new she realised she'd have to lower her sights and take whatever was on offer in Tiger Bay.

Rachael studied cards in shop windows looking for work as a cleaner, but all the local jobs seemed to be in pubs or the doss houses used by Merchant seamen.

It wasn't the sort of environment she was used to and the very idea of working in one of those places scared her. She didn't really want to do cleaning at all, but it seemed she had no option, since no one considered her suitable for anything better and she desperately needed the money.

When she finally did manage to get a job, a few months later, it was as a cleaner in a pub in Adelaide Street. She hated the idea, but she took it because the pay wasn't too bad.

For the first few weeks she was at The Crown, Rachael found that the smell of stale beer and tobacco when she arrived each morning made her heave so much that she could hardly bring herself to collect up the beer mugs, empty out the dregs and wash them. She found it even more distasteful having to empty and clean the ashtrays and spittoons.

'You can overcome that easy enough, my lovely,' Dai Pritchard the landlord told her, when he found her leaning over the brownstone sink heaving as she cleaned a pile of ashtrays.

'And how do I do that then?' Rachael snapped, as she wiped the back of her hand across her mouth.

'Have a mouthful of beer and a drag on a fag before you start.'

'If I could afford to smoke and drink do you think I'd be doing this sort of work?' she asked sarcastically.

'Dammo di! It needn't cost you anything!' he grinned.

'How do you make that out? Are you giving beer and fags away?'

'Help yourself to a mouthful of the slops and

74

have a drag on some of the stubs in the ashtrays,' he told her.

Bile rose in her mouth at the very thought.

Dai Pritchard laughed uproariously, his beer belly shaking like a monstrous jelly.

A week later, though, unable to face the enormous pile of beer mugs and ashtrays left after a particularly roisterous night, Rachael remembered his words. Tipping a mix of slops into a clean mug she raised it to her mouth, tried to ignore the obnoxious smell, shut her eyes and gulped down a mouthful.

To her astonishment, Rachael found she liked the taste. She took another mouthful and swallowed it more slowly, savouring the flavour.

Dai was right, she conceded. Once she'd had a drink, the smell from the used glasses didn't seem distasteful and no longer affected her. What was more, it seemed to give her a new source of energy and at the end of the morning she felt nowhere near as exhausted as usual.

It took her several more weeks before she added smoking to her daily routine. She couldn't face the idea of half-smoked cigarettes that had been in someone else's mouth and then discarded. Instead, she collected a handful of butt-ends and selected the best of them, then opened them up, collected the tobacco, bought a packet of Rizla papers and started rolling her own cigarettes.

At first her efforts were thin and ineffectual, and burned out almost the moment she lit them.

Dai laughed at her efforts and showed her the right way to string out the strands of tobacco and then roll them up, tapping the ends to make sure they were firm as well as fat.

Rachael found herself looking forward to her early morning drink and cigarette. They're like medicine, she told herself. The beer gives me energy and the fag calms me down and stops me worrying about Katie, that's why I can work better.

Gradually she realised she was relying on them. Even worse, she wished she had a drink and a cigarette to enjoy when she was at home. Knowing that she couldn't afford either, she began saving beer dregs in a bottle to take home with her, together with a pile of cigarette stubs.

'If you are as desperate as that for a drink and a ciggie then why don't you come and work in the evenings?' Dai asked her.

'I have a little girl to look after. I can't leave her on her own, she's only nine,' Rachael replied.

'Duw anwyl, why ever not? She's got plenty of friends to play with, hasn't she? Now the nights are lighter she's probably out with them after school, anyway.'

'No, I don't let her play out. I insist she comes straight home from school.'

'There's miserable for her. Kiddies need to play and have a little adventure or two.'

'She's far too young to be playing out on the streets!'

76

Dai Pritchard shrugged his massive shoulders. 'You've only the one child? So that's why you coddle her so much. It's a hard world, cariad, she's got to learn to stand on her own two feet sometime, mind.'

'Maybe,' Rachael conceded, 'but leaving her on her own at night isn't the right way to do that.'

'Darw! Who said anything about night after night, cariad? What I was talking about was a couple of hours of an evening, two or three nights a week. You pick your own nights. From half five when we open until, say, eight o'clock. Now, what do you say?'

'Do you really need me?'

'I wouldn't be asking you otherwise. I'm not a charitable man, you know.'

'Well, then why do you need me here? Mrs Pritchard helps out in the evenings, doesn't she?'

'That's the whole point, my lovely. It's a long night for her and my wife's not getting any younger, see! Now if you or a barmaid are here for a couple of hours a few nights a week, it will give her a chance to put her feet up. Give her a new lease of life as well as putting some extra money in your pay packet.'

Rachael agreed to give it a try. 'Only until half seven at night, though,' she insisted.

Dai Pritchard agreed to the compromise.

'Start next week, then,' he said as she was packing up to leave around midday.

'You'll have to dress up a bit more, mind,' he commented. He put two pound notes down on the bar. 'Take these and get yourself a new dress. Something a bit fancy, if you know what I mean.'

Colour flooded Rachael's sallow cheeks. 'Hold on, I'm coming in to serve pints, nothing else!'

'Duw anwyl, so I should hope! What else did yer think I was expecting you to do, my lovely?' he blustered angrily.

Chapter Eight

Katie found that life changed overnight once her mother started to go out to work in the evenings at The Crown.

For the first two or three nights she felt frightened returning to the empty room on her own after school each day. It was quite different to being on her own in the mornings. Then, she was always in such a hurry to get washed, dressed and gobble down a slice of bread and margarine sprinkled with sugar that her mother had left ready for her breakfast, that she hardly noticed she was on her own.

It had all started the Friday her mam had returned home with two crisp pound notes in her hand and announced that they were going into town the next day, shopping. Her mam said she needed something smart to wear because from now on she was going to work at The Crown in the evenings as a barmaid, as well as being a cleaner there.

It had been quite an adventure because it was the first time since Nana Roberts had died that they'd been able to go into a dress shop to buy something.

Katie was delighted by the new arrangement

because it probably meant that she would be able to see Juanita after school, or Megan and Ffion who always hung around down by the canal in James Street in the evening.

'I want you in off the streets by seven, and to find you washed and ready for bed when I get home, mind,' Rachael told her.

'What about tea, Mam?'

'We'll have it before I go out. I won't need to leave until five o'clock. You come straight home from school, mind, so that we can have tea together. Then you can clear the dishes away while I get ready to go to work.'

'And I can go out afterwards?'

'Well, yes, I suppose so,' Rachael said reluctantly.

'It is light in the evenings now, Mam,' Katie pointed out.

'I know that, but you are only just nine! Mind, you behave yourself and don't go getting into any trouble. And be home by seven. I mean it now! If I find out you aren't, then I shall stop you going out at all in the evenings. Oh, and keep away from the boys. Even from that Aled Phillips.'

'Aled's my friend. He always stands up for me, he won't do me any harm.'

'You hang around with the girls and leave the boys alone,' Rachael told her firmly. 'Otherwise you can stay in at nights. Do you understand?'

Katie knew better than to argue. She didn't want to spoil her chance of playing out each evening. She'd learned quickly from her new friends about the vagaries of grown ups and she was pretty sure that, once her mam was settled into her new job, it was more than likely that it would be later than half seven when Rachael came home at night.

In that she was right. After the first few weeks, the time Rachael reached home became more like nine o'clock, and not long after that she would often be out until after the pub closed. It all depended on how busy they were at The Crown.

On Saturday nights it was usually closing time before she came away and by then she had downed so many drinks herself that she was wobbly on her legs, and usually stayed in bed for most of the day on Sunday.

Katie made the most of her freedom. As she turned eleven and more and more months passed, her confidence grew in leaps and bounds and, instead of meekly doing whatever the others asked her to do, she was often the one who planned their adventures.

Since she had the least restraint on what time she had to be home at night, the friends she played out with were in constant trouble over the late hour they reached home and the state of their clothes when they did.

After a time, overtired and fuddled by drink, Rachael seemed unaware of Katie's torn clothes or the fact that she often went to bed without even troubling to wash her face and hands. Her shoes were down at heel and there were holes in the soles of them that Katie covered over with newspaper or cardboard. Her long fair hair, that Nana Roberts had brushed so lovingly each night, until it shone like spun silk, was lank, greasy and full of nits.

Katie was so tired in the mornings that she usually had to rush to get to school, often without stopping to wash. In class she spent more time flicking paper pellets or bits of chalk at the others, or whispering to whoever was sitting next to her, than paying attention, so that her schoolwork suffered as a result.

Her knuckles were raw from Miss Wells rapping them with her ruler. Instead of tears, as would have happened a few months earlier, Katie would put out her tongue as Miss Wells walked back to her desk. This would bring a titter of admiration from the rest of the class.

Matters finally came to a head when Juanita's father, who often came into the pub for a drink, confronted Rachael about Katie's behaviour.

'Your Katie is a bad influence,' he told her angrily. 'I can't stop my girl talking to her in school because they are in the same class, but I certainly won't permit them to play together after school anymore.'

Bemused, Rachael faced up to the huge black man belligerently. 'Who do you think you are, ordering me about?' she snapped.

'Mrs Roberts, I am trying to make it quite

clear that I want you to see that your Katie keeps away from Juanita.'

Rachael was taken aback that a black man should speak to her like that. How dare he dictate what she and her daughter could do! Her face contorted with anger, but before she could answer him he'd turned on his heel and walked out.

Rachael was home early that night, and her mood became even blacker when she found Katie wasn't in their room.

She tore back downstairs and into Alys Morgan's room. 'Have you got my Katie down here?' she demanded accusingly.

'What would I be doing entertaining a dirty, scruffy little urchin like that,' Alys Morgan sneered. 'You should be ashamed of her! She's probably out running wild in the streets as usual. You should hear the tales I get told about the way she carries on.'

'What do you mean?' The colour drained from Rachael's face. 'She's a good kid. She's in at seven every night, so how much mischief can she get up to in a couple of hours?'

'You'd better ask her that, though I wouldn't think she'd tell you. You've only got to look at her to see what a little terror she's become. I blame you, Mrs Roberts. Lovely little girl she was when you first moved in. You've let her run wild, especially since you've been out every night at the pub.' She sniffed the air. 'That's the trouble with you, when you've been on the drink you don't notice what's going on around you.'

'What the hell are you implying?' Rachael asked defiantly. 'Let me tell you, I never spend a penny piece on booze. Takes me all the money I get to pay for that one stinking room upstairs and have enough left over to buy food for me and Katie.'

Alys Morgan shrugged her massive shoulders. 'How you spend your money is your business. It's sad to see a pretty child turn into a little guttersnipe, though. Leaving a girl of that age to fend for herself night after night, with no guidance or anyone caring where she is or what she's up to, she's bound to end up a bad lot.'

'So you're blaming me because she's not as well dressed as she was when we moved in here?'

'You're her mother! I offered to keep an eye on her when you first came here, but you were too high and mighty to accept my offer, weren't you?'

'I'm not standing here listening to your vicious babble any longer,' Rachael told her angrily.

'Well, if you're going out to look for your daughter then you'd better try down by James Street canal or else Mount Stuart Square, that's where the gang she mixes with usually hangs out, or so I'm told. She's one of the ringleaders.'

Still raging at the implication behind Mrs Morgan's words, Rachael went in search of

Katie. She wasn't in Mount Stuart Square and none of the crowd hanging around there had seen anything of her that night.

Shivering in the night air, that was now turning cold and wet as fine rain started to fall, Rachael turned back towards James Street bridge.

Even before she reached the canal bank, she sensed something was wrong. There were flashing lights, crowds of people and half a dozen policemen.

Two barges were moored there and as she hurried towards them, Rachael saw that two policemen were questioning a group of Lascar seamen.

Her heart pounding, Rachael looked around wildly to see if she could spot Katie.

As she elbowed her way through the angry mob to try and find out what was going on, Rachael found herself pushed roughly from one side to the other and she fought back, causing further uproar. A policeman stepped in and took her firmly by the arm.

'Leave me alone, I'm not one of your rabble,' she argued. She tried to pull herself free only to find that the pressure on her arm was increased.

'What are you doing here? Get on home before you get hurt.'

'I'm looking for my daughter,' she told him.

'Hardly likely to find her amongst this lot! Gang of little hooligans of every creed and colour.' He frowned. 'Hold on a minute, she's not a skinny fair-haired kid is she?' he asked suspiciously. 'If so, she started this rumpus!'

Rachael didn't answer. She was too afraid of what his reply might be. She had already spotted Katie being interviewed by the other policeman. At her side was the tall gangly figure of Aled Phillips.

As she edged closer, Rachael heard Aled defending Katie.

'She didn't do anything, officer,' he protested. 'We were all larking about, mind, and then these Lascars got huffy. They seemed to think we were making fun of them, see.'

'And were you?'

'No, of course not. We were only walking along behind them . . .'

'Following them back to their boats and aping the way they were shuffling along, one behind the other,' the officer said grimly.

'No mun, it wasn't like that at all,' Aled protested quietly.

'Look, I'm letting you off with a warning, but if you cause any more ructions I'll have you both up in court. Now is that understood?'

Without waiting for Aled to say anything he turned to Katie. 'You shouldn't be out on the streets in the dark at this time of night,' he told her severely. 'Haven't you got a home to go to?'

'Yes! One crummy room in Lousy Street,' she told him with a cheeky grin.

The words stabbed Rachael like a knife. Was this really what their life had descended to, one scruffy room in a back street of Tiger Bay? She thought back to their comfortable home in Cathays, the polished furniture, the clean bedding, the crisp curtains and the good food that Nana Roberts had put on the table every day, and she felt an overwhelming sense of shame that she had reduced her daughter to this.

Timidly, she reached out and touched Katie's arm. 'Come on, cariad, I've come to take you home,' she said softly.

Katie spun around in shocked surprise, staring at her mam, as if she was a stranger she'd never seen before.

'So, is this your daughter?' the policeman frowned.

Rachael nodded, too choked to speak.

'This isn't the first time she's been in trouble, you know,' he said accusingly.

'I'm sorry ... I didn't know.'

'You didn't know!' he repeated in disbelief. 'She says you live in one room and you say you didn't know she was out after dark every night, running wild?'

Rachael shook her head. 'I didn't know what was going on because I work in the evenings. By the time I get home she is always at home, usually in bed and asleep.'

The officer chewed on his lower lip thoughtfully. 'If you don't want her to end up in trouble then I think you should either change your work, or find someone to keep an eye on her when you're not at home. Next time I won't be so lenient. Understand?'

Rachael nodded. 'There won't be a next time,' she assured him.

'Make sure there isn't. As it is, it's only because that lad spoke up for her,' he nodded in the direction of Aled, 'that I'm not going to take the matter any further.'

'Like I said, there won't be a next time,' Rachael repeated. 'Things are going to change. I won't be out working at nights ever again after this, I assure you.'

He grunted his acceptance of her promise. 'Come on, go along home with your mam and don't let me see you in trouble again,' he told Katie, as he pushed her towards Rachael.

Chapter Nine

Katie's misadventure brought Rachael to her senses. She took her home and made them both a hot supper. Before Katie went to bed Rachael made sure she stripped off all her clothes and had a good wash.

Not long after Katie was in bed, Rachael crept in beside her, but for a long time she lay awake, pondering on what had happened to them since they'd left Catherine Street nearly three years earlier. Then she began going over and over in her head the changes she would have to make in the future.

They couldn't go on living in this one shabby room and putting up with all the inconveniences. It was this that had started the downward spiral and she had to do something to change things.

The very next morning she handed in her notice at The Crown. Dai Pritchard was furious. He was losing both a cleaner and a barmaid and he knew he would never be able to find a replacement for either job for what he was paying Rachael. She'd been desperate for work and he'd taken advantage of the fact. Nevertheless, he resented her giving in her notice.

As she walked away from The Crown, Rachael decided that if she had to be a cleaner then she'd aim for something better than Tiger Bay. She remembered some of the lovely houses around Roath Park, Wyvern Road and Wood-ville Road, and finally plucked up the courage to go and look for a cleaning job there.

It took her some days to find a domestic agency willing to take her on their books because of her lack of experience. When she did, the money was so low that after paying her tram fares and handing over five shillings rent each week to Alys Morgan, she had less than a pound left to feed both herself and Katie.

The work was hard and some of the women she was sent to work for were extremely fastidious and demanding.

There were cinders and ashes to be cleared away and then the grates had to be black-leaded and polished before she laid a new fire. There were flagstones to be scrubbed on her hands and knees, and steps and windowsills to be scrubbed and then whitened with pumice-stone. The drains had to be cleaned and disinfected with Condy's Fluid.

After that, she had to take up the rugs and mats and carry them outside, hang them over the clothes line and beat the dust out of them. If there were wood-block floors then these had to be polished until you could see your face in them.

At some of the houses she had to clean the

windows. It was a job she hated because she was always afraid that the big casement windows, where she had to push the panes right up and sit out on the window ledge to clean the outside of them, might come crashing down at any minute and trap her.

She tried to avoid houses where she was expected to do the washing on a Monday. Some of the boilers were hard to light and the room was always full of soapy steam that made her throat raw. It was hard work using the dolly tubs and she found turning the handles on some of the big mangles so exhausting that she had to keep taking a rest. Afterwards, she had to hang out the huge sheets and all the other things onto the clothes line stretched between two poles in the back yard. By the time she'd finished doing that she hardly had enough energy to push the heavy wooden clothes prop into position.

So much hard work seemed pointless, because there was never any money left over for the new clothes they both so desperately needed and certainly not for luxuries of any sort. The last of the money she'd got for Nana Roberts's furniture had long gone, and now they were so desperately poor that she was worried what would happen when the summer was over and winter came around again.

Over and over again she wished she'd not sold the bulk of her and Katie's clothes, because there was no way at all that she could replace them.

She unpicked her own one good frock and turned it inside out to make Katie a new dress for school, because she'd outgrown the only one she had left.

For Rachael there was the added problem that she missed the drink and cigarettes that had come her way each evening when she'd been at the The Crown. Some days she felt completely drained of energy, every bone in her body ached and her head thumped so badly that she felt she couldn't go on.

By the August of 1930, when there was no school for a whole month, she was at her wit's end wondering what to do with Katie. She'd made her promise to stop seeing Juanita after the girl's father had come to the pub complaining about them being together. Megan and Ffion had both been told not to go around with her after the scene at the canal. Alys Morgan sniffed when she timidly suggested she could keep an eye on her.

'I grant you she's a different girl these days and you've cleaned her up a treat, but I still don't want the responsibility,' she told Rachael. 'If she gets into trouble again the police will be down on her like a ton of bricks, and you'd blame me.'

In the end, Rachael decided that she couldn't afford to lose her job, so if there was no other way out then Katie would have to come along with her each morning.

'You can help me with the polishing and

dusting,' she told Katie, who groaned at the prospect.

To her surprise, after the first morning, Katie seemed to quite enjoy accompanying her.

'They're such lovely houses, Mam,' she would sigh dreamily. 'They're even better than where we lived in Catherine Street with Nana Roberts. I'd like to live in a grand house like this.'

'If wishes were horses then beggars would ride,' Rachael told her. 'I can't see us ever living in a place anywhere near as good as one of these.'

'Perhaps when dada comes home,' Katie said wistfully.

'That's enough of that sort of talk,' Rachael said sharply. 'We don't know when he will be coming home and I hope you haven't said anything about him to anyone in Louisa Street or at school.'

'Of course I haven't,' Katie told her hotly. 'I'm not stupid. I know that whatever happens we mustn't let anyone know he's in prison.'

Rachael nodded, but said nothing. She was seeing Katie with new eyes. She was right, she wasn't a child anymore, and yet she still should be. In the past few years, since they'd moved to Tiger Bay, Katie had grown from the shy trusting child she had been, into a girl who had become sharp and calculating because of the need to look after herself.

Surprisingly, Rachael found that taking Katie

to work with her had some unexpected bonuses. Some of the women she cleaned for were taken by the pretty young girl, and if they had young daughters of their own they would often hand over some of their own children's outgrown clothes.

At first, Rachael had been stung to the quick at accepting what she regarded as charity from the people she worked for, but common sense prevailed. She knew she couldn't afford to buy such things for Katie, and Katie didn't seem to mind in the least that they were someone else's cast-offs.

'They're new to me and they're nicer than what most of the other girls at school are wearing,' she grinned delightedly the first time she tried on a skirt and blouse that had been passed on for her.

'The skirt will look even nicer when I've taken in a seam and I can move the buttons on the blouse to make it fit better,' Rachael told her.

After that, Rachael swallowed her pride and accepted everything she was offered. Over the years, things which couldn't be altered to fit, or which Katie didn't like, she sold in one of the local street markets and used the money to buy other things that they needed.

It was still very hard making ends meet. During the summer when they not only ate less, but didn't need to heat up food or hot water for washing themselves, they managed to scrape by, but once the weather became colder it was a different matter.

Rachael felt piqued that despite all her hard work they were still only able to live in the one squalid room in Louisa Street. The atmosphere between herself and Alys Morgan was strained and she had little or nothing to do with any of the other occupants. She knew this was partly her own fault, and that it dated back to the first Christmas when she shunned their company by refusing to join the Belazzios for a drink.

Alys Morgan lived on gossip and Rachael was well aware that she would have liked them to leave, and for someone else to be in their room; someone who would drop in on her at least once a day and confide in her.

She had tried countless times to lure Katie into her kitchen with bribes of cakes and sweets, but, although Katie ached to accept them, she knew that if she did she would upset her mam so much that she dared not do so.

She wished her mam would become friendlier with the mothers of some of her school friends, but she knew this was out of the question. Even though she earned her living by cleaning other people's houses, Rachael still considered herself to be better than any of her neighbours, and even after living in Louisa Street for over five years still regarded it as only a temporary measure. She kept promising herself that when she could save up enough money then she and Katie would move.

A chance remark by Lloyd Woodman, the husband of one of her employers, gave Rachael the opening she so desperately needed.

'I wish I had someone who cleaned as thoroughly as you do, Rachael,' he commented, as he was leaving the house one morning. 'Would you be interested? A couple of hours each evening. My offices are just off The Hayes.'

Spurred on by the thought of the extra money Rachael agreed to take on the work. She found cleaning offices was not only far easier than housework, but much better paid.

She tried hard to save the extra money she was earning, but occasionally she found herself dipping into it for cigarettes. Time and again she wished she had never listened to Dai Pritchard. His cure for the nausea she'd felt when dealing with the revolting smell of stale beer and cigarettes in the bar each morning had created an addiction.

As she cleaned out the ashtrays in the offices, the smell made her long for a smoke. She'd even started saving the butt-ends and taking them home, but there was rarely enough to satisfy her craving.

Katie enjoyed the extra freedom. She was now at senior school along with Megan and Ffion and she would meet up with them and a crowd of other school friends in Mount Stuart Square or by James Street canal. Often there were gangs of older boys there, but Aled

Phillips was usually amongst them and the three girls always felt safe when he was around, because he seemed to have a soft spot for Katie.

Megan and Ffion teased her about him but Katie didn't mind. It gave her a lovely warm feeling inside to know that Aled cared about her so much. He was still tall and thin and had the most unruly brown hair she had ever seen, but he had such a friendly smile. It made her feel safe simply knowing that he was around whenever any of the other lads tried to get fresh with her.

Although she was just thirteen she had learned enough from whispered exchanges between herself, Megan and Ffion to know that some of the older boys they met down by the canal were not content to simply lark around.

Her two friends were prepared to let them take limited liberties, but Katie refused to be kissed or mauled in any way and, as a result, it sometimes made her a target for daredevils in the gang to egg each other on to try and overcome her resistance.

As the winter of 1931 approached, and the nights began to get dark earlier and earlier, she readily fell in with her mother's suggestion that she went with her to give a hand with the office cleaning at night.

'With the two of us at it then we'd be finished in just over an hour,' Rachael told her.

'Yes, and it would make things a bit easier for you as well, Mam,' Katie agreed.

Rachael was pleased and relieved by her ready acceptance. What she had said to Katie was true, working together they would finish earlier, but there was more behind Rachael's suggestion than she had told Katie.

When she had first started cleaning Lloyd Woodman's offices the arrangement had been that she arrived there a few minutes before six o'clock, before the staff left. Then, when she had finished cleaning, she was to make sure that all the lights were off and slam the front door behind her as she left.

In the intervening year it had all worked perfectly until Bryn Evans, the office manager, had started working late.

The first time it had happened he'd explained that it was the end of the company's financial year and that he had work he must complete and suggested that she left his office until last.

The first few evenings he had been ready to leave by the time she went along to his office with her cleaning materials. Then he had started to stop and chat to her while she worked.

He was a fat, flabby, red-headed man in his early thirties, and she found his supercilious manner rather intimidating. She even wondered sometimes whether, for all his apparent friendliness, he was checking up on her and making sure she was cleaning the place properly.

He made her feel very uncomfortable. His green eyes seemed to follow her every movement as she polished the desks and cleaned the floor. There always seemed to be discarded balls of paper under his desk so that she had to bend and stretch to reach them.

He chain-smoked and his ashtray was always overflowing. She hated having to throw all the fat stubs into the large bag she carried around the offices to collect up waste paper and rubbish, but she hadn't the nerve to put them to one side, not when he was watching her so avidly. Sometimes the smell from the cigarette he was smoking as he leaned against the wall watching her work was so tantalising that she longed to have one herself.

It was almost as if Bryn Evans sensed her craving, Rachael mused, and seemed to deliberately exhale a stream of smoke in her direction. One night, when she thought she couldn't stand it any longer he had surprised her by offering her a cigarette.

She'd hesitated for a moment, wondering whether or not she should even admit that she smoked, then, overcome by her craving, she had accepted.

After that, the first thing he did the moment she went into his office was to offer her a cigarette. She could never bring herself to refuse, although each time she took one she felt that she was compromising herself in some way.

Her suspicions were justified. Once he had established the nightly routine it was only a few weeks before he made it clear that he was expecting something in return.

She steeled herself to accept the snatched kiss, the pat on the rump as she bent to pick things up, or leaned across the desk while polishing it. She tried to ignore his sly suggestions and sexual innuendos.

Bryn Evans didn't give in easily. When his persistence didn't have the desired impact he resorted to other tactics. When she resisted he used force, and when she angrily rounded on him he threatened to tell Lloyd Woodman that she was leaving early and that her work wasn't satisfactory.

'Lose your cleaning job here, and you'll lose it at his house in Woodville Road,' he warned.

Rachael shook her head. 'No I won't, he knows what a good cleaner I am. He asked me to come and do his offices, I didn't ask him for the job.'

'Oh, he'll sack you when he knows there's a question of honesty involved,' Bryn told her with a sneer, his mouth twisting into a cruel line.

'Honesty?' Rachael frowned, puzzled by his words. 'What do you mean? I wouldn't dream of taking anything and, anyway, there's nothing here I would want.'

'What about money?'

Rachael look bemused. 'As far as I know there isn't any money here, and if there was I wouldn't touch it.'

Bryn Evans pulled out the top drawer of his desk, took out a tin box and lifted the lid. Inside were some white five-pound notes, one-pound notes and a selection of small change. He lifted out the notes, waved them in her face and then stuffed them into the inside pocket of his jacket.

'Petty cash!' he leered. 'Supposing when I tell him that it has gone missing, I also tell him that I saw you take it.'

'How could I? That drawer is always locked.'

'So you've tried to find it before, have you?' he gloated. 'So if I am ever in a hurry and forget to lock the drawer, you'll be in there!'

'How dare you! I shall report what you have said to Mr Woodman.'

Bryn's green eyes narrowed. 'I wouldn't do that if I was you. It would be your word against mine and I know who he will believe.'

Without another word he turned on his heel and walked out of the office and she heard the front door slam behind him.

For a long time Rachael stayed where she was, clutching the edge of the desk and trying to control her shaking. He was right of course. If it came to his word against hers then he would win every time. But what was the alternative, she asked herself. She could give up her cleaning job there or she could give in to his demands.

It was only when she was walking home that a third way out came to her. She could take

Katie along with her in the evenings. He could hardly attack her if Katie was there with her.

Chapter Ten

Rachael had thought that taking Katie with her when she went to clean Lloyd Woodman's offices would save her from any further involvement with Bryn Evans, but she was disappointed.

He saw through her ploy immediately, and it seemed to make him more determined than ever to exert his power over her. Therefore, he stalked her more assiduously than ever. Instead of waiting in his office until she came to clean there he began to follow her around.

She tried remonstrating with him when he sneaked up behind her, kissing the nape of her neck, fondling her breasts or running his hands over her buttocks, but he only laughed, a contemptuous sneer on his face. Time and again she threatened to report him to Lloyd Woodman, but he always reminded her that if she did that then he would retaliate by saying he had caught her stealing from the petty-cash box.

Her dilemma increased when he started appearing without warning in the most unlikely places. She found herself scurrying along the corridors and peeping into the offices before she went in them when she wasn't sure where he was.

Whenever she could, Rachael tried to make sure Katie was with her, but it wasn't possible for them to work alongside each other all the time and Bryn Evans took advantage of this fact. It was a cat and mouse situation and Rachael began to feel so nervous and on edge the whole time she was working there, that she wondered if she would be better giving up the job.

The evening when he cornered her as she was cleaning the office toilets frightened her a great deal. He grabbed hold of her, and despite her efforts to push him away, savagely forced himself on her.

Rachael struggled wildly, but, despite his flabby appearance, Bryn Evans was strong and pinned her down. She wanted to cry out, but she was afraid of frightening Katie, so she resorted to kicking, biting and scratching in the hope that he would let her go.

Her efforts were completely ineffectual and only seemed to heighten his lust for her. Pushing her up against the wall he tore her dress from one shoulder and then lifted her skirts to her waist.

In sheer panic she wrenched one of her hands from his grasp and tore down his face with her nails, making him yelp with pain.

'I'll get you for this, you bitch,' he vowed, as he dabbed at the long bloody graze she'd made right down his cheek.

Rachael was too shaken to answer. Her legs were trembling, her heart beating wildly and she was shivering uncontrollably. To add to her distress, she saw Katie was standing in the doorway. From the shocked expression on Katie's face Rachael realised she must have witnessed most of what had happened.

Quickly, with trembling hands, she made an attempt to pull her dress together and straighten her clothes. She tried desperately to think of the right words to explain to Katie what had happened, but her mind was a complete blank. As Bryn Evans pushed past them, fastening his flies as he did so, all she could do was hold Katie in her arms and hug her close, their tears mingling, hoping she would understand.

She knew she had badly marked Bryn Evans's face, and when she discovered the next day that he was not feeling well and was taking a few days off work, she hoped he had learned his lesson and that from now on he would leave her alone.

It was well over a week before Bryn Evans returned to work. In the meantime, Lloyd Woodman waited behind each evening to let Rachael in, and she wondered whether she ought to tell him what had happened and that she couldn't go on working there any longer. Then, as the days passed and she'd still not summoned up the courage to do so, she reasoned that perhaps it was better to put the incident from her mind and try to forget it had ever happened.

She enjoyed the work; the money was good and no one objected to Katie being with her. They made a good team and if they were left alone to get on with things they were finished in little over an hour each evening.

The one thing that did trouble her deeply since the incident with Bryn Evans was that Katie had been very quiet and subdued.

When it came to the weekend and she made no effort to go out, Rachael felt very concerned. Usually, Katie wanted to spend as much time as possible with Ffion and Megan, and Rachael wondered if she had broken off her friendship with the two girls.

'Aren't you going up to The Hayes to have a look around the market with your friends, then?' she asked, when after breakfast on Saturday morning she found Katie curled up on the bed reading a magazine.

Katie shook her head, but offered no explanation as to why she was staying at home.

'You always go off with them on a Saturday morning, don't you feel well?' Rachael persisted.

'I'm fine.' Katie kept her head buried in the magazine but her voice was shaky.

'Come on, out with it. Have you fallen out with them?' Rachael insisted.

When Katie didn't answer, Rachael snatched the book out of her hands. When Katie went to grab it back, Rachael saw that her eyes were brimming with tears.

Rachael perched herself on the side of the bed and put her arm around Katie's shoulders. 'What's the squabble about?' she asked.

Katie shook her head and chewed on her lower lip. She wanted to confide in her mam, but she was afraid that if she told her why Ffion and Megan had refused to let her go with them, she would end up in deep trouble herself.

'Has it got something to do with what happened the other evening when we were cleaning the offices?'

Katie nodded. 'Yes, in a way,' she whispered.

She knew she should never have told Ffion and Megan about what she had seen take place between her mam and Bryn Evans, but she'd felt so confused and so upset that she'd needed to talk to someone.

Now, she felt so guilty about telling them that she wanted to talk to her mam about it, but she was so afraid she wouldn't understand and that they might have a terrible row. If she fell out with her mam as well as with Megan and Ffion she'd have no one.

She hadn't wanted to go with her mam to clean the offices the next night, but she hadn't been able to think of any way to get out of it. Her mam hadn't seemed to be very happy about going either, and Katie decided she ought to go to make sure Bryn Evans didn't attack her mam again.

She'd been so relieved when they found Lloyd Woodman waiting to let them in. When he told them that Bryn Evans wasn't well and would be off work for a few days, Katie hoped that would be the end of the matter.

She tried hard to put the incident out of her mind, but she found she couldn't. She wished her mam would talk to her about it, but Rachael remained tight-lipped. Katie suspected it was because she was also trying to forget what had happened.

She'd confided in Ffion and Megan because they were her best friends and seemed to know so much more about such things than she did. She'd been hoping that they would say it wasn't such a terrible thing as she thought.

Instead, they'd gaped at her open-mouthed as if unable to believe what she was telling them. Ffion had gone home and told her mother, who had immediately dashed around to see Megan's mam, and the two of them had decided that neither Megan nor Ffion were to have anything more to do with Katie Roberts.

She'd been utterly shocked when they told her that at school the next day.

'My mam says that your mam is nothing better than a whore,' Ffion said contemptuously.

'And mine says you probably don't have a proper dad at all, and that it's only a tale your mam has put about that he is working away. She says that your mam probably had a fling with some drunken sailor and you are the result,' Megan informed her.

She had hotly denied this and then, as they'd gone on taunting her about her mam, she'd gone for both of them. The three of them had ended up fighting.

It had been two to one and if Aled Phillips hadn't intervened she would probably have come off far worse than she did. As it was, she managed to pull Megan's long dark hair and tear a big rent in Ffion's smart red skirt before he separated them.

In return they had ripped a sleeve out of her blouse and one of them had kicked her hard on the shin, breaking the skin so that her leg was streaming with blood.

She refused to tell him why they were fighting like alley cats. She let him staunch the cut on her leg with his handkerchief and when she got home she told her mam that she'd fallen over.

It had led to one lie after another, she thought unhappily. She believed she had got away with it, and that her mam had accepted her story about falling over.

She had expected it to all blow over at school as well, but it hadn't. Megan and Ffion had cold-shouldered her, and since so many of the other girls started giving her queer looks she suspected that they had repeated to some of the others what she had told them.

It wasn't until after school on Friday evening,

when they usually made plans about what time they would meet the next day to go up to The Hayes, that she discovered the truth.

'I told you, my mam says I'm not to have anything more to do with you,' Ffion reminded her.

'And mine says you're a bad influence and I'm to keep away from you and not go out with you any more,' Megan added.

The two of them had linked arms and gone off giggling, leaving her to walk home on her own.

Aled Phillips had caught up with her and walked as far as the end of Louisa Street with her, but she'd been so choked by what had happened that she could hardly talk to him.

'Listen, Katie,' he said awkwardly. 'I heard what happened to your mam and I'm sorry. Anyway, it wasn't your fault so you shouldn't get upset about it,' he added gruffly.

Katie, her face scarlet, stared at him in disbelief. 'What are you talking about?' she demanded.

'I . . . know what happened,' he stuttered.

'No you don't. Besides, nothing happened to *me*. Who told you, anyway?'

'Rees Jenkins overheard Ffion telling his mam, and then he heard his mam telling Megan Edwards's mam.'

The colour drained from Katie's face. 'He's a liar,' she stormed, 'they're all liars.' With tears streaming down her face she ran the rest of the way home, feeling that her entire world had fallen apart.

She knew she should never have told anyone about what happened, but she'd felt so bottled up inside she'd thought she was going to burst. What was more, she'd really thought that since Megan and Ffion were her best friends they would understand how upset she was, and that she could trust them to keep her secret.

Chapter Eleven

Katie breathed a sigh of relief when school finally broke up for Easter. Her last few weeks there, ever since the news had spread about her mam being attacked by Bryn Evans, had been the unhappiest she could remember. In many ways it was even worse than when she had first come to the school, when she'd been only eight years old.

It was 1932 now, in another month she would be fourteen, and having been close friends with Ffion and Megan for such a long time, she found it very hurtful that neither of them would speak to her. Even worse was the fact that they were spreading all sorts of malicious rumours about her and her mam.

It wouldn't have been quite so bad, she thought, if she could have talked about it to her mam, but Rachael had been frightened by the incident that had caused all the trouble and she refused to discuss it.

By the time Bryn Evans had returned to work, the scratch on his face had healed completely and almost disappeared.

On their first night at work after he'd come back, both Rachael and Katie had been on edge, wondering what sort of retaliation he might make.

He kept them on tenterhooks, never saying or doing anything to upset them in any way. In fact, he practically ignored them and didn't speak to them at all unless he absolutely had to do so.

Nevertheless, there was a sinister atmosphere and for the rest of the week they'd both breathed a sigh of relief each evening when their work was finished and it was time to leave.

'I think that perhaps I should give up cleaning those offices,' Rachael said worriedly one evening, as they walked back down Bute Street. 'It makes my nerves jangle just to be in the same building as that man.'

'I don't think he'll ever try anything on with you again,' Katie told her.

'You don't know men, my girl. And he's a particularly nasty type,' her mother warned.

In that, Rachael was right. And so, in a way, was Katie. Bryn Evans completely ignored Rachael, but he began to take an avid interest in Katie. He never spoke to her, but he watched her every movement. He followed as she went from one office to the next. Sometimes he stood by the window, as if unaware that she was in the room. On other occasions he leaned against the door watching her work.

She tried to make light of it when Rachael became worried and again said that it might be better if they gave up the job, but she felt as jumpy as a cricket. For such a bulky man he was incredibly light on his feet and seemed to be able to come into a room without her hearing him.

The evening when he crept up behind her while she was stretching over, polishing Lloyd Woodman's massive mahogany desk, she was momentarily petrified. Then, as he slid his hands up under her skirt she screamed out at the top of her voice.

Rachael came running, as she knew in an instant what his intentions were. As she rushed at him, he picked up a chair and swung it at her. One of the legs caught her with a blow across the temple. The force not only floored her, but also knocked her almost unconscious.

Without a word, Bryn Evans walked out of the room.

Katie went down on her knees, cradling Rachael in her arms. She breathed a sigh of relief when she heard the outside door slam and knew that Bryn Evans had left the building.

For several minutes Rachael was too dazed to even get up. Her head was spinning and Katie could see a huge bump swelling up on her mam's temple, where the chair had caught her.

'I'll go and soak one of the tea-towels in cold water to put on your forehead,' she told her. 'It will help to get the swelling down. You'll probably have a black eye in the morning, mind!'

'No, don't bother doing that, you stay here where you're safe,' Rachael told her anxiously.

'He's gone. I heard the outside door slam, so I'm safe enough now, Mam,' Katie assured her.

'I'm not going back there ever again,' Rachael vowed later that evening, after they were safely at home, and Katie had made her a cup of tea and was fussing over her.

'He'll not try anything on again,' Katie argued. 'He knows he's no match for you, Mam.'

Rachael shook her head. 'I don't trust him.'

'Well, report him to Mr Woodman.'

'That would be a waste of time. He's an important member of staff, far more important than me, cariad, so Mr Woodman is going to take his word about what happened, not mine.'

'If you give up cleaning the offices then you will probably lose your job cleaning the Woodmans' house in Woodville Road,' Katie pointed out.

'I know, I've thought about that, my lovely, and I've decided I'd rather that happened than have any more run-ins with Bryn Evans,' Rachael said firmly.

And that had been the end of the matter as far as Rachael was concerned. She'd made sure she reached the Woodmans' house early the next day so that she would catch Mr Woodman before he left for the office. She told him exactly what had happened and that Bryn Evans had assaulted both her and Katie.

However, he had obviously heard a different side of the story from Bryn Evans and tried to dismiss the incident as a trivial matter of no great importance.

Rachael was hurt and angry by his attitude. She picked up the canvas bag with her apron in it, that she'd put down on the hall table when she'd entered the house, and opened the front door to leave.

'Come now, you can't walk out on us!' he said, with a placating smile. 'I'll find another cleaner for the offices, but you can't let my wife down like this!'

'Since you don't seem to believe what I am telling you, then I think it is much better that I do leave,' Rachael told him stiffly.

He studied her black eye and the huge bruise on her temple and tried another tack.

'Look, I know it has been rather an unfortunate episode and I will certainly talk to Mr Evans about it, but even if you prefer not to go back there to work, you can't let us down here,' he persisted.

Rachael shook her head. 'It's not as if it's the first time. Now he has attacked my daughter!'

'Look, we had a party last night and there's a draining board piled high with dirty glasses and dishes. Who's going to see to them if you walk out on us now?' he asked in a jovial tone.

Rachael shook her head. 'I'm not staying. Mrs Woodman will have to see to them herself.'

His mouth tightened and his manner changed.

'If you walk out then I shall send in a report to the domestic agency who sent you to us, and tell them that you are unreliable,' he threatened. 'And if I do that,' he went on when Rachael made no response, 'they will not only dismiss you, but take you off their books so you won't be able to get any other work from them. Do you understand?'

Rachael clamped her lips together to try and stop herself from saying anything, knowing that whatever she said it would be to her detriment.

'Let her go, Lloyd,' Mrs Woodman said sharply. 'I couldn't tolerate having her around when she can be so insolent. Cleaners are two a penny, darling.'

It had been equally difficult for Katie. Not only had she lost her two best friends at school, but she was constantly taunted by the rest of the class.

The one exception was Aled Phillips, but she refused to have anything to do with him in school. She knew that if he was seen talking to her then he would be teased and derided by the rest of the class, and she liked him far too much to let that happen.

She only talked to him when she saw him in the street and no one else was around. When she explained her reason for this Aled was indignant and then told her she was being daft, but she refused to change her mind.

'You're the only friend I've got,' she told him.

His long thin face went scarlet with gratitude and embarrassment. He stretched out a bony hand and awkwardly squeezed her arm. 'Thanks, Katie. Don't worry about any of the others, I'll always be there for you.'

There was such a devoted look in his soft brown eyes that Katie felt it was like gazing into the eyes of a faithful, loving dog. She was touched that he cared so much, and her appreciation deepened a few days later when Rees Jenkins waylaid her on the way home.

He was on his bike and he circled her menacingly as she walked along the pavement, his dark beady eyes shining maliciously.

She tried to ignore him and probably would have managed to do so if he hadn't started taunting her about what had happened to her mother.

'Bet you're a go-er just like her,' he said snidely, riding across her path and forcing her to stop.

She tried to walk around him, but he was not having it. Leaning over the handlebars he thrust his pimply face, with its big nose and beady eyes, so close to hers that she could smell the cigarette smoke on his breath.

Katie quickly stepped back. At the same time he reached out and grabbed at the front of her dress, ripping it open almost to her waist.

'Got great tits for a kid,' he leered. 'Going to give me a feel then?'

Before she could speak or scream a scrawny arm shot out and a bony hand grabbed at Rees Jenkins greasy dark hair, yanking his head back so hard that he lost his balance and fell sideways, his bicycle crashing down heavily on top of him.

Leaving Rees to untangle himself from the spinning wheels and twisted handlebars, Aled Phillips grabbed Katie's arm and pushed her clear, then escorted her over to the other side of the road and hurried her on towards Louisa Street.

'Stay out of his way, he's a bad lot,' he told her gruffly. 'He won't bother you again, though, I'll see to that.'

Katie tried to thank Aled, but she still felt so shocked by what had happened that she could only gulp and nod.

'Go on, you'll be OK now,' he told her, as they reached the corner of her street. 'I'll wait here until I see you go indoors.'

After that, although the evenings were growing lighter all the time, Katie felt too nervous to go out.

She knew Aled kept an eye out for her, but she couldn't expect him to always be there if anything went wrong and she didn't trust Rees Jenkins. She'd never liked him even when she'd been friendly with Ffion. He was always making suggestive remarks, but she knew he daren't do anything more than that, because he'd be in trouble if Ffion told her dad.

She wished she didn't have to stay in every night. The room was so tiny and there was nowhere to sit, except on the bed. Her mother wasn't very good company. She had become so depressed since the incident with Bryn Evans and found solace in smoking. Cramped as they were in the one room, the smell of cigarette smoke pervaded everywhere. Sometimes Katie thought she would choke if she couldn't have some fresh air, but her mam hated her opening the window.

'You let out all the heat when you do that,' she grumbled. 'It's cold enough in here as it is.'

As the evenings got longer and longer, Katie tried to persuade her mam to go for a walk with her, even if it was only around the neighbouring streets, but Rachael couldn't even summon up the energy to do that.

'Who wants to tramp around Tiger Bay, it's full of coloured people and ruffians,' she protested. 'It's not as though we have the money to go for a drink or even go to the pictures.'

'Now I'm fourteen I can leave school at the end of term and start work, and then we'll have more money. We'll be able to add it to the money we saved when we were cleaning those offices and then we can move to somewhere better,' Katie said hopefully.

'In your dreams, cariad. All that money is gone! We've been dipping into it for food and clothes.'

Katie stared at her mother in disbelief. How

could the money be gone? She'd helped to earn that money and her mam had promised that she would save every penny of it towards moving away from Louisa Street.

Her mother still had her daily cleaning jobs. Even though Lloyd Woodman had threatened to lodge a complaint with the domestic agency she worked for, he hadn't done so. Or if he had, then nothing had come of it. After she had stopped going to the Woodmans' house, the domestic agency had sent her somewhere else.

Katie felt resentful that they hadn't moved out of Louisa Street ages ago, since they both hated it there.

Most of the people who'd been living there when they'd first arrived had moved away, all except the Chinese family and they still didn't speak to anyone else in the house. Some of the new tenants were even worse than the previous ones. One family had a young baby that cried for hours on end most nights and kept them awake. The baby's mother was sluttish and often left the baby's soiled napkins on the worktop in the makeshift kitchen.

Katie couldn't put the thought that their precious hoard of money was all gone out of her head. They weren't living any better and neither of them had any new clothes. She still had to line her shoes with pieces of cardboard to cover up the holes in the soles, because her mam said there was no point in buying new ones while her feet were still growing so fast.

If the money was all gone then it meant that her mam must have spent it on cigarettes, Katie thought resentfully. She had promised to try and give them up, but as far as Katie could see she smoked more than ever these days. She couldn't understand why she did it. She said she got comfort from them, but Katie couldn't believe that.

She'd tried taking a drag on one of her mam's fags on the sly, and she'd found it horrible. The hot smoke had made her eyes water, seared her tongue and almost choked her. She'd been coughing for ages afterwards and vowed she'd never touch another one. Yet her mam smoked all the time, sometimes even lighting a new one from the stub of the old one.

To help pass the time until the end of term, Katie pinched a sheet of paper from one of her exercise books and brought it home and made a calendar out of it. Every morning she marked off the days until the time when she would be able to leave school.

She spent her evenings and weekends dreaming about the sort of job she would like to do. She didn't want to be a cleaner, she knew that for sure, and she didn't fancy working in a factory.

She couldn't believe her ears when Rachael suggested that at the weekend they should have a trip into town, to have a look around and see if there was a dress she fancied.

'What's the point when we can't afford it?

You didn't buy me a birthday present because you said we'd spent all the money we'd saved up,' Katie reminded her.

'I know that, cariad, but I'll take out a Provvy cheque.'

'Oh, Mam! You said you would never do a thing like that,' Katie protested. 'You always said it was asking for trouble to take out one of those because they charge so much interest. You always said you ended up paying back double what you'd borrowed.'

'Yes, I know all about that, my lovely, but leaving school is a milestone in your life. Anyway, it won't cost anything to look at a new dress and you must have some new shoes ready for when you start work.'

They were both so excited by the prospect of the forthcoming trip, deciding which shops they would go to, that they were startled when there was a rapping on the door of their room.

Rachael frowned. 'Who can that be?' she whispered. 'We're not making a noise and I gave Alys Morgan her rent first thing this morning.'

Katie shook her head. 'Shall I go and see?'

Before Rachael could speak, the door opened. A man stood there. A stocky broad-shouldered man with a shock of black hair, a square chin, and grey eyes set in a deeply-lined face. He was wearing a dark navy suit and white shirt. Although the suit fitted across his wide shoulders it hung loosely as though he had lost weight, or as if it had been made for a man with a fuller figure.

He strode into the room, his grey eyes disdainful as he looked around.

'Christ, this is a tip! It's hardly any bigger than my cell was in Cardiff jailhouse!' he sneered.

'Lewis!' Rachael gasped. She stared at him in disbelief. 'I didn't think you'd be out for ages yet.'

'Extra time off for my good behaviour,' he said laconically.

Katie stared at him uncertainly. 'Dad?' she gasped.

'That's right! Does your old dad get a welcome home kiss, then?'

Chapter Twelve

Five and a half years in prison had left a marked impression on Lewis Roberts. Gone were his smooth good looks. Instead, his face was etched with lines and furrows. Gone was his smooth manner and charm. Now he was an embittered man who was determined to get back from life what justice and society had taken from him.

Six years had also made their mark on Rachael. He remembered her as slim, fresh-faced and bandbox neat. Now, although she wasn't yet forty, she looked grim with despair. Her hair was streaked with grey, her face was lined, her mouth turned down and there were dark shadows under her once bright hazel eyes.

He also found it hard to take in that Katie was so tall and attractive, and no longer the little girl he'd seen clutching at her mother's skirts when they'd taken him off to prison.

His first impression of the small, squalid room his wife and daughter were occupying stayed with him, and he was continually carping on about the fact that he'd had more space in his prison cell.

Katie had fantasised for so long about her father's homecoming, although her memory of him was now a childish blur. The picture she had built up of what he was like had a dreamlike quality to it. She now found that, in so many ways, her real dad was nothing like what she had imagined him to be.

He was still good looking in a hard brash way with his shock of black hair and chiselled features, but his grey eyes had a cunning gleam in them and his face was deeply lined.

She hated the way he swaggered about the place and bullied her mam all the time. Like her mam he chain-smoked, and she shivered whenever he touched her with his nicotine-stained fingers.

Worst of all, she resented the fact that he insisted on sharing their bed. Her mam slept in the middle and she kept as far over to her edge of the bed as she possibly could, but she still found it distasteful.

He not only snored noisily, but every night she was aware of him pawing her mam. At first he had waited until after he thought she was asleep, but after his first week at home he no longer troubled to do that, especially when he had been out drinking.

There were constant rows between him and her mam. Two months after he'd come out of prison he was still refusing to even look for work, because he was still getting public assistance money.

'I mean to let the buggers keep me for as long as I can,' he boasted. 'They had to keep me when I was inside and they can do the same now.'

'If you got a job then we might be able to afford to move, and Katie could have her own bedroom,' Rachael pointed out.

'What's wrong with where she sleeps now?'

When Rachael made no answer he swung her around to face him. 'Bloody well answer when I speak to you, woman,' he bellowed.

Katie tried to intervene, but he pushed her roughly aside. 'Keep out of this. If you were working as you should be, you great lollop, then with your wages we'd be able to afford a better place.'

'Katie leaves school in a few weeks time, so she will soon be working,' Rachael told him placatingly.

Knowing there was nothing further he could say on the matter, Lewis stomped out of the house, and Katie and Rachael breathed a sigh of relief because they knew that they wouldn't see him again until almost midnight when he would come rolling home drunk.

On occasions like this, Katie always tried to make sure she was in bed and even if she wasn't asleep she pretended to be so.

Lewis would burst into the house and stumble up the stairs to their room, singing at the top of his voice. Alys Morgan would yell out to him to make less noise as he was disturbing everyone. Lewis would retaliate by shouting drunken abuse. Others in the house joined in the melee until a thumping on walls from the adjoining houses quietened them all down.

Next day, both Rachael and Katie felt ashamed to show their faces. Once Lewis recovered from his hangover he would saunter down to Alys Morgan's overcrowded kitchen, and apologise with such charm for having caused a disturbance that she would invite him in for a drink. The two of them would sit there gossiping and smoking until Rachael arrived home from her cleaning jobs and Katie came in from school.

However, the minute they were back in their own small, cramped space, his temper would rise and unless they moved quickly out of arm's reach, one of them, or sometimes both, would be on the receiving end of his clenched fist.

He never apologised for his behaviour. Instead, he expected them to placate him. Rachael would scurry around trying to prepare a meal in the confines of their one room and the shared kitchen on the landing. Knowing that, no matter what she cooked, Lewis would not find the results very appetising, more often than not Rachael sent Katie out for fish and chips.

The minute he'd finished eating, if he had any money in his pocket, Lewis would take himself off to one of the nearby pubs. Otherwise, he'd go downstairs and spend the rest of the evening playing cards with Alys Morgan.

She'd taken a great liking to Lewis and even

kept a supply of his favourite beer and cigarettes handy. They'd play cards late into the
evening. When he had money to bet, he did.
When his pockets were empty, he used IOU's,
but his skill was such that he invariably won.
Often, the stakes, and his resultant win, were
high enough to cover the rent for the coming
week.

He tried not to let Rachael know about this.
Since he insisted on being the one to take the
rent downstairs to Alys, it invariably went into
his own pocket. Whenever Rachael found out,
and asked him what would happen if he didn't
win, there were rows between them that more
often than not ended in blows.

Katie looked forward more and more to
leaving school and finding work. She had
already tried for several jobs, but each time
someone who was a friend or was related to the
owner was given preference.

'I don't know why they bother putting cards
in the window saying they need an assistant,'
she would grumble when she came home,
disappointed to find that once again the job had
already been taken.

'Go into town and look for something,' Lewis
told her. 'You'd get better money there for a
start.'

'I'd have to pay tram fares,' she pointed out.

'You've got to spend to accumulate,' he
grinned. 'Take my advice, set your sights as
high as you can.'

'That's rich, coming from you,' Rachael told him bitterly. 'You haven't contributed a penny piece to the housekeeping since you came out of prison.'

'All in good time,' he told her. 'I've got a nice little project in mind. Just waiting for it to develop.'

'So, what is it?' Rachael demanded.

Lewis tapped the side of his nose with his index finger. 'I don't want to build your hopes up yet,' he told her evasively.

Lewis's great scheme was not work for himself, but for Katie. In many ways he was proud of his daughter. At fourteen she was well developed and very appealing, with her big grey eyes and heart-shaped face. Her long straight hair was as fair now as it had been when she was a toddler. She still wore it in plaits, although every week she threatened to have it cut short in one of the fashionable bobs as soon as she had the money to do so.

In his opinion, the only thing she lacked was nerve. She was far too shy and restrained to make an impression. His spell in prison had taught him that you had to be bold and face up to people if you wanted to get anywhere.

He blamed Rachael for being over-protective. He knew nothing about the incident between Rachael and Bryn Evans and so he had no idea why Katie was snubbed at school. Consequently, he blamed it on her reticence.

'Shut up in this one crummy room, the pair of

you have lost contact with the outside world,' he'd sneer, when he was in one of his disparaging moods. 'Look at you both! I've seen long-stretch prisoners who had more spirit in them than either of you two. You never go anywhere or do anything.'

'How are we supposed to go places and live it up, when it takes us all our time to put food in our bellies?' Rachael asked him bitterly.

'Ambition! That's what you need, mun! As long as you're content to scrub and clean for other people, you'll never get anywhere. I'll make damn sure Katie doesn't end up as a skivvy. You wouldn't catch me kowtowing to my so-called betters, I can tell you!'

'Never catch you working at all,' Rachael told him sourly.

These arguments usually ended in a row. Lewis would backhand her for answering back. Katie would try and stop them fighting. The two women would end up in tears. Lewis, if he could find any money in Rachael's purse, would go to the pub to get blind drunk.

Lewis meant what he said when he insisted that, whatever happened, Katie wouldn't become a cleaner like her mother.

The week before she was due to leave school, he came home at tea-time with a grin on his face and an even greater swagger in his step.

'I've got a job all waiting for you, cariad, when you leave school next week,' he told Katie.

'What sort of job?' Rachael asked worriedly.

'One she'll love. It's all fixed. She'll need a new dress and some shoes though, but a Provvy loan will take care of that, and she can pay it back herself out of her wages.'

'Putting the kid in debt before she even starts to earn,' Rachael sniffed disparagingly.

'I've told you before, you've got to speculate to accumulate.'

'So where is this wonderful job then? In James Howell's emporium?'

'No! It's not far away from there, though!' He laughed as he saw the puzzled looks on their faces, playing with their hopes like a dog with a bone.

'So where is it I'm going to be working then?'

'The Hayes!'

He paused again, watching the hopes and bewilderment that flickered over their faces.

'Doing what?' Rachael demanded.

'Serving on one of the stalls!'

'You call that a good job, out in the open in all weathers!' Rachael said in disgust.

'Better than on your knees scrubbing some snotty woman's kitchen floor,' he snapped angrily.

'It sounds good, Dad,' Katie said quickly, hoping to forestall the row she could see was about to flare up between the two of them. 'What will I be selling?'

'Bits and bobs! You know, reels of cotton, ribbons, stockings, material, that sort of stuff.'

Katie looked relieved. 'You mean I'll be working on the haberdashery stall?'

'That's right. You won't even be getting your hands dirty.'

'She'll be on her feet all day and she'll be working out of doors in all weathers,' Rachael repeated.

'No, she won't! They've got a bloody great canopy over the stall so that none of them or their stuff gets wet when it rains.'

'And what about in winter when it's freezing?'

'She'll bloody well have to wrap up warm, won't she. A bit of fresh air won't kill her, do her good in fact. She certainly doesn't get any in this sodding place. It stinks to high heaven most of the time.'

'Yes, especially when you've been out on the beer and come home belching all over the place,' Rachael told him in withering tones.

'And what about your cigarettes. Place stinks of tobacco smoke.'

'You smoke as well!'

'If I get this job then perhaps with your wages and mine we'll be able to afford to move, Mam,' Katie intervened. 'I hate it here, all of us cramped together in one room.'

'Oh, you'll get the job all right, Katie. It's all arranged, you start next Saturday morning.'

Katie looked startled. 'I can't, Dad! I don't finish school until the end of the following week.'

'Sod that! I'm not having you buggering things up, my girl!' he warned her angrily. 'I've said you'll start work next Saturday so just make sure you're there. No one is going to care if you miss the last few days at school. You start next Saturday morning at eight o'clock, like I've arranged it. Understand?'

Chapter Thirteen

In spite of the doubts her mam had expressed, Katie found she was thoroughly enjoying going to work at The Hayes.

The big open market was a bustling focal point, because it was the start of the real shopping area. The two huge departmental stores, David Morgan's and James Howell's, were both within a stone's throw, but the market, with its colourful stalls and bright awnings, drew people like a magnet.

Even though both of the departmental stores stocked everything from ribbons to evening dresses, from furniture to scrubbing brushes, people still liked to browse in the open market looking for bargains. They seemed to enjoy listening to the sales pitch and cheery banter from the cosmopolitan collection of stall-holders.

The stall Katie was working on was a favourite with women of all ages. The owner, a swarthy Sikh, Nino Patel, had business connections with some of the leading wholesale houses. He was always ready to take their surplus stock, cancelled orders, and any goods which had defects of some kind and were therefore not suitable to be sold in stores of repute.

Lewis insisted that he would be going with Katie on the first morning and introducing her to Nino.

'You don't have to do that, I'm not a kid,' she told him. 'It's not like the first day at school.'

'No, it's the first day at work for you, though, and I want to make sure you start off right. For one thing,' he went on, 'I want you to be dressed properly.'

'What's that supposed to mean?'

'You'd better get your mam to go shopping with you. Buy yourself a plain dark skirt, one that covers your knees, and a couple of blouses. They don't have to be white, pick colours that look smart and won't show every mark. You'll need some stockings as well, you can't go off to work in ankle socks.'

'Are you going to pay for all this lot?' Rachael asked.

'I thought we agreed you were going to get a Provvy cheque and let her pay it off out of her wages?'

'If I've got to pay for them myself then I'll pick them,' Katie told both of them.

'Oh no you won't!' Lewis told her. 'I want you to make a good impression. Nino's brother is an old friend of mine, we got to know each other when I was inside. You need to look smart, but not flashy.' He handed her a pound note. 'Here, see how you get on with that.'

'I'm not going to be able to buy a skirt, blouse and stockings out of a pound,' Katie argued.

Reluctantly, Lewis handed her another ten shillings. 'If you haven't enough for two blouses then get one and wash it and dry it overnight, or make it last all week.'

Although she knew she looked smart in her new clothes, Katie felt anything but confident on her first Saturday because she wasn't at all sure she'd be any good at selling things.

She knew the stall her father was talking about, because she often stopped and looked at all the things displayed there when they went to town.

When she told him she was ready to leave, he surveyed her critically.

'Duw anwyl, wear your hair loose, cariad! Fasten it back into the nape of your neck with a slide,' he told her. 'Having it in plaits makes you look like a schoolgirl!'

'Well, that's what I was until today,' she reminded him.

'Well you don't look like a schoolgirl,' he snapped. 'More like twenty than fourteen, judging by the shape of you.'

'How do you know this Nino Patel so well that he's agreed to give me a job without ever having seen me?'

'I told him you were my daughter, that was good enough.'

'Did you tell him I had no experience at all,

that I've never sold a thing in my life?' she asked worriedly.

'You do what he tells you, he will train you in next to no time,' he told her calmly.

'What if I don't like working on his stall. I mightn't like him,' she protested.

'You don't have to like him. You are there to work. You arrive there at eight o'clock in the morning and you do what he tells you until six o'clock at night, that is all there is to it.'

'I don't even know how much I shall be earning.'

'That is all taken care of. I have arranged everything with him.'

'So what are my wages to be, and when will I get paid?' Katie persisted, as they got off the tram at the junction of Bute Street and Bridge Street and started to walk the short distance to The Hayes.

'Duw anwyl! Will you listen to yourself! You are asking how much money he is going to pay you before you have even done a day's work,' Lewis snapped. 'I've told you, I've taken care of it all. I'll come and meet you on Friday night and I'll see he pays the right amount for the work you have done.'

Katie stopped dead in her tracks. 'Oh no! I know exactly what you are up to. You are going to come and collect my wages and then you're going to give me a couple of shillings for myself and keep the rest.'

'You ungrateful little bitch! I go to the trouble

of finding you work and now you think you can keep all you earn for yourself, do you?'

'No! I want mam to have it. She has to buy our food and my clothes, and even your beer and ciggies. She's the one who is going to get my paypacket, not you!'

Although inwardly she was trembling, Katie refused to back down. She had never stood up to him before because she was always afraid of what he would do, but here in the open street she was pretty sure he wouldn't hit her.

Lewis, realising there were people around who might overhear their argument, backed away from any open confrontation. Turning on the charm, he put his arm around Katie's shoulders and gave her a fatherly squeeze.

'That's what I like to see, a girl who knows what she wants from life,' he said jocularly. 'Now come on and meet Nino. I've told him how keen you are and promised him you'll do a good day's work. Remember, I was the one who found this job for you so don't let me down.'

'If I'm to do a good day's work then I don't want you hanging around watching me. That will only make me nervous.'

Lewis didn't answer, but his grey eyes narrowed angrily and Katie wished she had said nothing. Knowing it was too late to do anything about it, she tried her best to be as polite and nice as possible to Nino Patel.

Living in Tiger Bay, Katie had grown used to

seeing people of every colour and nationality, but even so, she was taken aback by Nino Patel.

He was very tall, very thin and his aquiline features stood out in sharp relief against his snow-white turban. When he smiled, which she discovered he did quite a lot, his strong, even teeth shone out as white and as gleaming as his turban. His jet eyes were like two polished marbles as they darted from side to side, watching everything going on around him, yet, at the same time, seeming to concentrate piercingly on the person he was addressing.

Even while Lewis was introducing them, Nino was alert to the people passing by his stall, especially if they paused or showed the slightest interest in what was on display.

It seemed to Katie that Nino managed to serve customers, wrap up their goods, take their money and hand over their change without a pause, while still listening intently to what her father was telling him.

As soon as Lewis had taken his leave, Nino explained the layout of his stall to Katie. Most items were arranged in a strict order. Silks, cottons and ribbons in a special colour sequence. Socks and stockings were in different piles according to whether they were for men, children or women, and then segregated into their sizes. Materials in type and then in colour order.

It was so straightforward that Katie had no difficulty in picking it all up. Everything was marked with a code denoting its category. Although his system intrigued Katie, it presented no problems as it was so simple to understand. The only thing that puzzled her was the enormous trunk at the front of the stall, filled with everything from off-cuts of material to odd socks or scraps of ribbon.

'That,' Nino Patel told her, 'is where everything and anything that doesn't sell goes. Let people rummage in it to their heart's content. Everything in it is very cheap and each item carries a price tag. If a customer finds something they want in there, then they think they have a real bargain. Keeping customers happy and making sure they come back time and time again is what selling is all about.'

Katie could see the sense of what he was telling her and nodded in agreement.

'Now, I want you to wear this money-bag around your waist. I have already placed some money in it that you will use for change. I want you to count it right now in front of me and tell me exactly how much is in there.'

Her hands shaking, Katie checked it. There were three one-pound notes and a mass of silver and coppers in the bag. 'There's five pounds here,' she exclaimed in awe. 'That's a lot of money to trust me with on my first day.'

Nino's teeth gleamed. 'That is why you must never take it off or put it down anywhere. When you go for your snack at midday, I want you to hand over the money-bag to me for safekee-ping.'

'Very well, Mr Patel,' Katie nodded.

'And call me Nino. All the customers do and it will confuse them if you don't.'

'Very well, Mr Pa— Nino.'

'Good! Now listen carefully and I will tell you what you have to do when you sell something. Everything, even the bits and pieces in the trunk, has its price marked on it. You will see it is always done twice. When you make a sale, you take off one of the price tags and drop it into the front pocket of the money-bag. That way, I can count up what you have sold each day. Also, I will know from the code what the item is, so I can check my stock at the end of the day.'

'And I leave the other price ticket on the item?'

'Indeed, yes. Then, should the customer come back and say he has changed his mind, or that the garment doesn't fit, we know exactly how much money to give them back.'

'So what happens if they come back and they have taken the ticket off?'

'Then we don't change the item!'

'But . . .'

'They all know that is Nino's rule and so none of them will argue about it. Is that all clear, or do you have some questions to ask?'

'No, it sounds perfectly clear,' Katie admitted.

'So, you think you could manage here on your own if I went to see a wholesaler?'

'You mean right now, today?' Katie exclaimed.

Nino smiled, his white teeth sparkling in the early-morning sun.

'No, not today. First I need to see you talk to customers and handle a sale. Anyway, it is far too busy on a Saturday for me to leave the stall.'

There was not very long to wait. A woman on her way into town dropped by to see if they had any lisle stockings, and Katie was able to find exactly what she was asking for and complete her first transaction without any problems.

'That was good,' Nino praised. 'One thing though, never hand over the goods until you have the money in your hand.'

'Oh! I'm sure she wouldn't have walked off without paying,' Katie assured him.

'That lady might not do so, but there are many who will, especially if you are busy.'

By the end of her first week of working for Nino Patel, Katie felt very much at home there. She found the other stall-holders were a cheery, friendly bunch of people, and always ready to help each other.

They kept an eye on each other's stall whenever necessary and helped out, whether it was over change or alerting each other when they spotted someone pilfering stock.

Katie found herself intrigued by all the different things on sale. She loved the colourful fruit

143

and vegetable stalls and the stand where they sold exotic rugs. She was fascinated by the smells from the bakery stall with its array of breads and cakes, and the aroma from the cheese van.

She was slightly repelled by the sight of great chunks of raw meat and by the smell from the stall that displayed mounds of glistening, scaly fish.

The noise and bustle as some of the stall-holders hailed passers-by, and their sales patter as they touted their goods and prices amused her, but she made sure they didn't distract her when there were customers at her own stall.

Nino seemed to be pleased with her progress. 'I agreed with your father to pay you five shillings a week while you are learning,' he told her. 'After that, if you work well, I will be paying you seven shillings and sixpence. However, you have shown such enthusiasm that I am going to pay you six shillings for the first two months, and then we will talk further.'

'Thank you, Mr Patel!'

'Ha!' He frowned at her in a ferocious manner. 'I shall deduct sixpence from your wages every time you forget to call me Nino!'

'Sorry Mr . . . Nino!' Katie said quickly.

'You must remember or else I'll sack you!' he said sternly, but his wide smile softened his rebuke.

'Yes, Nino, I will,' she promised. 'It's just that

I feel I should call you Mr Patel because you are my boss.'

'And because I am so old and ancient that you feel it is a mark of respect to address me so,' he said with a deep sigh. 'It is working here on this stall that makes me old. You too will look old and haggard in a few weeks, Katie!'

Katie wrapped up the money he had paid her for her first week's work in her handkerchief, and slipped it into the pocket of her skirt. As she did so she looked around nervously, to see if her father had carried out his threat to be there when she collected her wages. She breathed a sigh of relief when she found there was no sign of him.

On the tram on the way home she was tingling with excitement as she unwrapped her money. Six shillings, and Nino Patel had told her dad she would be getting five shillings. That meant a whole shilling that no one else knew about. She could hand over five shillings and keep the other shilling hidden away.

Mr Patel had said he would be paying her six shillings for the first two months, so that meant she would be able to save up eight shillings without anyone knowing.

Wrapping one of the shillings back up in her handkerchief, she put it back in her pocket. The other five shillings she clutched in her hand ready to give her dad the minute she went in the door, if he was there waiting as she expected him to be.

Chapter Fourteen

Going to work each day became the focal point of Katie's life. She was often the first to arrive and was certainly the last to leave.

The others who worked at the market always seemed eager to get home each night to their families, but going home held no delights for her.

Katie dreaded the thought of returning to the one squalid room in Louisa Street, knowing that if her dad was there he and her mam would be bickering or shouting at each other. If her dad wasn't there then her mam would be whining on about his drinking and the fact that he still hadn't found any work.

The promise that once she was working they would be able to move to somewhere bigger, where she could have a bedroom of her own, was still only a dream. Whenever she brought the subject up, her mam said it would remain just that until her dad found work.

Her mam looked so tired that Katie hadn't the heart to make an issue about it. They were no longer very close; the evenings when they curled up in bed with a mug of hot cocoa and shared their hopes and dreams had long gone.

The atmosphere since her dad had come home from prison was far too fraught for that. If he was there they barely spoke, either to him or to each other, for fear of saying something that would spark a row.

When he wasn't there then her mam would snatch an hour or two of sleep, while Katie read a magazine she'd borrowed from one of the women at the market, or laid out her clothes ready for the next morning.

When her two-month trial came to an end and Nino increased her wages to seven and sixpence a week, Katie was no longer able to hoard her shilling a week, because her father knew she had been promised this amount and expected her to hand it over in full. Her mam, however, insisted that she should be allowed to keep one and sixpence, and by careful budgeting she was able to save a shilling out of that some weeks. When the weather was fine she walked from Louisa Street to The Hayes, instead of paying a penny on the tram from the Pier Head.

Katie was also very popular with the other stall-holders, because she was always so willing to keep an eye on their stalls if they nipped away for a few minutes. As a result, she often found herself being given an apple or an orange from the fruit stall, a cooked sausage tucked inside a bread roll, or cakes and sweets from some of the other stalls.

Nino, too, saw that she had biscuits or cake

whenever it was their tea break, so she found she never needed to spend any of her own money on those sorts of things.

Since she'd been working on Nino's stall she'd taught herself to sew, and had made herself two new blouses out of lengths of cloth that had been in the trunk, and which Nino had said she could have.

They were not very successful, and Nino had shaken his head regretfully when he saw her efforts.

'Perhaps it would be better if you tried knitting a warm jumper for the winter,' he suggested.

The next day, when he went to the warehouse, he came back with a consignment of wool, knitting needles and knitting patterns.

'Can you knit, Katie?' he asked, as he handed her a pair of needles and a ball of red wool.

'At school we used to have to knit squares that the teacher made up into blankets,' she grinned.

'Perhaps you should try again and this time make something for yourself. You can knit here on the stall if we are not busy,' he told her, as he priced up the rest of the wool and knitting paraphernalia and put it on display.

Katie found that she liked knitting far more than sewing. She enjoyed the challenge of following a pattern and the satisfaction of seeing her work take shape.

At first she worked slowly and laboriously,

concentrating on every stitch, but in next to no time her speed increased, and she could knit and even talk to people at the same time.

Her first effort at knitting a jumper was a reasonable success. The sleeves were a little bit too long, but she turned back the cuffs and felt quite proud of her achievement.

Seeing her standing there knitting fascinated many of the customers. When she'd shown them the pattern and said how easy it was to do, several of the women who had never done any knitting before agreed to give it a try.

'Do you reckon I could knit a jumper for my young boyo to wear to school?' one woman asked her.

'Of course you could,' Katie assured her. 'It would be much cheaper than buying a ready-made one, and would wear much better, too.'

So many other women decided to follow suit that Nino increased his stock of wool.

'Perhaps you should also start knitting children's jumpers and we can sell them on the stall,' he told Katie. 'You can have the wool at cost price and we will share the profit when you sell the garments.'

Rachael was impressed. 'Don't tell your dad or he'll have it off you,' she warned.

'Why don't you knit some jumpers as well, Mam?' Katie suggested.

'No!' Rachael shook her head. 'I haven't the energy, cariad. It takes me all my time to do my cleaning jobs these days.'

By the beginning of December, Katie had managed to save almost ten shillings including the money she'd earned from her knitting. It was a small fortune and since she was afraid to hide it in her room in case her dad found it, she carried it in a little leather bag which she hung around her neck and was able to conceal under her clothes.

She spent a lot of her time dreaming about how she would spend it. She wanted to buy something special for her mam for Christmas, but couldn't decide what it should be.

She knew if she picked something from one of the stalls at The Hayes she would get a good discount on it, but she wanted the present to be really special.

If she bought her mam something from David Morgan's or James Howell's then she would be able to give it to her still in its fancy bag.

In the run up to Christmas all the stalls were particularly busy, especially Nino's. People trying to make their money go as far as possible were looking for bargains, and they knew that there was no better place to go than the market on The Hayes.

Nino warned her that she must be extra watchful, both of the takings and their stock. 'At this time of year there's always a lot of thieving,' he warned. His sharp eyes were everywhere and, when they were very busy, he made sure that the money-bag she wore around her waist was emptied regularly.

'If you get a big order then come to me with the takings immediately,' he cautioned. 'You never know who is watching. If they think that a slip of a girl like you has twenty or thirty pounds in their money-bag, they may well try to snatch it off you.'

'I'd like to see them try,' Katie told him spiritedly.

He smiled. 'Some of them are such clever pickpockets that you wouldn't even notice it was gone until afterwards. It is going on all the time. If you watch the crowd you will see people bumping into other people and very often it is so that one of them can take money from the other person's pocket.'

'Really?' Katie looked astonished.

'It is the same on the stalls. People pretend to look at the goods while all the time they are sliding something else that is on the stall into their pockets. Keep your eyes open and you will see it going on all the time, especially at this time of the year when there are crowds about.'

At first, Katie didn't believe him. She thought he was telling her this simply to keep her on her toes. Then she started to witness it happening with her own eyes and it astounded her how people got away with it.

Sometimes the stall-holder realised what was happening and did something about it. On several occasions, though, she saw people help themselves and walk away. Once they'd mingled with the crowd they were lost to sight before she could raise the alarm.

Her most upsetting experience took place less than a week before Christmas. She saw a man filch a watch from an adjacent stall and, to her horror, realised it was her own father who had done it.

The stall-holder, Pedro, a big swarthy Spaniard, also witnessed the incident and, abandoning his stall, gave chase. He made such a hue and cry, and threatened to call the police, that everyone stopped what they were doing to watch what was happening. Katie glanced at Nino and from the look on his face she was quite sure that he had recognised the thief.

Her face burned and her heart thudded with embarrassment. She didn't know what to say or do. If Nino had recognised her father, then the chances were that he would tell Pedro who it was when he came back with the police.

Quickly, she decided what to do. Without asking Nino if she could leave the stall she raced after Pedro, grabbing him by the arm just as he stopped two uniformed policemen who were patrolling along St Mary Street.

'It's all right, Pedro, there has been a mistake. I know who took the watch,' she gabbled. 'It was meant to be a surprise, that is why he dashed off with it. Look, I have the money for it here.' She pulled the little leather bag from around her neck and rattled it. 'There's no need to involve the police. You tell me how much the watch is and I will give it to you, right now.'

Pedro spread his hands in a gesture of bewilderment. 'You know the thief and you are offering to pay for what he took?'

'Yes, I know who took the watch, and he isn't a thief.' She bit her lip, then with a great effort admitted, 'It was my dad, he wanted to get it as a surprise and he saw me look across as he picked it up.'

Pedro scratched his head in disbelief. 'Are you sure? It is a very expensive watch.'

'Quite sure. It's all a silly misunderstanding. Let me pay you and that is the end of the matter.'

The two policeman stood there, grinning widely as they listened to the conversation and looked from Pedro to Katie and back again.

'So, is this the end of the matter?' one of them asked Pedro, 'or do you still wish to press charges?'

Pedro shrugged his massive shoulders and waved his hands in dismissal. 'Perhaps it has all been a mistake. I do not really understand,' he said vaguely.

'As long as you are being paid for your goods, that will do, won't it?' the policemen persisted.

'Yes! If I am paid I will say no more,' Pedro agreed.

'And you are prepared to pay for the watch, Miss?'

'Yes, of course I am. And I'm sorry you've been troubled,' Katie told them primly.

They waited as Katie counted out the money and handed it over to Pedro before they moved off. Pedro counted and re-counted the money and was still shaking his head in a bewildered manner as Katie went back to her own stall.

Nino looked at her sharply, as if waiting for an explanation, but since she didn't know what to say she said nothing. Although outwardly she tried to remain calm, inwardly she was seething. It meant that almost all of her carefully hoarded money was gone.

For the rest of the day she was keenly aware that the other stall-holders were looking at her and whispering amongst themselves. Instinctively, she knew her dad's action had ruined things for her at the market and that, from now on, no one was going to trust her.

She caught a tram home that night. The incentive to walk and so save the penny to add to her hoard of money was no longer there. As the tram bumped and lurched its way down Bute Street, she battled with her own thoughts about what she would do when she got home.

She didn't want to upset her mam, yet, at the same time, she felt she ought to know what had happened. There were times when she wished her dad had never come back to them when he'd come out of prison, and she wondered if deep down her mam felt the same way, because he'd changed so much.

If he'd left them to get on with their own lives she was sure that by now, with both of them working, she and her mam would have been able to move to somewhere better than their one dismal room in Louisa Street.

Sharing a bed with her mam had been bad enough, but now having to sleep three in a bed was unbearable. Her dad's snoring kept her awake most nights. There was nowhere to sit, not even to eat their meals, except on the bed. On Sundays, when all three of them were at home, they could hardly move without falling over each other, and she had no privacy whatsoever.

Having to wash in the makeshift kitchen was horrible as well. When it had only been the two of them, her mam used to heat up some water and bring it into their room, and they'd take it in turns to have a good wash. Now, with her dad there, they couldn't even do that.

By the time she reached home, Katie's mind was made up. She would tell her mam what had happened and demand an explanation from her dad. What was more, she'd tell him that he had to sell the watch and pay her back her money before Christmas.

All her brave intentions drained from her when she walked into the room and found her dad was there, but not her mother.

They stood staring at each other, each waiting for the other to speak.

'Where's Mam?' Katie demanded.

'Never you mind where she is, I want to hear from you where you got that money from today.'

'You mean the money that saved you from being arrested as a thief and being sent back to prison?' she sneered.

'Don't you take that tone with me, young lady!' Lewis Roberts snarled.

He grabbed hold of Katie's arm and twisted it behind her back. 'Nine pounds you handed over, so where did you get that from, eh?'

'Well, I didn't steal it like you tried to pinch the watch. In fact, I worked for it.'

'You had that much money hidden away, did you? And how much more have you got?'

'None, well, hardly any. Cleaned me out, keeping you out of the hot water you'd have ended up in if I'd let Pedro report you to the police and had them arrest you!'

'Hand over the money you've got left straight away, and less of the lip,' Lewis demanded, twisting her arm still harder.

'No! You go and sell that watch and pay me back my money. I need it! I'm saving up to buy something special for Mam.'

'Oh you are, are you?' Lewis taunted. He gave Katie a violent shove that sent her sprawling onto the bed. As she fell, the leather bag suspended around her neck was jerked outside her dress.

Lewis spotted it immediately and grabbed at it.

Katie tried to fight him off, but he was far too strong for her. Pinning her down on the bed, he plunged his hand into the neck of her dress and grabbed at the bag.

As he pulled it free, his hands brushed against her firm breasts. The contact with her warm flesh roused him into a frenzy of rage and anger.

Abandoning the money, he concentrated on her warm, nubile body. 'I'll teach you to defy me,' he panted. Lifting her dress, he rolled her over, and raising one arm he brought his hand down in a resounding slap on the bare flesh of her backside.

Katie kicked and screamed. When he slammed a hand over her mouth to silence her, she sank her teeth into it.

'You bloody little vixen!'

He slapped her again, and as his hand came into contact with her bare flesh he grabbed hold of her legs, pulling her towards him, turning her onto her back and ripping away her underclothes at the same time.

Panting with the exertion, and still holding her pinioned down on the bed, he began to undo his trousers. Realising what he was about to try and do Katie yelled out at him to stop.

Frightened by his heavy breathing, she looked up into his glazed eyes, horrified by what was happening. She couldn't believe that this lust-crazed creature was the same man she had once idolised, and who had carried her on his shoulders to the park when she'd been little.

Her screams were so loud that they reverberated not only through the house, but could even be heard in the street outside.

She heard people shouting and running up the stairs, and then the bedroom door crashed open and someone grabbed Lewis by the back of his neck and hauled him off her.

Sobbing with fright and shame, Katie hastily tried to cover her nakedness. As she looked up to see who had come to her rescue and saw that it was Aled Phillips, she felt she would die of shame.

Chapter Fifteen

The decision about whether or not they should go on living in one room in Louisa Street was decided for them by Alys Morgan.

The moment she heard Katie screaming she guessed that there was serious trouble of some kind, so she rushed outside to look for help. When she spotted Aled Phillips circling round and round on his bike, as though waiting for someone, she entreated him to come in and help her.

'Come on, boyo, will you help me sort things?' she begged. 'I don't know what's going on, but it sounds as though murder is being committed.'

Aled jumped at the chance. He often waited by the tram stop at the Pier Head, hoping to see Katie on her way home and have a chance to talk to her. Tonight he'd missed her so he'd been hanging around outside Louisa Street in the hope that she would come out again to go to the chip shop, as she sometimes did to get their evening meal.

He'd heard the screams and it had made his blood run cold, although he hadn't thought that they were from Katie.

Now, when Alys Morgan said, 'Go on then, get up those stairs and see what's happening, it's the room at the back, the Roberts's,' his stomach turned over.

If that was Katie screaming then she must be in some sort of terrible trouble, and he couldn't think what might have happened to her.

When he burst open the door and saw Katie prone on the bed and her father leaning over her, both of them with their clothes in disarray, he guessed what was happening and he felt physically sick.

He thought the world of Katie, and had done so ever since her first day at school. He'd tried to protect her then, and he was more than ready to do the same now.

Grabbing hold of Lewis Roberts by the scruff of his neck, he hauled him clear and pushed him against the far wall.

'Are you all right, Katie?' he asked, averting his eyes and giving her time to cover herself over.

Her sobs tore at his nerves. He wanted to gather her up in his arms and rush from the house with her, but he was afraid to touch her in case she pushed him away.

He looked around the cramped, sordid little room and shuddered. Surely all three of them didn't live and sleep in this one room, he thought, in shocked surprise. There was only one bed! The implication of what that meant seared into his brain, but he refused to let himself think about it.

'Where's your mam, Katie?' he asked gruffly.

'I don't know!' She pulled the bedcover tighter around her thin body.

'Then you'd better get yourself tidied up and come down and stay in my room until she gets back,' Alys Morgan puffed. She was leaning against the door having followed Aled up to their room, and her face was red with the exertion of climbing the stairs.

Katie nodded. Gulping back her sobs she tightened the bedcover around her, picked up her clothes, and moved ahead of Alys Morgan out of the room.

'Give her a minute or two to sort herself out and make herself decent, and then I'll make you both a cup of tea,' Alys Roberts told Aled. 'You know her, don't you?'

'We were at school together,' Aled mumbled.

'I see. Well hang on in the passage until she's dressed. I'll call you.'

'What about Mr Roberts? I think I may have hurt him. I pushed him up against that wall pretty hard. I was in a bit of a temper, see!'

Alys Morgan gave a look of contempt towards where Lewis Roberts was still lying on the floor, moaning and holding his head in his hands.

'Don't worry, boyo, he'll live, more's the pity. I don't want to know what was going on,' she told Lewis angrily, 'but I want you out of my house before the end of the day. Understand?'

Lewis groaned and shook his head.

'Come on, boyo,' Alys Morgan took hold of Aled's arm. 'Get back downstairs before you're tempted to thump him again. Not that he doesn't deserve it, but I don't want you landing yourself in trouble because of the likes of him.'

Alys Morgan was puffing and panting so much that Aled thought she was going to pass out.

'Here, you sit on the stairs for a minute and get your breath back, and I'll go and make that cup of tea,' he offered.

'Oh no, boyo, you're not going into my room until I know young Katie is decent,' she wheezed. 'I'll soon get my breath back when I've had a chance to sit down. Wait here until I call you.'

Katie was white-faced and red-eyed as she sat sipping the tea Alys made for the three of them. Aled longed to put his arm around her shoulders, and assure her that he would protect her and wouldn't let anything like that ever happen to her again.

He thought back to when she'd been a little girl on her first day at the school in Bute Terrace. He had never forgotten how frightened she'd been when the other kids had teased her. She'd had a special place in his heart ever since that day and he wanted to be more than just a friend.

He was afraid to say or do anything in front of Alys Morgan. He was worried about what she might think, and he didn't want to make things any more awkward for Katie than they were.

He was relieved when they heard the front door open and a woman's step sounded in the hallway.

'If that's you Rachael Roberts, then you'd better come on through here and see to your Katie,' Alys called out sharply.

'What's she doing down here? Has there been an accident or something?' Rachael asked, as she came into the room. Then, as she saw Katie huddled in a chair, she pushed past Aled to get to her.

'Katie, my lovely, what on earth has happened to you?' she asked anxiously.

Dropping to her knees she cradled the girl in her arms and turned angrily towards Aled. 'Is this something to do with you?' she said accusingly.

'Hold on a minute,' Alys Morgan warned. 'You've got this boyo to thank that your girl isn't in a far worse state. Attacked, she was, by that man of yours! He tried to rape her by the looks of things!'

The colour drained from Rachael's face. 'Duw anwyl! What are you saying, you wicked old witch? He's her dad!'

'He may be her father, but from what I've just witnessed he's the wickedest sod I've ever met,'

163

Alys Morgan told her. 'He attacked her all right! Ripped the clothes off her back. Screaming her head off, she was. Frightened me to death, I can tell you. Half naked, she was, when we got upstairs. If it hadn't been for this boyo here then I don't know what her fate would have been.'

Rachael shook her head in dismay. 'There must be some mistake,' she persisted. 'Lewis wouldn't do anything as disgusting as the sort of thing you're implying,' she added tersely.

Alys Morgan shrugged her fat shoulders. 'I'm as shocked as you, but facts are facts! I know what I saw and I've got a witness. You can always ask the girl herself if you don't believe either of us.'

'Katie?'

'It's all true, every word of what she's said,' Katie admitted numbly.

Rachael shook her head in bewilderment. Her thin face looked haggard with dismay. 'Is Lewis still up there?' she muttered.

'He is for the moment,' Alys told her.

'I'll go up and talk to him,' Rachael told her. 'Can Katie stay down here with you?'

'She can stay here while you pack up your belongings and then I want the lot of you out, bag and baggage,' Alys Morgan told her.

'Out? What are you talking about?'

'I've already told that piece of scum lying on the floor upstairs holding his head and groaning, that I want him out of my house, and I think it's best if you all leave,' Alys repeated.

'We've nowhere else to go!'

'Then you'll have to find somewhere. I'm not standing for that sort of carry on, not in my house. I've always prided myself on having respectable lodgers. I've turned a blind eye to the three of you living in one room and sleeping in one bed because I felt sorry for you with him not working. If I'd ever for one moment thought that anything like this was going on, then I'd have had you out of here long before now.'

'I don't know what you are talking about,' Rachael replied quickly, the colour draining from her face.

Alys Morgan gave a dry cackle. 'I think you bloody well do. I know you've tried to hide from everyone that your old man has just come out of prison, but it's a well-known fact. And let me tell you, he'll be back in there as sharp as a knife in your back, if I tell the bobbies what's been going on here.'

Rachael shook her head in bewilderment. 'I don't know what you think has been happening, but there has been nothing wrong going on.'

'Oh no? So what about today then? Your girl was screaming her lungs out because her dad was trying to rape her! And all this time you've been pretending that it's because you're such a respectable woman that you don't want anything to do with the people living here. Nose stuck up in the air, even though your old man has been in prison.'

'I never said he wasn't.'

'No? You've never said why he was in there either,' Alys Morgan sneered. 'I bet I can guess. Who did he try and rape last time?'

'It was nothing at all like that,' Rachael said stiffly.

'You don't get put inside for nothing. I can soon find out. The bobby who came round to check up if he was living here just after he was released will tell me.'

'What on earth are you talking about?'

'Ha! You didn't know about that, did you? You were out at work and young Katie was at school when the police called around. I was shocked then to discover I had a jailbird living under my roof. I waited for one of you to say something, but you've never breathed a word.

'Now, after what has happened today, and I know what sort of a criminal he is, I want you out, the lot of you. I won't feel safe in my bed at night while there's a rapist still under my roof.'

'My husband is not a rapist,' Rachael defended. 'That is not the reason he was in prison. It was something quite different, and anyway, it was all a misunderstanding.'

'Pull the other one!' Alys replied mockingly.

'If you must know the reason he was in prison, it was because he was wrongly accused of stealing something. It was all a big mistake,' Rachael added lamely.

'I'll bet!' Alys Morgan gave a derisory laugh. 'And I suppose what me and this boy saw happening up in your room just now, when he was trying to rape young Katie, was all a misunderstanding as well, was it?'

'I've already told you that there is probably some very simple explanation for what you saw,' Rachael said wearily. 'So do we have to keep on going over it!'

'You can't brush something like that under the carpet and forget it,' Alys blustered.

'I'd like to have a chance to talk to Katie on her own, and ask her exactly what happened.'

'You mean you want the chance to talk to her so that you can tell her what she has to say, so as to keep her dad out of trouble, don't you?'

'Of course not!'

'I know what I heard and what we saw, and there's no doubt in my mind about what was going on. And don't let us have any misunderstanding about the fact that I want you all out of here now, right this minute,' Alys told her firmly.

'We've nowhere to go. Surely you can give us a few days to find somewhere else?' Rachael begged.

'Until the end of the week. And then if you're still here, I'll tell the police all about what has happened here today. It wouldn't be very good for him upstairs if I did that, now would it, not with the sort of record he has.'

Chapter Sixteen

It felt strange to Katie, leaving Louisa Street later that evening with all their possessions in an assortment of bags and cases. It had been her home for over six years, and the only friends she had lived in the surrounding streets.

Katie was as surprised as her mam was when her dad said he knew of somewhere in Loudon Square where they could go. She really had expected that they might have to spend the night sleeping in a shop doorway.

She and her mam stood on the pavement, huddled over their possessions and shivering in the cold night air while Lewis went to negotiate with the owner. They both felt too upset by all that had happened that evening to even talk to each other.

Katie felt almost as if it was happening to someone else and she was an onlooker. She started quivering and taking in great gulps of air. She wished her mam would put a reassuring arm around her and tell her it was all a bad dream, like she'd used to do after the nightmares Katie had had when she'd first started school in Tiger Bay, and had been teased and bullied.

Instead, Rachael simply stood there, tight-lipped and frowning as if she was in some kind of a trance, her thin shoulders hunched and her arms wrapped around her own skinny body as if holding it together.

I wonder if she thinks it is my fault that all this has happened, and that's why she doesn't want to talk about it, Katie thought miserably.

If only she would let me explain exactly what happened, she'd realise that I was powerless to stop my dad and that I'm not to blame, Katie told herself over and over again.

She still couldn't understand why her dad had acted like that. She wondered if it had something to do with him being in prison all those years. Perhaps it had turned his brain. All her memories of him when she had been little were of someone who'd been kind and loving, so perhaps it really had changed him.

She felt so ashamed, especially about Aled Phillips seeing her with all her clothes ripped off like that. If it had been anyone else, a complete stranger, then she might never have seen them again, but she could hardly avoid Aled. He followed her like her own shadow. She didn't know what she would say or how she would face him the next time they met.

When Lewis came back and said there were three rooms they could have, both Katie and Rachael breathed a silent sigh of relief.

'They're up in the attic,' he warned, as he picked up as many of the bags as he could carry. 'Just follow me. There's a separate entrance we can use up an iron staircase at the back of the building, so we'll take our stuff in that way.'

The three rooms seemed like paradise to Katie as she took stock of her surroundings. For the very first time since they'd left Nana Roberts's house in Cathays, she was once again to have a bedroom to herself.

It was a very small room, and the single bed took up almost all the floor space. However, there was a built-in cupboard she could use to store her clothes, and a shelf with a mirror over it so that she could see to comb her hair and put on the pale pink lipstick she had started using.

The other bedroom wasn't much bigger, but her mam seemed to be happy enough with it.

The living area was a long narrow room that had a sloping ceiling and only a small window at the far end that looked out over the backs of the houses. In one corner there was a shallow brown-glazed sink and, alongside it, a cooker. In the rest of the room there was a square wooden table and four chairs, and a dark brown Rexine-covered sofa with two matching armchairs.

'There you are, everything you could dream of,' Lewis told them. 'There's a lavatory and a washbasin on the next floor. We have to share that, of course, but this is all ours. Are you both happy, now?'

'Can we afford it?' Rachael asked in a bewildered voice.

'We'll manage,' Lewis told her. 'We're in now so let's make the most of it.'

'And get turned out into the street in a couple of weeks because we can't find the money for the rent?' Rachael questioned dolefully.

'We'll find it some way or other,' he told her. 'You can take on some extra cleaning and Katie can ask for a rise.'

'Or you could go out and find yourself a job,' Katie suggested. Now they'd found a place where she had her own bedroom, and felt safe right away from her father, she didn't want to be uprooted again.

'Katie!' Rachael shot her a warning glance. There had been enough upsets for one day. Her head was already spinning and she didn't want Katie to stir up a fresh row with Lewis. 'You've got a nice little bedroom all to yourself, cariad, just as you've always wanted,' Rachael murmured placatingly.

'Sorry, Mam,' Katie said truculently. 'I was only thinking out loud.'

'Well, stop thinking and help us get unpacked and settled in,' Lewis ordered. 'You can take your belongings into your room for a start and then come and help your Mam get us something to eat.'

For the first few days Katie felt ecstatic. She had dreamed of having a room to herself for so long that for the first couple of evenings, all she wanted to do was shut the door, lie on her bed and daydream about the future.

Grateful that she no longer had to share a bed, or even a room, with her mam and dad, Katie struggled to push the incident with her dad to the back of her mind, and hoped that nothing like that would ever happen again. She knew she would never be able to completely forget about it, or ever forgive him for what he'd done, but it was a tremendous relief not to have to go on sharing a bed with him and her mam.

He seemed to realise that she would never trust him again and kept his distance, so for her mam's sake she was determined to come to terms with the situation and not to let it ruin the rest of their lives.

Every day helped. The fact that so far she'd not seen anything of Aled Phillips was an important factor. With the passing of time, his part in the episode seemed to be less and less important and her feeling of acute embarrassment subsided.

'Have you done anything about asking Nino to give you a rise?' Lewis demanded, when she handed over her paypacket at the end of their first week in Loudon Square.

'How can I? You agreed what my wages were to be when I first went to work for him.'

'For Christ's sake show some guts, girl! Stand up to him, tell him you are worth more.'

Katie shook her head. 'I can't do that. He's

having a hard time at the moment. We're not nearly as busy as when I first started.'

'Duw anwyl! That's not your fault!'

'I know that,' Katie told him. 'If I ask for a rise, though, he might decide he can manage without me and then I'd have no money at all.'

'You dopey little cow! I'd come and talk to him myself, but after the fuss you created over that bloody watch you know I can't show my face anywhere near The Hayes.'

'That's your own fault, you shouldn't have been thieving, should you!'

'What did you say?' Lewis's handsome face turned ugly and Katie felt a jolt of fear as he adopted a menacing manner. Her memories of his attack on her were still vivid in her mind. She knew that if he did turn on her he was so much stronger than her that she hadn't a chance of warding him off.

'I won't ask Nino for a rise, but I will ask around and see if I can find a job that pays more money,' she told him placatingly.

'Mind you do, then, and do it pretty sharp or else I will be finding a new job for you, and you'll take it whether you want to or not,' he threatened.

Katie's good intentions to find a new job went completely out of her head the next day, when Aled Phillips called at the stall. He was dressed in the navy and red uniform of a Telegram Boy and, with his navy and red peak cap covering his lank hair, for a moment she didn't recognise him.

'I thought you had a job in a factory,' she said in surprise.

'I got the sack! Been out of work. I was even thinking of going on the hunger march to Hyde Park in London, I was so fed up. Then I got this job at the Post Office and I've been away on a week's training. As soon as I'm eighteen I can apply to become a postman. There's even a pension scheme. You have to work there for thirty years in order to qualify, but it's real security, isn't it.'

Katie smiled in agreement. The thought of doing the same job every day for thirty years horrified her, but she was afraid it might hurt Aled's feelings if she said so. She waited for him to ask her how she was, and was relieved when he appeared to be too embarrassed to do so.

'Mrs Morgan told me you'd moved out of her place, but she didn't know where you'd gone, so I hoped I'd find you here so that I could tell you my news.'

'Yes, we've moved away from Louisa Street.'

'So where are you living? Still in Tiger Bay?'

'Oh yes! We've got a place in Loudon Square.'

Aled stared at her, bemused. 'Loudon Square?'

'That's right! Number 32. We've got three rooms, right at the very top of the building. I've even got my very own bedroom.' She flushed as she said it, remembering the scene Aled had witnessed in the seedy little room where they'd lived in Louisa Street.

'Is . . . is the house owned by someone called Betti Davies?' he asked.

Katie frowned. 'I think so, but I'm not sure. My dad made all the arrangements. Why?'

Aled chewed on his lower lip. 'It doesn't matter,' he said, avoiding her eyes.

'It must matter or you wouldn't have asked.'

'Well, I could have the address wrong. Anyway, I must go, I've got two telegrams to deliver.'

'Then they can wait,' Katie told him, grabbing hold of the handlebars of his bicycle. 'I want to hear whatever it is you know about Loudon Square, so come on, tell me.'

Aled avoided her eyes and looked uncomfortable. 'I may be wrong,' he parried. 'Give me time to check it out before I say anything else.'

'Until tonight, then? We can meet when I finish work.'

'All right. See you on James Street bridge at eight o'clock.'

Katie frowned. 'It will be dark by then and I don't like wandering around Tiger Bay on my own at night.'

'Do you want me to come and meet you here, and walk you home when you finish work, then?'

Katie hesitated. 'All right, that would be better. See you at six o'clock, then.'

Chapter Seventeen

Although she was kept fairly busy on the stall for the rest of the day, Aled's comments about where she was living were never far from Katie's mind.

She kept wondering why he had looked so taken aback when she had mentioned the address in Loudon Square, and what on earth he could have heard about the place to make him so uneasy.

She was more than a little relieved to find him waiting for her when she finished work that evening. 'Well?' she asked, anxiously. 'Was it the house you thought it was?'

He looked at her dolefully, as if reluctant to answer her question. 'I'm afraid so, Katie.'

'Go on then, tell me what is wrong with the place,' she said impatiently. 'Has it some kind of bad name, or is it something to do with Betti Davies?'

'Both really.'

'I'm waiting.'

'I'm surprised you should be asking,' he said awkwardly. 'Most people down the Bay already seem to know.'

'For goodness' sake, Aled Phillips, stop beating about the bush and get on with it,' Katie said crossly. 'Let's hear whatever it is you have to say, and then I can judge for myself whether it is anything to worry about or not.'

'Have ... have you met any of the other people who live there yet, Katie?' he stuttered, his long face bright red.

She shook her head. 'No, not even Mrs Davies. We've only been there a few days, remember, and I'm out most of the time. It seems quiet enough when I leave for work in the morning. There aren't any screaming kids or crying babies around the place ...'

'What about during the evenings and at night?'

Katie shrugged. 'I don't know. We're right at the top of the house so I don't know who comes in or goes out.' She frowned. 'Why are you asking all these daft questions?'

Aled cleared his throat and avoided her eyes. 'Betti Davies is well known down at the docks. A lot of sailors visit her house in Loudon Square when they're in port,' he told her awkwardly.

Katie was silent for a minute trying to work out exactly what he was trying to say. Then, when the truth dawned on her, she stared at him in wide-eyed disbelief. 'Are you trying to tell me that she entertains seamen?' she asked accusingly.

He nodded. 'I'm afraid so. Her place is a brothel, see. She employs half a dozen girls.

They work most of the streets around there and then take the sailors, and anyone else they pick up, back to her place.'

Katie stared at him, horrified. 'I'm sure my mam and dad don't know about this!' she protested indignantly. 'My mam will be really shocked. Are you sure you haven't made some mistake?'

Aled shook his head vehemently, his lank hair flopping wildly. 'No. I checked again today. The chaps at the Post Office sorting office know all about Betti Davies and what goes on at her place.'

Katie felt both alarmed and angry and wished that Aled hadn't told her. It spoiled all the lovely feelings she'd had for the last few days, that they were at last moving up in the world. Having a bedroom to herself once again had been such an achievement, something she'd been longing for, ever since they'd moved to Tiger Bay, and now suddenly it all seemed so sordid and wrong.

She didn't want to believe Aled. Yet, the more she thought about what he'd told her, the more she knew instinctively that he was right. The fact that there were no children or babies living there had struck her as strange.

The house was always so quiet in the mornings, as if everyone was still in bed asleep. And they probably were, she thought cynically. And, if she was completely honest, she had to admit that she had heard lots of comings and goings at night. She'd simply put that down to the other people who lived there coming home or going out, or having friends or family visiting them.

She couldn't believe that some of the tarty-looking girls she had seen hanging around the Pier Head and outside the Seaman's Mission, who sold themselves to men, were living in the same house as she did. The thought was so distasteful to her that for a moment she didn't even want to go back to her new home.

She wondered if her mam knew, or whether she'd be horrified when she found out. She wasn't sure about her dad. He not only mixed with so many more people than she and her mam did, but he frequented the pubs around the dockside so he must have heard something.

She started wondering how he had known that there were rooms available at 32 Loudon Square in the first place. Were they vacant because no one else would take them, because they didn't want to live in a house of ill-repute?

There must be more to it than that, she reasoned. He'd taken them straight there when Alys Morgan had told them to leave Louisa Street. How could he have known they were not only empty, but that Betti Davies would let them have them?

It was almost as if it had all been pre-arranged! If that was the case then it meant that her dad must know Betti Davies pretty well.

'I wish you hadn't told me, Aled' she blustered.

'I didn't want to, but you kept on at me, cariad,' he protested uncomfortably.

'I know. It's such a nasty shock though!'

'I suppose it is,' he shrugged, 'but you were bound to find out sooner or later now, weren't you?'

'Yes, but now I know the sort of reputation the place has, I feel I don't want to go back there!'

His long, thin face brightened. 'Well why don't we go to the pictures then. Come on, Katie, my treat. Anywhere you like. There's a smashing western on at the Odeon.'

She shook her head. 'I hate westerns!'

'All right, you choose. Anything you like. I'll even take you to see a mushy Clark Gable film, or Marlene Dietrich in *Blonde Venus*, if that's what you want.'

'No thanks, Aled,' she told him stiffly. 'It would be a waste of your money, see, because I couldn't keep my mind on the screen, not when I've so much churning around inside my head.'

'That's being daft,' he said huffily. 'A night out would do you good and help to take your mind off it all. You'll see things differently tomorrow.'

Katie's lips tightened as she shook her head. She was too upset to even try and explain to Aled how she felt.

'You can't do anything to change the situation,' he persisted, 'not unless you move out and I don't see that happening. In fact, the chaps at work say you'd probably never have got those rooms if your dad hadn't been in so thick with Betti Davies, and working for her.'

'Working for her? What's that supposed to mean?' The colour drained from Katie's face as she stopped and turned to face Aled. 'No,' she held up her hand as he was about to speak, 'don't say another word, Aled Phillips, you've already said more than enough.'

'Well things like that do get around, Katie. You'd be bound to hear it yourself sooner or later,' he protested defensively.

'For goodness' sake, can you stop saying that, Aled! I really thought you were my friend,' she added, as tears rolled down her cheeks, 'but if you believe what other people say when they talk about my dad like that, then you can't be.'

'Katie, I am! It's because I care for you so much that I'm telling you all this.'

'Care for me! You have a funny way of showing it, telling such outrageous lies about my dad.'

'After the way he treated you a few nights back, I don't understand why you are sticking up for him!'

Katie shook her head, her shoulders heaving. 'He's my dad, isn't he,' she wailed. 'He must have been drunk or something the other night, otherwise he wouldn't have acted like that.'

'That's bloody rubbish and you know it,' Aled shouted. His face was red and he was as angry and as upset as she was.

'Your dad's a bully most of the time. Look at the way he treats your mam. These days she looks half-dead most of the time, yet he expects her to go out skivvying while all he does is strut around in his best suit!' he said scornfully. 'He has no respect for women, not for you, or your mam, or for the young girls he corrupts by luring them to Betti Davies's brothel.'

'Aled!'

Aled was now so worked up that he hardly noticed that Katie was white-faced and shaking.

'I do care for you, Katie. I always have!' He reached out to take her hand, but she pushed him away.

'I don't want to ever speak to you again after what you've just said,' she told him bitterly, 'so stop following me around.'

'Katie, I'm worried about you. I'm only trying to warn you to watch out. Living in that house could be dangerous . . .'

'All the more reason, then, for you to keep away, in case you get hurt,' she snapped.

Taking to her heels she hurried off. When she reached the next corner she looked back and saw that he was still exactly where she had left him.

As she continued on home his revelations rang in her head, and she felt a frisson of unease. Would Aled have said such things unless he knew for sure?

One half of her mind wanted to believe he'd

made it all up, the other half was convinced that every word he had said was true.

Chapter Eighteen

The full implication of Aled Phillips's information became unpleasantly clear when Katie brought the matter up later that evening. They had almost finished their meal and Lewis was reading the *South Wales Evening Echo* while Katie and Rachael were about to clear away and wash up, when she dropped her bombshell.

'How did my dad manage to find these rooms for us, Mam?'

'I don't know, cariad.' Rachael put down the cup of tea she was still drinking and looked at Katie in surprise. 'He's sitting right there so why don't you ask him yourself?'

'Well, Dad, what's the answer then?'

'What you blabbering on about, girl?' Lewis lowered his *Echo* and looked at Katie from over the top of it.

'I asked how you managed to find these rooms for us?'

'What sort of daft bloody question is that! We're in, and that's all that matters, isn't it?'

'Yes, but how did you know there were any rooms empty here?'

He frowned. 'I was told about them,' he said coldly. 'Satisfied?'

'No, not quite,' Katie persisted. 'I was informed today how people say you got the rooms, and I didn't like what I heard.'

'That bloody Nino been opening his great gob again,' Lewis said dismissively as he returned to his paper.

'It wasn't Nino who told me. It was someone else.'

'What are you on about, my lovely?' Rachael asked in a bewildered voice.

'What do you two know about Betti Davies?' Katie asked, looking first at Lewis and then at her mam.

Rachael frowned. 'You mean the landlady?'

'That's right! Is she a special friend of yours, Dad?'

'I don't know what the hell you are prattling on about, girl!' Lewis muttered sullenly from behind his newspaper.

'I heard today that you work for her and that was how you got these rooms. Is that true?'

'What is it to you if it is true or not,' Lewis blustered. 'You've got what you always wanted, somewhere better to live than that crummy little room in Louisa Street, and you've got a bedroom of your own into the bargain. Are you never satisfied?'

'It's the sort of work you're doing, Dad, that bothers me,' Katie persisted.

Rachael stood up and began clearing the table. 'What are you talking about, Katie? Your dad hasn't found a job yet.'

'Oh yes, he has! Not the sort of job that most men would take on, so that's probably why he's never said a word to us about it. Other people know what he's doing, though. Today, when I was told what it was, I couldn't believe my ears,' she went on.

Rachael tried to concentrate on the dishes in front of her. Her heart was pounding as she wondered exactly what Katie had heard. Surely Lewis had more sense than to start thieving again. Six years in prison should have shown him the error of his ways. Katie had told her about how he had tried to pinch a watch from one of the market stalls but she had hoped that was just a silly lapse.

'Well? What sort of job is he supposed to be doing?' Rachael asked nervously.

'Go on, Dad, I'm sure you will want to tell her,' Katie jibed.

'Duw anwyl! Let it drop,' Lewis growled, shaking the newspaper angrily.

'He's working for Betti Davies as a pimp, that's the sort of work he is doing,' Katie said in a disparaging voice.

'Katie!' Rachael's eyes widened in horror. 'I don't like to hear you saying such a thing about your dad!'

'Well, it's the truth! That's right, isn't it, Dad?'

Lewis lowered his newspaper again. 'Did you have to open your big mouth and upset your mother?' he asked angrily.

'You mean that what she is saying is true?'

Rachael gasped. 'You mean all those nice young girls I've seen around this place, and passed the time of day with, are prostitutes?'

'Yes, they're on the game,' he said calmly. 'They live here and work for Betti. This place is popular with sailors and with other men . . .'

'Men you've cajoled into coming here to meet these young girls you've lured here,' Katie interrupted scornfully.

He laughed cynically. 'None of them need much enticing, I can tell you!'

'Lewis, tell me that what she's saying is not true! I can't believe it,' Rachael said in a shocked voice.

'Oh it's quite true! He goes out looking for young girls and then persuades them to come and work for Betti Davies,' Katie repeated scornfully.

Lewis's grey eyes narrowed and he squared his broad shoulders as he regarded them both balefully. 'And what's wrong with that? Both of you could earn a damn sight more working for Betti than either of you do at the moment,' he snapped.

'Lewis!' Rachael's face turned a dull red as she stared at him in disgust.

He shrugged, and looked directly at Katie. 'You've got a nice figure on you and you're pretty enough, so think about it, my lovely. If you dropped that prim attitude you could score, all right.'

'You mean you'd like me to do that for a

living, I suppose,' Katie retorted. 'You're a wicked man, do you know that?'

'That will do Katie,' Rachael interposed quickly. 'You've said enough, cariad. It's been a shock for you as much as it has for me, but don't start saying things you'll regret later on.'

'No, let her have her say,' Lewis intervened, a malicious smile on his face. He turned and looked straight at Katie. 'I'll tell you something now, cariad, unless you start handing over more money than you are doing at present, you'll find yourself working for Betti whether you want to or not. Understand?'

'Lewis! How can you say such a thing,' Rachael gasped. 'To threaten your own daughter in that way! I've never heard anything so immoral in my life. It's enough to make your poor mother turn in her grave!'

'The same goes for you, you stupid cow,' he told her scornfully. 'You could earn a damn sight more on your back, than you do on your knees, so think about it.'

'How dare you suggest such a thing!' Rachael exclaimed furiously. She'd tried so desperately hard not to take sides, but now she felt guilty that she hadn't been more outspoken about Katie's ordeal at his hands.

Anger brought two high spots of colour to her pallid cheeks and her chest heaved as she faced him. 'You talk about us earning more money yet you've never handed over a penny piece since you came out of prison. You've lived on what I earn, even if it has been on my knees scrubbing other women's homes, and what your young daughter has earned on that market stall ever since she left school. You've not contributed one penny piece, Lewis Roberts. In fact,' she stuck her chin in the air and looked at him defiantly, 'we were better off when you were inside. Then, at least everything I earned went on food and clothes for Katie and me, and we didn't have you sponging off us. You even cadge my cigarettes!'

Lewis shook out his newspaper dismissively and turned to the racing pages. 'Have you finished?'

'No, I haven't! Not yet,' Rachael blazed. 'I want to know what you are going to do about it. You find work or I'll kick you out. I don't see why we should work hard to keep you, when you are as fit as a fiddle and could be out there working like the rest of us.'

'Kick me out, would you?' He raised one eyebrow and looked amused. 'You're living here rent free, remember, and you'd have a job to go on doing that without me.'

'Let me remind you that I managed to keep a roof over our heads while you were in prison, and now that Katie is working we'd have no trouble in managing on our own again,' Rachael told him.

'Not here you couldn't.'

Rachael's face flushed furiously. 'Don't push your luck, Lewis, or I'll throw your stuff out onto the street, and you along with it,' she told him angrily.

Lewis tilted his chair back on two legs and laughed. 'If anyone leaves here it will be you two, not me,' he pointed out. 'These rooms are for my use, not yours. They are part of the perks of my job. If you make a scene, or cause any trouble between me and Betti Davies, and I have to go, then you'll be out on the street along with me.'

'I'm quite sure Mrs Davies wouldn't put me out as long as I pay her the rent,' Rachael argued.

'That's where you are wrong. As I've told you, there is no rent. Don't you understand, Betti provides me with this accommodation in return for what I do for her.'

The colour drained from Rachael's face. 'So everything Katie has been saying is true, then,' she said in a strangled whisper. 'You really are acting as one of her pimps.'

Lewis grinned broadly. 'Amongst the many other things I do for her, yes, you could say that I am one her pimps. I prefer to describe it as being her Manager, helping to rustle up clients, and recommending the services she can offer. In addition, I also provide protection for the girls who work for her.'

'And what other services do you perform for her?' Rachael demanded, her eyes blazing and her lips trembling.

Lewis tapped the side of his nose with his

forefinger. 'I don't think we should discuss that in front of our innocent young daughter, do you?' he asked in mocking tones.

Katie felt acutely embarrassed as she listened to the exchange going on between her parents. She didn't want to believe what she was hearing, even though it was what she had accused him of doing. Now, she was very much afraid that however distasteful it may sound, every word that Aled had said about her dad had been the truth.

She couldn't bear to look at her mother's face. She could hear her breathing in deep harsh gulps as though she was going to choke at any moment. She wanted to go to her and put her arms around her, and hug her and tell her everything was going to be all right, but she felt rooted to the spot and unable to do so.

It was as if their entire world was collapsing around them and she wondered how she would ever hold her head up again. How was it that she'd been so slow to realise the sort of place they were living in, she asked herself over and over again.

The clean, neatly furnished hallway and the complete lack of children about the place had seemed a bonus when they had first moved in. The fact that there was never anyone waiting to use the bathroom at the same time as she did in the mornings should have told her something.

The trouble was that she was so happy up in her tiny attic bedroom that she took no notice of what went on anywhere else in the house. She'd not even paid very much attention to the constant comings and goings during the evenings, not until Aled had opened her eyes to it.

In the evenings, once she'd finished helping her mam to clear away the remains of their meal and to wash up the dishes, she'd been quite happy to seek the seclusion of her own room. She hadn't given a thought to what her mam and dad were doing.

Thinking back, she realised that often when she went into the living room to make herself a drink before going to bed, her mam was sitting there on her own. She'd never questioned where her dad was. The less she saw of him the happier she was these days. She always felt on edge when he was around.

The two of them would sit there chatting over their cup of cocoa, and then both of them would go off to their separate bedrooms. Next morning, there was the usual rush to get to work. Her mam went out before her so she cleared up the remains of their breakfast and left the place tidy before she set off for The Hayes.

She'd always assumed that her dad was still in bed because he had come home late from the pub. Now she wondered if he was there or if he hadn't even come home the night before.

The more she thought about how they came to be living in Loudon Square, and how involved her dad was with Betti Davies, the more upset and muddled she felt. She would have liked to leave right that minute, but where could she go?

She remembered her mother's struggle to pay the rent on the room they had in Louisa Street, and how horrible, cramped and smelly it had been there. At least this house was well kept. It was the way they were paying the rent that was so contemptible, and she knew it was distressing her mam because she'd never seen her looking so upset.

Despondently, Katie thought about the wonderful picture she'd built up of her dad while he had been in prison. She'd put him on a pedestal and looked forward so much to the day when he would come home again. Once that happened and they were a proper family again, she'd imagined that everything would be fine.

When he had come home from prison he'd been almost a stranger. It wasn't simply that his face was lined or that he looked so much older than she remembered, it was his manner that was so different. He was so hard and cynical; so bitter and sarcastic about everything they said or did.

In the beginning she tried hard to recapture some of the rapport there had been between them, by telling herself that six years was a long time to have to live shut away from the world. She also kept reminding herself that in his eyes she must have changed quite a lot as well. The last time he'd seen her she had been a trusting little girl who had idolised him, and who had hung round his neck and clung onto every word he said.

All three of them having to live and sleep in one room hadn't helped, but, until the day he'd almost raped her, she really had tried her hardest to like him and to please him. After the attack, though, she'd felt humiliated and now she was suspicious of his every move.

Even so, after they had moved to Loudon Square she'd had great hopes of everything sorting itself out. It was wonderful to have so much space and a bedroom all to herself. Such a relief to be able to sit down at a proper table for their meals instead of perching on the side of the bed, balancing their plates on their knees.

Now, after what she had been told by Aled Phillips about the place they were living in, and it had been confirmed by her own dad, all that wonderful feeling of elation was gone. All she could think about was how she could get away from Loudon Square.

She'd heard her mam and dad talking long after she went to her bedroom, and as she was dropping off to sleep she'd heard their voices raised again in anger.

Her mam was leaving for work as Katie walked into the living room the next morning, so there was no time for them to talk. She looked pale and unhappy and her face was puffy as though she'd been crying, and Katie was sure it was because her mam felt as sickened by the revelations as she was.

All the dreadful things her dad had said and the threats he had made went round and round in her mind. She couldn't believe that he wanted her, his own daughter, to work for Betti Davies. It made her feel hot under the collar every time she remembered him saying it.

She also felt frightened every time she thought about it, because she knew from the look on his face and the tone of his voice that it was no idle threat. He'd meant it!

There was only one way to change things and for her and her mother to live in safety, Katie decided, and that was to get a better paying job so that she could move right away from Loudon Square.

If only she could be certain that her mam would be willing to come with her, then she was sure they could manage to afford a room between them.

In the meantime, she thought unhappily, there was no alternative, but to put up with things the way they were.

Chapter Nineteen

Katie was in despair about finding another job. She visited most of the larger stores in St Mary Street and Queen Street and asked if there were any vacancies. On several occasions she even managed to get as far as being interviewed by the head of one of the departments, only to be turned down when they discovered that she was, at present, working on a market stall in The Hayes.

The people working on the stalls were such a close-knit bunch that it wasn't very long before news reached Nino that she was looking elsewhere for a job.

'What is the reason?' he asked, his dark eyes puzzled. 'Do you not like working here with me anymore?'

'Yes, of course I do,' she told him awkwardly, her face red with embarrassment. 'I love working on your stall and I like working with you, but my dad has said that I must find work that pays me more wages.'

'Aah!' he breathed a sigh of relief. 'That is different. Perhaps I can help you in some way.' He spread his hands wide and gave a deprecating shrug. 'I wish I could pay you more money, but it is out of the question. You know well that trade is bad, especially since Christmas. People have used up all their money on festivities, so now they have to watch what they are spending.'

'Yes, I know that,' Katie agreed. 'I wasn't even going to ask you if you could give me a rise. In fact, I thought you might even be glad if I told you I was leaving.'

He shrugged. 'That is possibly true, but I would never ask you to leave, Katie. You have been such a good worker and I like you very much. So where is it that you have been looking?'

I've been to all the big stores in St Mary Street and Queen Street, but I've been turned down by all of them.'

Nino looked surprised. 'So why is that? You are young, pretty and very polite.'

When Katie told him it was because she was working on a market stall at present, he became very annoyed.

'These people, who do they think they are,' he said angrily. 'You should have told them to come and speak with me. The work you do here is the same as you would be doing behind one of their counters. You have to deal with the same people! You have to sell. You have to take the money. And you are good at all of that!'

Katie shook her head sadly. 'I never even got as far as giving your name as a reference,' she told him.

'Then that is a very bad thing, very bad, but do not worry. Nino will solve everything for you. Wait with patience and you will see. I will speak out for you. What sort of work is it you would most like to be doing?'

'I don't really know,' Katie admitted. 'I came here straight from school. The only other work I know anything about is housework. My mother goes out cleaning, but I wouldn't like to have to do that.'

'Of course, it is not right for you to do that sort of work!' Nino exclaimed shaking his head emphatically. 'Don't you worry anymore. Nino will find you a job you will like, something you will be good at, you wait and see.'

Nino was as good as his word. A week later he told her of an opening that he thought would be just right for her.

'It is as a waitress, working at a café in Bridge Street that is owned by my good friend, Mario, and his wife, Gina,' he told her. 'They will be happy to have you there and you can start working as soon as you like.'

'That's very kind of you, Nino, but I know nothing at all about being a waitress. I mightn't be any good at it!'

'What rubbish you talk,' he exclaimed. 'Of course you will be good at it. Gina will tell you what to do and poof!' he snapped his fingers, 'in a flash you will be doing it, yes?'

'I will certainly try,' Katie smiled.

'Then everything is settled. You can start working there next Monday, yes?'

Katie looked uncomfortable. 'You didn't tell me what the wages would be,' she said hesitantly.

Nino slapped his hand against his forehead. 'Stupid man. That is the most important thing, yes?'

'It is!' Katie nodded.

'Well, the news is good. Mario, he provide you with the clothes you must wear, the black dress, the white frilly apron and the starched little white hat for your head. He will pay you ten shillings a week to start, and in a month's time, when you have learned what to do, then it will be twelve shillings a week.'

'Really?' Katie couldn't believe her ears. 1933 looked as though it was going to be lucky, in spite of all that had happened.

'Aah! There is more! You will also earn money from the tips. If you smile at the customers and serve them pretty damn quick, then a lovely looking girl like you will earn tips, yes?'

'It gets better and better,' Katie smiled.

'The work is hard,' Nino warned her. 'You have to dash around all the time. First thing each day is getting the tables ready for the morning coffees. Then it is time to whip everything away and prepare them with knives and forks and serviettes, ready to serve the lunches. Before you get your breath back from clearing those away, the tables have to be re-laid ready for the ladies who come to take tea.'

'Do I have to help with all the washing up as well?' Katie asked in alarm.

'No, no, no! Your job ends once you carry the dishes back into the kitchen. Someone else does all that,' Nino assured her, patting her arm. 'All the time you are serving, though, remember you have to put on a smile, Katie. Even when the customer shouts, or complains about being kept waiting.' He tilted his head on one side and looked at her. 'That should be no problem for you, Katie, because you smile a lot and you never lose your temper with difficult customers, no?'

'I try not to,' she admitted.

'It will work well,' Nino said confidently. 'I will tell Mario you will be there promptly at eight o'clock on Monday morning, yes?'

'Yes, Nino, and thank you very much for finding this job for me. I'm sorry to be leaving you, but I won't let you down, I promise.'

'And I shall miss you, Katie. You have been a good worker.'

Mario and Gina were as fat as Nino was thin. They were both very voluble and at first Katie found it unnerving when they started shouting and screaming at each other. When it was in Italian she had no idea what they were saying, but often when it was in English she was so shocked by the ferocity of their arguments that she expected them both to walk out at any minute. Seconds later, though, they would be all smiles, singing together, or slapping each other on the back.

They never shouted at her. Mario was kind and courteous and Gina went out of her way to show Katie the right way to do things. She even altered the uniform that Katie had to wear, so that the dresses fitted her better and made her look smarter. She helped her to put her hair up in a French pleat so that it looked elegant under the starched frilly cap. Most importantly of all, Gina taught her the skills she needed to know to become an efficient waitress.

Katie was eager to comply and learned very quickly. Even the grumpiest of customers seemed to mellow when she flashed them one of her sweet smiles and apologised when she kept them waiting.

As Nino had warned her, it was a very busy café. Women stopped by in the morning for coffee, either before or after doing their shopping. At midday it was packed with men who had limited time to spare and who wanted quick, efficient service. In the afternoon it filled up with ladies exhausted after their day's shopping. They liked to dawdle over their tea and cakes as they sat gossiping, or discussing their day's purchases with each other. This could sometimes make it a very late finish for Katie.

After everyone had left and the 'Closed' sign

went up on the door, there were still the dishes to be cleared from the tables and all the tablecloths to be stripped off and replaced by crisp clean ones ready for the next morning.

'Appearance is everything,' Mario explained. 'The tables must look attractive even if we are closed, so that people looking in through the windows as they pass by will want to come back and eat here when we are open.'

Katie quite understood this, but there were some evenings, when she was tired and her feet ached, that she felt annoyed about it. Sometimes she would try and chivvy up some of those ladies who were lingering longer than she thought necessary, by starting to clear the tables near them. It usually worked. The women would immediately check on the time, exclaiming that they wouldn't be home before their children got in from school, or their husbands from work. Then they would gather up their parcels and leave.

She knew Mario didn't approve of such tactics so she was very careful only to do it very discreetly, or when he was not there.

She was astute enough never to rush customers who left her tips. The afternoon ladies rarely did, but the men who came in at lunchtime could be quite generous.

It was not long before she recognised the regular customers and knew where they liked to sit. Whenever possible she would save their special spot for them. She often knew in advance what they were likely to order and would make sure it was ready to place onto the table almost the moment they sat down.

At home, if her dad was there when she talked about her job, Katie never mentioned anything about the tips.

'He'll be ever so angry with you if he ever finds out about them, cariad,' Rachael told her worriedly.

'Why should he be, Mam? I hand over all my wages and you don't even have to keep me in food, I get my meals at the café.'

'You know how he is about such things,' Rachael reminded her. 'He feels that since he is the man of the family it is only right that he handles all the money that comes in. He's bound to realise that as a waitress you'll be getting tips.'

'If he wants to handle money then he should go out and earn some himself, not rely on us bringing it home.'

'Katie! Don't talk so bitter, cariad. Not when everything is going so well for you. You've got a lovely job and you're friends with that Aled Phillips. He's turned out to be a hard-working boyo and I can see he thinks the world of you, cariad.'

Katie sighed. 'I know I should be content, but it worries me that things are not going so well for you, Mam. Even though I've been saving all my tips since I started at the café there's nowhere near enough for the two of us to leave here and get somewhere of our own.'

'I'm all right, my lovely, just a bit tired, that's all,' Rachael responded with a dry laugh.

'Then why don't you stop working, Mam?'

'That's right out of the question, cariad, and you should forget about us having a place of our own. You go on saving up, though, you'll be needing it for your own bottom-drawer. When Aled becomes a fully-fledged postman he'll be popping the question, you mark my words!'

'No, Mam!' Katie shook her head emphatically. 'He's a friend, that's all. He's got his mam and gran to take care of, remember. He wouldn't leave them.'

Rachael smiled wanly. 'We'll see. I'm sure he thinks there is more than friendship between the two of you. And you could do a lot worse, cariad!'

Katie shook her head dismissively. 'Anyway, stop changing the subject, Mam. We were talking about you and I asked you why you don't take some time off work if you are feeling so tired.'

Rachael shook her head. 'It's the money, Katie. We need my money as well as yours to get by.'

'Why?' Katie persisted. 'Is it to do with dad?'

Rachael's face crumpled, her lower lip trembled and tears rolled down her cheeks.

'He's started smoking,' she sobbed. 'That's where all the money is going.'

Katie frowned. 'He's always smoked, ever since he first came home.'

Rachael rubbed her eyes with the back of her hand. 'That was only cigarettes. Now he's smoking opium. And if he gets caught I don't know what will happen. It would certainly mean another prison sentence.'

'Perhaps that's the best thing that could happen. Now I'm working we could manage. Think about it, Mam. It was better when we were on our own.'

'Ssh!' Rachael shook her head. 'He's my husband and your dad. I have to stick by him.'

Chapter Twenty

The thought of her dad smoking opium troubled Katie dreadfully. She knew her mam was right and that if the police found out he would end up back in prison.

Although her feelings for him had changed so much since the night he had almost raped her, she was still concerned because she knew that her mother would be deeply distressed if such a thing happened.

She was so worried, that in the end she confided in Aled Phillips.

As usual, Aled did his best to allay her fears. Being a lot more streetwise than she was, he knew all about the Tiger Bay opium dens and even knew which one her father visited.

'Will you take me there?' she begged.

Aled looked alarmed. 'It's not the sort of place women go to,' he told her.

'I want you to take me there when my dad is there,' Katie insisted. 'If I actually catch him there he can't deny what he is doing, and I might be able to get him to stop before he gets caught.'

'It's not a good idea for you to go there,' Aled

argued. 'If anyone sees you they might think you were there for other purposes.'

'Other purposes?' she looked puzzled. 'Do you mean they might mistake me for a prostitute?'

Aled looked embarrassed. 'Well, yes, something like that,' he admitted.

'I live in a brothel as it is, so what difference does it make?' Katie asked bitterly.

He shrugged non-committally. 'Betti Davies's place is considered to be high class and quite respectable. Anyway,' he rushed on, 'your rooms are at the top of the building so it's not as though you have anything to do with what's going on in the rest of the house.'

'I'll remind you of that if there's ever a police raid!' she grinned.

'That's pretty unlikely to happen, since several of the top police use the place themselves,' he said wryly.

'I don't know anything about that and I don't want to talk about it,' Katie told him impatiently. 'What I do want to know is where does my dad go to smoke opium. I'm pretty certain he doesn't do it here at home.'

'I'm sure he doesn't, or you'd know by the smell. It lingers everywhere and there's no mistaking it.'

'You seem to know a lot about it?'

Aled flushed. 'I get around in my job,' he said evasively. 'I know where most businesses are.'

'Then in that case, you can take me there. When are we going?'

Aled tried hard to persuade Katie that there was no point in her seeing where her dad went, but she was so insistent that in the end he capitulated.

'It could be dangerous, it's where all the Chinese live. They don't like being spied on so you'd be much better forgetting all about it,' he stressed, as they set out for the heart of Tiger Bay.

'I've got you to protect me,' she said, taking his arm and smiling up at him as they walked down Bute Street together.

Aled was still as tall and as gangly as he'd been as a young boy, but there was an air of self-assurance about him that made Katie feel she was quite safe.

The opium den that he knew Lewis Roberts used was situated in a small grimy court. To reach it they had to walk past a public house called the Coalman's Arms, and Aled warned her that it had a terrible reputation. It was popular with the roughest sailors of every nationality under the sun, and one of their first ports of call when they came ashore.

There were drunken brawls there most nights of the week and a squad of police attended regularly on Saturday nights, knowing there was bound to be trouble.

As Aled had warned Katie, both the pub and

the court alongside it was the haunt of prosti-tutes. They were not dolled-up, well-dressed, buxom young girls like the ones who flaunted themselves at Betti Davies's place. These were bleary-eyed, raddled, tousled-haired women of indeterminate ages, who were lolling in door-ways or squatting on doorsteps waiting for trade. They eyed Katie up suspiciously.

The 'den' was the third house along in the Coalman's Court and consisted of three rooms and a washhouse. A tired-looking Chinese woman answered the door and, when Aled told her they had arranged to meet Lewis Roberts there, she let them in without asking any questions.

The dark sloe eyes in her yellow-skinned face were inscrutable, as she took them down a dark hall and led them up a narrow dirty staircase. There was a subtle, sickening smell that made Katie's stomach churn, and if Aled hadn't been right there by her side she knew she would have turned and run.

The room they were taken into was dingy and dilapidated. There were rain stains on the ceiling and the walls were grimy with smoke and grease. The small window let in hardly any light, because several of the panes were broken and covered over with brown paper.

A large bed, that was covered with a grubby patchwork counterpane, took up most of the floor space. On the table alongside it was a metal pot, and a small brass lamp.

Katie's eyes were drawn to the bed where her father lay sprawled, sucking greedily on a very long bamboo pipe, a rapturous look on his lined face.

A gurgling sound came from the pipe, but there was hardly any smoke, only a faint purple vapour rising into the air from the bowl of it.

He seemed to be in another world and he was completely unaware that they were standing there, right beside him.

As they watched, he stopped sucking on the dark-coloured bamboo tube, and as it dropped from his lips his head lolled back against the greasy pillow.

Katie moved closer, and clutching at his shoulder tried to shake him back to the present. Slowly, he opened his eyes and stared at her glassily, but with a faraway sublime smile on his face.

Aled caught her by the arm and tried to pull her away. 'Leave him alone,' he whispered. 'You can't reach him, he isn't conscious of anything that is happening at the moment. I think we should go now, Katie,' he added uneasily.

'No!' She shook Aled's restraining hand away. 'I'm going to wait here until the effects of what he's been smoking wears off, and he comes round.'

'And what then?'

She looked at him helplessly, her big grey

eyes dark with concern. 'I don't know. Tell him to stop doing it, I suppose.'

Aled was suddenly aware of some sort of commotion going on downstairs. Before he could warn Katie, a Chinaman burst into the room, followed hot on his heels by the woman who had let them in. They were both arguing furiously, and the man moved towards Katie, waving his hands angrily and shouting at her in Chinese.

'I think he's saying that you shouldn't have been allowed to come up here and that he wants you to leave,' Aled whispered.

'You're making that up, you don't understand Chinese,' Katie said accusingly.

'No, but I bet it's what he means. He doesn't like us being here, you can see that for yourself.'

'Isn't there some way of telling him that it is my father who's lying there on that bed and who has been smoking that horrible pipe?'

Aled shook his head. 'I don't know. Perhaps if we tell the woman she can translate for us.'

'He already know, but he still want you to go,' the woman said in a flat nasal voice. 'Mr Roberts is a valued friend. He no want him upset by seeing you here when he come round, in case it causes scene.'

Katie bit her lip. She understood their concern, but she wanted her dad to know she'd been there, and had seen for herself what he got up to.

'I have a message for him, it is very urgent,' she told the woman.

'You tell it to me and I tell it him later,' the woman promised. 'Shock not good for him, make him sick up here,' she added, tapping her head with one finger.

'Come on, Katie,' Aled urged. He didn't want to be involved in a scene either. He'd heard plenty of scurrilous stories about what happened if the Chinese became upset. In no time at all it could degenerate into a fight, and that meant knives.

'Will you tell Mr Roberts that his daughter was here, right here in this room, and that she will talk to him when he gets home,' Katie said firmly.

The Chinese woman's face remained inscrutable as she bowed her head in acknowledgement. Then, with a hurrying gesture, she waved them towards the stairs.

'We should have insisted on waiting until he was awake,' Katie said, as they made their way out of Coalman's Court.

'Those Chinese people wouldn't have let you,' Aled told her. 'It was better to leave quietly than find ourselves thrown out, or involved in a brawl.'

'You could have stood up to a little man like that! And I could have held that woman off, I'm sure.'

'If we had refused to leave then they would have raised the alarm, and before you know it there would have been half a dozen more of them on the scene.'

'Which means that we've left my dad to their mercies!'

'Don't worry, he'll be OK. He's a long-standing, regular-paying customer, they certainly won't want him to come to any harm!'

'He'll come to some harm from me, though, when he gets home,' Katie vowed. 'To think that my mam goes out scrubbing other people's floors and doorsteps so that he has the money to indulge in that filthy stuff,' she said angrily.

'Do you think she knows?'

'Oh, she knows all right. It was my mam who told me he had started smoking it.' She laughed bitterly. 'At first I thought she meant cigarettes! The trouble is she's too scared to say anything to him.'

'Does he take your money as well for it?' Aled frowned.

'I hand over every penny I earn, I always have,' Katie told him heatedly. 'Well, except for the tips,' she grinned. 'He doesn't know about them and I make sure I keep that money well hidden. Someday,' she went on dreamily, 'I'm planning to rent a couple of rooms somewhere nice, as far away from Loudon Square and Tiger Bay as possible, just for me and my mam.'

Aled shook his head. 'I don't want you to go too far away, Katie.' He squeezed her arm and his long face went beetroot red. 'You're very special to me, Katie, and I'd miss you something dreadful if you did!'

'You've been the best friend I've ever had, Aled,' she assured him, 'even if we do fall out now and again.' She reached up to kiss him, but even though she stood on tiptoes her lips barely grazed his chin.

He stopped and looked down at her in astonishment. 'Does that mean you really do care for me, Katie?'

'Of course I do, you great silly!' She grinned. 'Don't I always turn to you when I'm in trouble?'

'I know that, but I mean do you care for me enough to go out with me?'

'I do go out with you, and I go to the pictures with you sometimes. I'm out with you now,' she teased.

'I know, but I mean something more serious. I want you to come out with me, as my girl-friend,' Aled told her emphatically.

Katie's face sobered. 'I don't know about that,' she said hesitantly. 'Aren't we both a bit too young to be serious about each other? I don't want to tie myself down yet, anyway.'

He pulled back and began walking on, so fast that she had to run to keep pace with him.

'Look, we can give it a try if you like,' she said hastily, as she saw how his face had clouded over and knew she had hurt him. 'Why don't we go somewhere together this Saturday night?'

His face brightened. 'You mean on a date, a real date? Oh, Katie, I'd like that,' he beamed.

Chapter Twenty-One

If one thing in her life was going well, then there was always something else happening to cause problems for her, Katie decided.

She was enjoying being a waitress at Bridge Street Café very much, but at home things were far from calm. Her dad had found out about her following him to Coalman's Court with Aled, and although he had said nothing to her he'd vented his fury on Rachael.

Katie had been horrified when she'd come home from work the following evening to find her mother had a black eye as well as a cut lip, and that her arms and shoulders were covered in bruises.

'My dad did this to you?' she gasped in disbelief.

'You shouldn't have spied on him, cariad. I've never seen him in such a terrible rage,' Rachael told her.

'Where is he now?' Katie demanded. She felt so furious that she had trouble keeping her voice steady, and she couldn't wait to attack him both verbally and physically.

Rachael shook her head. 'It's best if you ignore what has happened, my lovely. There's no point in stirring up more trouble and you don't want your own pretty face marked for life now, do you?'

'I'd like to see him try!' Katie fumed, bristling with anger.

'Oh, make no mistake about it, cariad, he will if you rile him. He's so angry about what you've done he'll stop at nothing.'

Katie felt scared. This was a side of her dad she knew something about. She would never forget the attack he had made on her, or how scared she'd been of him for a long time afterwards. Even so, she refused to let her mother see how frightened she was.

'You should report him to the police, Mam,' she blustered.

Rachael sighed. 'What good would that do? The damage is done.'

'He's hit you before, remember!'

'Only since he came out of prison.' She sighed heavily. 'Before that, he was a lovely man. Kind, gentle and a perfect gentleman. I don't know what happened to him while he was in there, but it's changed him completely. Made him into an animal.'

'Oh, Mam!' Katie felt a chill shiver down her back as she studied her mother's black eye and swollen face.

Rachael shrugged dismissively. 'No point in drawing you into our squabbles now, was there, cariad. As long as the bruises weren't visible there was no need for you to know anything about it.'

'Oh, Mam, I'm so sorry. If you'd told me then I would have been more careful about the way I spoke to him. I feel it's all my fault that you've ended up like this.' Tenderly, she wrapped her arms around her mother, hugging her very gently.

'Where is he now, then?' she asked, fighting to keep her voice steady.

'Downstairs enjoying tea and sympathy with Betti Davies, I imagine.'

'You mean he's telling her about your quarrel?' Katie looked stunned. 'Why ever would he want to do that?'

'He probably has told her about what's happened, but that's not the only reason he's down with her.' Rachael's mouth tightened, but her face was inscrutable as she confided, 'They've been close for ages, see. Really close, I mean.'

'Are you saying that there's more between them than dad acting as one of her pimps?' Katie asked in disbelief.

'Oh yes, a lot more, cariad, but don't worry your head about it. I suppose it's partly my own fault. Since he came out of prison I've not been as good a wife to him as I should have been. I've been feeling a bit run down, cariad, so being the virile sort of man he is, he's looked elsewhere for his pleasures.'

'Oh, Mam! I can't believe I'm hearing this.'

Fear gripped Katie's insides making her stomach churn. 'Why didn't you tell me that you weren't feeling well? Have you been to see a doctor?'

She studied her mother as if seeing her for the first time. She'd been so busy with her own life ever since she'd left school, that she had taken her mother's health for granted. Her scalp crawled with sweat as she noticed how thin and frail her mam had become.

'Now don't worry about me, cariad,' Rachael said gently. 'It's just this old cough of mine that leaves me breathless and exhausted. The trouble is it won't seem to go away.'

'Of course I'm worried about you, Mam. You shouldn't be working. You're out at the crack of dawn every morning, scrubbing and cleaning, when you should be resting and taking things easy.'

'Life's not like that, is it, my lovely,' Rachael sighed. 'We all have to work if we want to eat and pay our way.'

'Except my dad,' Katie said bitterly. 'He seems to manage to get other people to do the work and he sits back and enjoys the results!'

She studied her mother's lined face and careworn hands, roughened by years of cleaning work. She thought back guiltily to earlier days, and remembered how her mam had given her whatever food was available and often made do with just a cup of milkless tea herself.

At the time, childlike, she'd thought it was

because that was all her mam had wanted. Now, she realised that it was probably a case of her mam doing without so that there was more for Katie to eat.

It was probably all those years of being undernourished that were taking their toll on her mam's health now. It wasn't only that she was painfully thin, but she looked so lacklustre in every other way. Her hair was lifeless, her eyes red-rimmed, and even her skin was an unhealthy yellow colour.

Katie was pretty sure that her mam didn't eat properly, even now. The sort of meals that were being put on the table was something she gave hardly any thought to, because she was able to eat her fill of whatever she fancied at work. Mario and Gina were both splendid cooks and produced such a variety of mouth-watering dishes every day that she was spoiled for choice.

She was sure it was the sort of food that would tempt her mother's appetite and perhaps put the colour back into her cheeks. She wondered if she could persuade her to come to the café for a meal one day.

Rachael smiled thinly when Katie suggested it. 'I don't think you'd want them to see me looking like this!'

Katie nodded understandingly. She'd leave it for a few days until her mam's face was better and then she'd mention it again, she decided.

'I'm so glad you like your job at the café so much, cariad,' Rachael murmured.

'Oh, I do, Mam!' Her face lit up, her mother's illness and other problems momentarily forgotten. 'Mario and Gina are lovely people to work for. Mario sings all the time he is working and Gina joins in with him sometimes!'

'And what about the customers? Are they nice to you?'

'Most of them are, especially the regulars.' She smiled, thinking of one man in particular, Mr Thomas. He was in his thirties, good looking with straight dark hair that he wore brushed back from his broad forehead and eyes that were such a deep shade of blue they were almost navy-blue. He was well spoken, expensively dressed and very polite. He came in each lunchtime, promptly at twelve-thirty. He was always in a hurry and she knew he liked the single table tucked away in the corner by one of the windows, so she made a point of keeping it free for him.

The first time she'd put the 'Reserved' card on it she'd seen the look of dismay on his face. She'd left the customer she was serving to rush up to him and explain that she had reserved it for him, and had been rewarded with a warm smile.

After that, he made his way straight to that special table and she made sure she was on hand within minutes to serve him.

They gradually exchanged more than the

mere formal greetings. The day he told her that he was in business in St Mary Street, which was why he found it so convenient to come to this particular café every lunchtime, she'd been quite touched, because she felt that confiding in her like that made them friends.

That was all she did know about him, but she conjured up all sorts of scenarios in her mind and dreamed of the day when she would get to know him better.

'And what about Aled Phillips, then? You seem to have no time for him or any of your other friends from around Louisa Street.'

Her mother's question brought her back to the present.

'I don't see very much of Ffion and Megan but Aled is still a good friend.' She smiled dismissively. 'You know he's always looked out for me, ever since the first day I started school.'

Rachael sighed. 'Yes, he's grown up into a very nice boy. I used to see him around on his red bicycle delivering telegrams.'

'He's training to be a postman now he's old enough,' Katie told her. 'He's been looking forward to it because it means he'll earn more money, of course. He's asked me to go out with him to the pictures on Saturday night,' she added, her face flushing.

'You've been to the pictures with him before, haven't you?' Rachael frowned.

'Yes, once or twice. This is more like a proper

date though, at least that's what he says, because he will be paying for me.'

Rachael looked worried. 'You will be careful now, won't you, cariad. You are too young to start being serious about boys and he's older than you and probably looking for a steady girlfriend.'

'I know that, Mam. I told Aled I wasn't ready to be serious, but he said he still wanted us to go out together.'

'That's all right, as long as you're not filling his head with too many hopes.'

'No, don't worry, Mam. I like Aled as a friend but nothing more than that. I'm certainly not interested in being his regular girlfriend, even though he asked me to be. I don't intend marrying the first chap who asks me,' she went on thoughtfully. 'I want something more than that out of life. When I settle down it will be with someone who can afford a lovely house and can buy me nice clothes, and has enough money for us to live on so that I will never have to work again!'

'That sounds so wonderful, my lovely. I only hope it comes true,' her mother smiled. 'We all dream of marrying a handsome husband and living like that.'

'You mean you had those sort of dreams, too?'

'Of course! And I thought they'd come true when I met your dad. Everything was so blissful when we were first married.'

'You never had your own home though, did you, Mam?'

'No,' Rachael sighed, 'it didn't seem to matter, though. My own mam and dad were both dead and Lewis's mam was kindness itself. Once I got used to her, and let her do things her way, we got along well enough, even after you were born.'

'Then why did everything go so wrong?'

Rachael sighed. 'The shock of your dad being caught stealing and sent to prison was too much for his mam. You were only a little girl but I know you remember her having a heart attack. Leastwise, that's what the doctor claimed she died from.'

'Do you think it was something different then, Mam?'

Rachael nodded. There were tears in her eyes. 'I'm quite sure she died from a broken heart because Lewis had been sent to prison,' she said sadly. 'He was her only child and she thought the world of him. She was widowed when he was quite small so he'd been her whole life, see!'

'My dad's caused a lot of heartache, hasn't he?' Katie said bitterly, anger in her grey eyes. 'Why do you stay with him, Mam?'

Rachael reached out and stroked Katie's long fair hair. 'I've told you before, cariad, he's my husband, so it is my duty to stand by him.'

'We were better off when we were on our own in one room in Louisa Street!'

'Not really, cariad.' Rachael shuddered. 'That was a dreadful place to live, all boxed up in that one dingy room. At least here we have a separate living room and you have your own bedroom.'

'It's what goes on downstairs that bothers me,' Katie frowned, her mouth stark with distaste.

'We're well away from it up here,' Rachael said consolingly.

'Not really, not if my dad is mixed up in it all and carrying on with Betti Davies into the bargain,' Katie said bitterly, unable to suppress her overpowering disgust about what was happening. 'I wish I could take you away from all this, Mam. It would be really lovely, just the two of us in a place of our own.'

Chapter Twenty-Two

All through 1933, life for Katie seemed to divide itself into sharply different compartments: work, home, and the time she spent with Aled.

At home she was engulfed by pity and concern about her mother's deteriorating health. She found her father's nonchalance about it all both irritating and unreasonable.

His philandering with Betti Davies didn't help matters and Katie wanted so much to point this out to him. She would have done so, only her mam had begged her not to interfere.

'It will do more harm than good if you do,' her mother insisted, 'and he'll only tell you it is none of your business.'

Katie now spent most of what little leisure time she had with Aled, or very occasionally with Ffion or Megan. Both of them were now working at Curran's factory along the Taff Embankment. They didn't work on a Saturday so they would sometimes call in at Bridge Street Café when they were in town shopping, purely for the fun of ordering tea and cakes from Katie. The minute she had taken their order and moved off to get it for them she could hear them giggling, and knew they were talking about her.

At first it had hurt, but when she thought about how much better off her working environment was than theirs she shrugged it off.

She was happy at the Bridge Street Café, whereas they seemed to grumble most of the time about their jobs because making aluminium pots and pans was such dirty, smelly work. What's more they were working with a bunch of loud-mouthed men who spent their time calling after them or making suggestive remarks.

That was so totally different to the kind of people Katie encountered each day that she decided she was the one who should be laughing at them, not the other way around.

Far from dreading the start of a new week, Katie looked forward to it, knowing she would be seeing Mr Thomas each lunchtime. His warm smile and friendly greeting always set her heart pounding and her blood racing.

No matter how busy they were, Katie made sure she found time to stop by his table to make certain that everything was to his liking. They would chat for a few minutes, even if it was only about the weather. It was not what he said, or the sound of his voice, but the expression on his handsome face as his dark blue eyes met hers that she carried with her for the rest of the day.

She studied every detail about him. She couldn't make up her mind whether he was married or not, and she had no way of finding out. If he was, then his wife didn't look after him nearly as well as she should. Often, there was a button missing on his shirt, or his tie clashed with it or with his suit. Sometimes he wore the same shirt for three days running, and once, to her amusement, she'd noticed that he was even wearing odd socks.

She wondered if perhaps he lived on his own and that he was absent-minded. Or was it that he was so absorbed in his work that he didn't notice things like that?

The day she found he had left his wallet behind she decided that he was absent-minded, and that it was because he was so wrapped up in his work.

She didn't find the wallet until she was clearing his table and she decided that it was too late to run after him. She also knew that the right thing to do was to hand it over straight away to Mario or Gina, but she couldn't resist the temptation to look inside and see if there was any clue as to where he lived.

As she had expected, his business card was inside the wallet. She scanned it eagerly, but it only told her what she already knew:

Roderick Thomas
Sales Manager
SOUTH WALES BOOT & SHOE COMPANY
19A St Mary Street, Cardiff

As she returned it to the wallet she noticed another smaller card and her heart raced as she realised that this gave his home address:

> *Roderick Thomas*
> 15 Cathedral Close
> Cardiff

For the rest of the afternoon, Katie battled with her conscience over what she knew was the right thing to do and what she wanted to do.

Every time she walked into the kitchen and saw Mario or Gina in there she knew she ought to hand the wallet over to them, but she couldn't bring herself to do so. She wanted to return it to him herself.

Her only fear was that Roderick Thomas might discover his wallet was missing and come back to the café to see if he had dropped it there. If he did, then she knew she would be in trouble. She would have difficulty explaining to Mario why she'd held onto it, instead of handing it over to him for safekeeping. He might even think she had been trying to steal it. If that happened, then he might sack her on the spot.

The thought sent shivers through her, yet, although she knew she was taking a considerable risk, she couldn't bring herself to abandon the idea of returning the wallet herself.

The thought of doing so as soon as she finished work stayed with her for the rest of the day. It wouldn't take long, she kept telling herself. Cathedral Road was in the opposite direction to the way she went home, but it wasn't all that far away, only the other side of Cardiff Castle.

The moment the café closed at five o'clock, Katie scurried around clearing the tables and re-laying them ready for the morning, then she shot off, eager to undertake her self-imposed task.

All the trams were packed and there were long queues. She wasn't quite sure which ones went right down Cathedral Road. Some of them only passed along Castle Street and Cowbridge Road which was at the top end of it. She wasn't sure, either, whether Cathedral Close was at the top end or towards the bottom of Cathedral Road, so she decided she might as well walk.

It was a bright July evening and it felt good to be out in the fresh air. As she cut up Westgate Street to Cathedral Road the wallet almost seemed to be burning a hole in her pocket.

Perhaps she should have called at his office in St Mary Street first to see if he was there, she thought guiltily. She tried telling herself that it was too late in the day and that he was bound to have left for home, but the real truth, she knew, was that she wanted to see where he lived.

Cathedral Close was a cul-de-sac. The houses were all double-fronted and imposing. They reminded Katie of the houses where her mother cleaned. No. 15 was a handsome house, well built, solid, with large bay windows on the ground floor and deep sash windows above. With its black and white paintwork, neat front garden, laurel hedge and fancy wrought-iron fencing, it symbolised well-to-do family living.

Katie walked past it, then turned around, took a deep breath, and walked back again. This time she opened the wrought-iron gate and walked up the pathway to the front door, which was recessed inside a glazed porch.

As she pressed the bell and listened to it ringing deep inside the house, she admired the brilliantly coloured leaded-light glazing on either side of the porch. The bright blues and vivid reds were blended with darker blues, yellows and greens, to form striking flower patterns that spiralled from ground level right up to the top of the panes. A similar pattern was etched into the centre panel of the front door.

Katie was surprised when no one came to answer the bell, because she was sure Roderick Thomas would be home by now. She pressed it again, but still no one opened the door, although she thought she could hear a move-ment in the hall.

She wondered what to do for the best.

She could simply push the wallet in through the shiny brass letter box. He'd be sure to find it when he got home. Or she could try the next house, just to make sure he did actually live here. It would be a disastrous state of affairs, she told herself, if she pushed the wallet in and then found out he had moved or something.

'Third time lucky,' she murmured aloud, as once more she pressed the bell.

This time the door did open, but only the merest crack, and Katie found herself looking down into the scared face of a very young boy.

For a moment they both stared at one another in shocked surprise. 'Hello!' She smiled down at him. 'Does Mr Roderick Thomas live here?' she asked.

The boy nodded, pushing his straight dark hair back from his brow. His dark blue eyes were wary, his square chin jutted almost defensively.

'Is he in? I would like to speak to him, please.'

'He's not home from work yet,' the boy told her.

From behind the boy a small girl, who was even younger, appeared. She, too, had straight dark hair which was caught back in a slide. Her oval face was streaked with tears and she was holding a hand to one side of her face, which appeared to be bright red and slightly swollen.

'Whatever is the matter with your little sister?' Katie asked. For a moment she thought perhaps they had been quarrelling and that he had hit her, but when he put his arm around the little girl's shoulders as though trying to comfort her she realised it was something more than that.

'Rhia's got earache,' he explained, 'and she won't let me put any camphorated oil in her ear to make it better.'

'I want my daddy to do it, not you,' Rhia sobbed.

'Can't you let your mam do it?' Katie suggested.

'We haven't got a mother,' the boy scowled. 'She's dead!'

'Oh!' Katie felt so taken aback that for a moment she didn't know what to say or do. Then common sense took over as she saw how distressed Rhia was. 'Would you let me put some drops of camphorated oil in your ear, Rhia?' she asked gently. 'I'll do it very carefully,' she promised.

The child studied her for a long moment, then slowly she nodded.

'I'd better come in then, hadn't I?' Katie said.

The boy stood there, not moving and making no attempt to open the door any wider.

'Are you going to let me in?'

He shook his head doubtfully. 'We don't know you,' he blurted out. 'You haven't said why you are here.'

'My name is Katie and I know your father,' she told him quietly. 'He comes into the café where I work for his lunch every day.'

'So why have you come here to see him?'

'He left his wallet behind at lunchtime so I was bringing it back to him.' Katie put her hand into her pocket, brought out the wallet and held it out for the boy to see.

'Yes, that is his wallet,' he said slowly. He chewed his lower lip between strong little white teeth for a second, while he considered the matter. 'I suppose it's all right to let you in,' he said rather reluctantly as he pulled the door back.

'Thank you!'

As Katie stepped into the hallway, Rhia grabbed hold of her hand. 'Are you going to make my earache go away?' she whimpered.

Katie squeezed the little girl's hand. 'I'll try to do so, Rhia,' she promised. She turned to the boy. 'Can you bring me the camphorated oil, then? And I need some cotton wool if you can find any.'

'Take Katie into the sitting room, Rhia, while I fetch them,' he instructed. He paused. 'Is there anything else you need, Katie?'

'I don't think so. It would be nice if you could tell me your name, though,' Katie suggested.

'Sorry,' he mumbled, looking uncomfortable. 'My name is Barri, and I'm ten. Rhia's only six,' he added as an afterthought, before he headed off to fetch the cotton wool and camphorated oil so that she could attend to Rhia's earache.

Rhia, still clutching Katie's hand tightly, took her along the hallway to a door on the left that led into the sitting room.

Katie gulped back a gasp of astonishment. She had never seen such an elegant room, not even when she had gone to big houses cleaning with her mam.

The French doors at the far end were framed by blue velvet drapes and looked out onto a neat paved terrace that separated the house from a lawn edged with flowerbeds. At the far end of the garden was a huge tree, pink with blossom.

The room itself took Katie's breath away. The delicately patterned blue wallpaper shimmered in the evening light and there was a deep gold carpet on the floor. It was comfortably furnished with a big sofa and two immense armchairs, and they were all upholstered in blue and gold patterned moquette.

A walnut bookcase ran the full length of one wall and Katie had never seen so many books. There was also a handsome walnut display cabinet holding pretty china figurines and other pieces of decorative pottery and glassware.

Over the marble fireplace was a huge mirror with bevelled edges and it reached right up to the ceiling.

For a moment, Katie wondered if the children were allowed in such a splendid room. Then, on a low table in the middle of the room, she saw there was an assortment of picture books, some of them open, and some colouring crayons.

Despite being so elegant, the room had such a warm, welcoming atmosphere that as she sat down in one of the armchairs and took Rhia on her lap, it brought a lump to Katie's throat.

Chapter Twenty-Three

There was a look of astonishment on Roderick Thomas's face when he arrived home twenty minutes later, let himself in with his doorkey and found Katie in an armchair in the sitting room nursing Rhia, who was almost asleep.

'Whatever is going on?' he asked in mild surprise. 'Katie! What are you doing here? And what is the matter with Rhia, why has she been crying?'

'Katie brought your wallet back, she said you'd left it in the café. Rhia had earache and was crying and she wouldn't let me put camphorated oil in her ear, so Katie did it,' Barri exclaimed nervously. 'After that, Rhia started crying again and said she wanted to be cuddled and so Katie said she'd stay until you came home,' he ended breathlessly.

'I see! And where was Mrs Clarke when all this was happening?'

'She went home at five o'clock as usual.'

'I asked her to stay on until I got home,' Roderick said angrily. 'I explained I had a meeting that wouldn't finish until six o'clock. Mrs Clarke is my daily housekeeper,' he explained to Katie, 'but she also acts as a baby-sitter when I am going to be late getting home.'

'She said she had to leave on time tonight because it was Mr Clarke's birthday. She said to say sorry she forgot to tell you this morning,' Barri told him. He grinned widely. 'She's left a casserole in the oven for our meal, though, and I'm starving.'

'Well, that's something, I suppose. She should have phoned me and reminded me though,' Roderick sighed. 'It isn't right for the children to be on their own when they're so young,' he told Katie earnestly.

Katie smiled understandingly. 'Barri did explain all that to me, which was one of the reasons I thought I had better wait for you to come home,' she said shyly.

'And I was crying and didn't want her to leave,' Rhia piped up sleepily.

'How is your earache now, cariad?' he asked tenderly, as he took Rhia from Katie's arms and hugged her.

'Gone!' She clapped her hands. 'Katie made it all better!'

'Clever Katie!' Roderick smiled at Katie over the top of his daughter's head.

'Can Katie stay and have some of Mrs Clarke's casserole with us?' Rhia begged.

'Well ...' Roderick Thomas paused awkwardly and looked questioningly at Katie.

Colour flooded her face as she shook her head. 'No, I really must be getting home, but thank you all the same. I only came to return your wallet. You left it behind on your table at lunchtime,' she explained, as she stood up and prepared to leave.

'Thank you very much for doing that,' he said with obvious relief. 'I was going to report it to the police but I didn't know whether I'd accidentally dropped it, had it stolen or left it in your café.'

Rhia insisted on kissing Katie goodbye as Barri opened the front door for her. The three of them stood on the doorstep waving to her until she turned the corner into Cathedral Road.

All the way home Katie's mind was filled with what she'd seen and heard. Now she understood why Roderick Thomas sometimes looked dishevelled or appeared to be absent-minded.

The house was beautiful and very well looked after. However, it must be very worrying for him to have to care for such young children on his own, Katie reasoned, especially since the woman who came in daily did not appear to be as responsible as she might be.

They were very sweet children, she decided. Barri was such a sturdy little chap and it was touching to see how hard he was trying to look after his little sister. Rhia was a pretty, winsome little thing and Katie felt sure that when she was feeling well she could be mischievous and quite a handful. There was a sparkle in her deep blue eyes and Katie loved the way her cheeks dimpled when she smiled.

Katie felt attracted to both children, and as she made her way home she very much hoped she would be seeing them again.

It would be so lovely if her own mam could go and work for Roderick Thomas and look after the two children, she mused. The work would be so much easier than scrubbing floors and general cleaning.

She wondered if she dared talk to her about it. It would mean telling her all about Roderick Thomas, of course, and she wasn't sure if she wanted to do that. She didn't want her mam getting the wrong idea or thinking that she was running after him.

Katie did nothing to further her plans that night, because when she reached home she found her mam in tears and her dad in a furious temper.

At first, Katie thought that it was because she was so late, but neither of them seemed aware of the fact. They were far too engrossed in the row that was going on between them.

'I'll tell you this,' Lewis Roberts stormed as he banged out of the room, 'either you do it or that daughter of yours can. Duw Anwyl! The money you two bring in is pitiable! A young kid could earn as much doing a paper-round! This is the last chance for the pair of you, otherwise you can both bugger off.'

'What on earth is going on?' Katie asked in

alarm, as she heard her father pounding down the stairs and guessed he was going to see Betti Davies.

Rachael was too upset to answer. She sat with her arms folded across her body, hugging herself and rocking backwards and forwards.

'Mam, come on, tell me what has been happening?' Katie insisted, as she put her arms around her mother and held her close. 'Is it because I'm late home?'

She felt saddened as she realised how frail her mother had become lately. It was like holding a skeleton; she could feel every bone in her mam's body.

'No, cariad, it has nothing to do with that,' Rachael told her. 'You are late though, I was beginning to worry.'

'You shouldn't do, I can take care of myself. Come and sit and talk to me. Would you like me to make some tea?'

Rachael nodded.

'Come on, what was my dad on about,' Katie asked, as she put the kettle on to boil and reached down two cups and saucers. 'What did he mean when he said that if you wouldn't do it, then I would have to?'

'He wants me to go and work for Betti Davies,' her mother whispered. Her hazel eyes were filled with despair as she looked up at Katie. 'She wants us both to work for her, but I told him I'd see you dead before I'd let that happen.'

'Mam!' Katie stiffened. 'He's said all that before but he doesn't really mean it.'

'Oh, he meant it all right, every word!' her mother said bitterly.

'So why has he brought it up again now?' Katie queried.

'I lost my cleaning job today, so that's probably why.'

'Oh, Mam, however did that happen?'

'The agency said they'd had complaints about my work. They said some of the women thought I shirked the heavy jobs because I wasn't up to it. They're probably right,' she added gloomily. 'I do find it hard work cleaning out kitchens and scrubbing and pumice-stoning front doorsteps, especially when it means carrying buckets of water up and down flights of steps. I haven't got the energy I used to have.'

'You certainly don't look well,' Katie agreed. Her mind was racing round and round like a clockwork car. Was this Fate playing into her hands? Should she suggest to Roderick Thomas that her mother would be the ideal person to work for him? Was it the time to tell her mother about him and his two lovely little children, and ask her if she would be interested in working as his housekeeper?

Katie opened her mouth to speak and then shut it again. Was it fair to raise her mother's hopes? She wasn't at all sure that he would be willing to employ her mam when she looked so wan and frail.

The fact that she had just been sacked because she wasn't strong enough to do her work wouldn't impress him either. Perhaps it would be better to wait a week or two to let her mam have a rest and regain some of her strength. In the meantime, though, there was her father's threat, and it was easy to see that her mam was taking it seriously.

'Why don't you go and lie down, Mam,' she suggested. 'Have an early night and everything might look different in the morning. You can sleep in my room tonight if you like?'

'No, no, my lovely,' Rachael said quickly. 'If I did that it would only rile him all the more. Anyway, the chances are he'll stay downstairs with her so he won't bother me any more tonight.'

Tears filled Rachael eyes as she squeezed Katie's hand. 'Try not to hate your dad, cariad. He's changed so much since he's been in prison, he's not the same man at all.'

Katie shook her head. 'I can't help feeling as I do about him, Mam. Why does he have to be so hateful and say such dreadful things to us both? Why does he have to smoke opium and act as a pimp for Betti Davies?'

'A lovely man he was, when I first knew him,' Rachael told her dreamily. 'So handsome and so kind and gentle. His own mam indulged him, mind. Cosseted him and made sure he had everything of the best. It broke her heart when he was caught stealing. There was no need for it; she would have given him the moon if he'd asked her for it. I think he did it for the excitement.'

'Excitement?' Katie stared at her in astonishment.

'That's right, cariad. You see, all the time he was growing up he had everything so easy. He never had to work or struggle. His dad died when he was only a boy and after that his mam took care of everything. They had a nice home and enough money to live on . . .'

'And she spoiled him?' Katie questioned bitterly.

'I'm afraid so. Even after we were married she ruled the roost, and like a fool I went along with it. I never stood up to her. She ran the house her way and handled all the money. That's why things were in such a dreadful state after she died. I had no idea about coping and I'd never had any money of my own. The money she had coming in each week was some kind of pension that her husband had arranged and, of course, when she died the pension simply ended.'

'We managed though,' Katie said with a wry grin.

'Not really, cariad. If I had my time over again I would have done things in a very different way. Still,' she let go of Katie's hand and stood up, 'it's too late to change things now. We have to get on with our lives and make the best of what we have.' She smiled weakly.

'Weren't you supposed to be going out with Aled Phillips tonight?'

Katie's hand flew to her mouth. 'I'd forgotten all about that,' she gasped. 'I should have met him over half an hour ago.'

'I'm sure he'll still be waiting,' her mother smiled. 'That boy is besotted by you. I hope you're not leading him on, it will break his heart if you are.'

'I've told you before, Mam, I don't think of Aled in that way. He's just a good friend, that's all. And he knows that. We were only going for a walk and perhaps down to the new Milk Bar that's opened near the Pier Head.'

'Well then, you'd better run along and meet him or he'll be standing on the corner waiting all night for you.'

Katie hesitated. 'Will you be all right here on your own for a couple of hours?'

'Of course I will. I've already told you, I won't see any more of your dad tonight because he'll probably stay downstairs with Betti Davies.'

Katie still hesitated, reluctant to leave her mother alone. She wanted to see Aled though, because he was the only one she could talk to about this latest trauma. He was so pragmatic about such things that she was sure he would be able to offer her some good advice. Even talking to him would help her to see the right way of dealing with the situation.

'I won't be late, Mam,' she promised.

Chapter Twenty-Four

Weeks passed, and still Katie couldn't bring herself to tell her mother about Roderick Thomas, because she wasn't at all sure how she would react. She was in such a strange mood since she had lost her cleaning job, as if she was unable to settle.

Katie worried constantly about her. She noticed that she had started wearing clothes that she had never seen before and which didn't fit very well or suit her. She was also wearing silk stockings instead of her lisle ones and using a strong musky perfume, vivid red lipstick, darkening her eyebrows and applying rouge. Sometimes it made her face look hard and raddled, at other times almost clown-like.

When Katie commented on this, Rachael snapped at her. 'What's wrong with making the best of myself? You are always saying I should get out more, so that's what I'm doing while the nice weather is still here. It will be winter soon and then I won't want to go out.'

The atmosphere between her mam and dad had also changed. They were no longer bickering or fighting and yet there was a coolness between them as though each of them lived their lives in a separate compartment.

Her dad seemed to spend more and more time downstairs in Betti Davies's part of the house. Her mam seemed to be in a constant daze, as though her mind was on something else all the time.

In the evening, as soon as they started to clear away and wash up, her dad would disappear. As soon as the last of the dishes had been put away, her mam would start looking anxious and question her about what she was going to do for the rest of the evening.

Usually, Katie was tired from being on her feet all day at the café. Often all she wanted to do was sponge and iron her uniform so that it was ready for the next day and then go to bed with a book and read until she fell asleep. Occasionally she would go out with Aled to the pictures or for a walk, but even then she was usually home again well before ten o'clock.

'Well, I'm off to bed,' her mother would tell her, 'so make sure that if you do go out you don't make a noise when you come in, cariad?'

'Of course I won't, Mam. Anyway, apart from you, who else is there to disturb? I always come in the back way up the metal staircase.'

'And mind you do!' her mother told her sharply. 'You don't want to get mixed up with anything that goes on downstairs at night and you might well be if you are seen approaching the front door.'

'I know all about that. It's been drummed into me ever since we found out what goes on down there!'

Once or twice she had asked, 'Would you like me to make you a hot drink and bring it to you in bed?' and her mother had almost snapped her head off.

'No! I want to be left alone and I don't want anyone coming in my bedroom and waking me up!'

Her dad had been in the room at the time and when she'd seen his mouth curve in a snide smile she'd felt her flesh creep.

Two nights later, unable to sleep because of the suspicions racing around in her mind, she'd crept along to her mother's bedroom and stood outside the door, straining her ears to see if she could hear any sound coming from inside. Then, very very cautiously, she turned the handle.

As she inched the door open she held her breath. As her eyes grew accustomed to the darkness within she could see that the bed was empty, and sweat rivered down the nape of her neck.

'She can't sleep either so she's gone to make herself a hot drink,' Katie whispered out loud.

The sound of her own voice increased the whirling panic inside her. She took a deep breath and exhaled it so slowly that she almost choked.

In an agony of nervousness she padded into

the living room. It was in darkness and she sensed as soon as she stepped over the threshold that it was empty.

Making her way over to the worktop she felt the kettle, but the moment her hand touched the metal side she knew it hadn't been used since they boiled up hot water to wash up the dishes after their evening meal.

Her legs were shaking so badly that she had to perch on the edge of a chair, or she was sure she would have fallen over.

If the bedroom was empty and there was no one here in the living room, then where was her mother? Instinctively she knew, but she felt much too scared to confront her suspicions.

The row that had taken place a couple of weeks earlier, and her father's ultimatum, resounded over and over again inside her head.

Surely her mother hadn't given in to his demands?

Katie knew the answer even before the question had formed in her mind. All the probing each evening about where she as going and what time she would be home again, her mother's instructions that she didn't want to be disturbed, they all fell into place like the pieces of a jigsaw. It was obvious that her mam didn't want her to go into her bedroom during the evening or when she came home because she wouldn't be in there!

The more she thought about it, the more distressed Katie became. She hadn't really taken her dad's ultimatum seriously. Surely he wouldn't want either of them to become involved with Betti Davies in that way. It was unthinkable! And that her mam had given in to his demands was equally unbelievable. Losing her job and not being able to find another was the reason, she supposed. Even so, her mother wasn't well. With her terrible cough she was not fit for any kind of work, most certainly not to go along with her dad's despicable suggestion.

Even if she had been well, that was not something she would have wanted to do anyway, Katie told herself indignantly. She wondered which of them she should talk to about it. She was sure her mam was frightened of her dad, so even if she pleaded with her not to give in to his demands she'd be afraid to tell him she wasn't going to work for Betti Davies. She should speak to her dad directly, but she didn't think he would listen to her. Perhaps the right person to talk to was Betti Davies herself.

Katie spent a sleepless night trying to work out what she ought to do. In the end she resolved she would speak to Betti Davies next morning. Perhaps if she explained about her mother's ill health she would listen and agree to 'sack' her.

The plan, which had seemed to be so logical and so easy when she was lying in bed in the dark, took on an entirely different aspect next day. Even so, with her mind made up, Katie was determined to go though with it.

She knew it was useless trying to speak to Betti until after midday as she seldom put in an appearance until then. Which meant leaving it until she got home from work, before the evening clientele arrived.

She felt so worried that she found it hard to concentrate on her work and her usually warm smile was mechanical and forced. She even avoided Roderick Thomas when he came in at midday, afraid that if she indulged in her usual chat she might let something slip about the dilemma she was facing.

Twice during the day, Mario asked her if she was feeling all right or whether someone had said something to upset her. Gina raised her eyebrows each time and gave her an understanding smile.

'Stop embarrassing poor Katie, it is probably women's problems making her feel out of sorts,' she scolded laughingly. 'You'll be bright as a button again tomorrow, yes?' she grinned at Katie.

Katie gave her a wan smile. 'I hope so,' she agreed.

She could have hugged Gina when at about half past four, as the café was emptying of the afternoon customers, she suggested, 'You run along! I can see to things. Hope you feel better tomorrow.'

Katie accepted gratefully. Arriving home early would give her a better opportunity to speak to Betti. For the first time since she'd moved into Loudon Square she used the front door instead of the metal staircase at the back. This way, she hoped, neither her mam or dad would know what she was about to do.

Betti heard the front door open and close and came sashaying out into the hall like a galleon in full sail. She was already dressed, ready to greet her clients in a swishing red and black taffeta dress, cut low to show off her ripe figure. Her face was powdered and painted, her hard green eyes outlined with mascara and she had her hair piled up in an elaborate style, so that the long, red earrings she was wearing dangled unimpeded from her ears.

Her heavily defined eyebrows shot up in surprise when she saw who it was. 'What are you doing coming in this way, Katie?' she asked frostily.

'I wanted a word with you,' Katie said hesitantly.

Betti surveyed her craftily. Katie was wearing a three-quarter-length light brown swagger coat that hung loose from her shoulders over the black dress and frilly white apron that she wore at the café, yet she still managed to look attractive.

If she was dolled up in a low-cut sleeveless silk or velvet dress, or a pretty taffeta with puffed sleeves, she'd be very eye-catching since she was so very young, Betti mused. She could see her now, teetering on high-heeled court shoes, flashing her flesh-coloured artificial silk stockings, winning lustful glances from every man who set eyes on her.

She had been suggesting to Lewis for months that he should persuade Katie to come and work for them. They had numerous clients who would pay handsomely for the services of such a fresh and innocent young girl. He'd promised to speak to her and Betti had been most hopeful, but instead it had been Rachael, his faded skinny wife, that he'd pressed into service.

Betti had too much experience to refuse to have Rachael on the payroll, but she was careful to see that she was allowed to entertain only the least important of her clientele. Rachael might have been pretty once, but now her looks had faded to such a degree that she looked time-worn and decrepit.

The thought that Katie was, at last, about to capitulate excited Betti. She led the way towards her lavishly furnished office and insisted that she sit down in a comfortable chair and have a glass of sweet white wine before they began to discuss whatever it was Katie had come to see her about.

Her apparent kindness and friendliness disconcerted Katie. She had arrived on the doorstep her mind full of all the things she intended to say, and now Betti's charming manner was undermining her determination.

As she sipped the wine and answered the seemingly innocuous questions Betti was asking her, she found it harder and harder to raise the real issue.

Finally, she drained the last of her wine, refused point blank to have her glass refilled, and confronted Betti Davies.

'It's about my mam,' she said unsteadily.

'Oh yes?' Betti's heavily made-up green eyes narrowed.

'I . . . I know she's working for you and I don't think she should be.'

'Really?' Although the woman's voice was bland and faintly amused, her mouth tightened.

Katie had a vague sense of unease as she blundered on. 'She's not well. She's lost an awful lot of weight recently, see . . .'

'So what are you trying to say, cariad?' Betti asked softly. 'Do you want to take her place?'

'Take her place?' Katie looked horrified. 'No, of course I don't want to take her place. I'm trying to tell you that she shouldn't be working.'

Betti smiled dismissively and shook her head. 'Surely that's for her to decide, not you?'

Colour stained Katie's cheeks. 'I'm sure she doesn't want to.'

Betti shrugged. 'Then it's up to her to tell me.'

'She's afraid to do so because she knows dad wants her to work for you, because he says we need the money. I'm sure we don't. No . . .' Katie stuttered in embarrassment. 'He works for you, and I hand over all my wages . . .' Her voice broke and she looked appealingly at Betti, hoping she would help her out.

Betty remained ominously silent, her carmine lips set in a grim, unrelenting line.

'I'm sure we could manage without my mam having to work,' Katie repeated lamely.

Betti shook her head. 'I doubt it. Your dad owes so much money that he needs every penny he can scrape together,' she observed. 'In return for working for me he pays no rent for the flat you are living in, but he has several bad habits. He spends a great deal on opium, on drink and on cigarettes.'

Katie shook her head and held her lower lip steady between her teeth to stop herself from breaking down and crying. It all sounded so hopeless.

She knew from the visit she had made with Aled to the house in Coalman's Court, where they'd found her dad smoking opium, that Betti was telling the truth, but why did her mam have to be punished for her dad's misdeeds? The thought of her mam being housekeeper to Roderick Thomas flashed through her mind. She wished she'd mentioned it to her mam before she'd got involved with Betti Davies. Now, if Roderick Thomas knew what she'd been doing for a living he wouldn't want her near his children.

He mightn't even want me near them, or wish to have anything further to do with me if he knew the truth about my background, she thought apprehensively.

'You could help them both, you know,' Betti's

oily tones cut across her thoughts. 'If you came to work for me you would be earning double what you are paid at that old café, cariad. Think of that. Imagine what a help it would be to your mam and dad. In time, if you proved to be popular with my clients, then you might even be able to afford for your mam to retire!'

As Katie opened her mouth to make a blistering retort, Betti smiled coldly and held up her hand in warning. 'Think about it, Katie. Don't speak out recklessly. If you turn down my offer I mightn't give you another chance!'

Chapter Twenty-Five

Katie found Christmas 1933 in Loudon Square dismal, but once New Year's Day 1934 was over and things were back to normal, she found talking to Roderick Thomas every day helped her to briefly put her own problems from her mind.

It was also one of the highlights of her day to hear his report of what Barri and Rhia had been doing, or the things they'd been saying.

Tentatively, she told him that if he ever needed someone to stay with Barri and Rhia in the evenings she would always be willing to do so, provided he gave her a day's notice.

His handsome face lit up at the news. 'That would be a tremendous help, Katie,' he told her. 'They would both be absolutely delighted if you did. They are always talking about you and asking when you are going to come and see them again. You would have to let me pay you, of course.'

Colour flooded her cheeks. 'No, no, don't do that, it wouldn't seem right,' she told him. 'I think they're lovely children, so it would be a real pleasure for me to be able to spend some time with them.'

'And I wouldn't dream of not paying you,' he insisted. 'Mrs Clarke doesn't mind staying on for half an hour or so, but she has her own family coming home from work for their evening meal which is why she likes to get home as promptly as possible.'

Between them they came to an amicable agreement about the arrangement that left Katie feeling that at least something was right in her world, and going the way she wanted it to do.

Aled was far less enthusiastic when she told him the news.

'So does that mean you're not going to have as much time to come out with me as before?' he asked glumly.

'I shouldn't think it will make any difference. We don't go out together all that often,' she protested, 'and it will only be once in a blue moon that he will ask me to look after them.'

'We could go out a lot more if you wanted to, but whenever I suggest it you always say that you are busy at home, or that you're tired or something,' he argued, his long face solemn.

'Well, I'm not too busy or too tired to go to the pictures with you on Saturday night,' Katie grinned.

His scowl vanished. 'Great. So what time shall I pick you up?'

Katie hesitated. Ever since she'd found out what her mother was doing every evening she'd made a point of discouraging Aled from coming to Loudon Square to pick her up. She was afraid that if he did, he might see or hear something that would lead him to guess what was happening. To her mind he knew far more about what went on in her family than she really liked.

She knew he often hung around in Loudon Square hoping to catch her if she went to the chippy or came out of the house at all during the evening, so that they could have a chat. It worried her that he did this and she wished he wouldn't, but she didn't see any way of stopping him.

She couldn't forget that Aled had taken it upon himself to follow her dad and find out all about his opium smoking. Because of this she was quite sure that, if he saw her mam in Betti Davies's doorway with one of the fellows who visited regularly, then he'd become suspicious about what she was doing. He'd probably make it his business to find out exactly what was going on and that was the last thing she wanted!

'Why don't we meet outside the Gaumont?' she suggested.

'If you like. If that's where you want to go,' he agreed.

'Jean Harlow in *Red Dust* is on there at the weekend, isn't it?'

'I don't know. I haven't bothered looking at the *Echo* because I didn't think you'd be coming out this weekend,' he said tonelessly.

'Whatever gave you that idea?' Katie snapped indignantly.

Aled shrugged his shoulders. 'Oh, I don't

know. You are so wrapped up in this Roderick Thomas and his kids that I don't know where I stand in your scheme of things half the time. You seem to be afraid to make any plans to go out with me, in case he needs you to babysit. I think it's just an excuse not to see me.'

'Don't talk daft, Aled. We're friends. Why would I try to avoid going out with you?'

He thrust his hands deep into his trouser pockets. 'Friends? Is that all we are ever going to be, good friends?'

He looked so doleful that Katie didn't know whether to laugh at him or hug him. 'Isn't that enough?' she teased.

'Darw! You know it isn't! I'm in love with you, Katie, and I want a damn sight more than just sitting next to you in the pictures.'

Katie frowned uneasily. Aled was getting far too serious for her liking and far too persistent with his attentions every time they went out together. He was no longer satisfied with a friendly goodnight kiss, but that was all she was prepared to give him. He must either accept that or else she would stop seeing him altogether, she told herself.

'Well, is Saturday night still on, or isn't it?' she demanded. 'No fumbling in the dark, mind, and a goodnight kiss and nothing else. All right?'

Aled pushed his badly cut dark hair back from his forehead and she looked away quickly as she saw the rebellious look in his dark eyes.

'I've not got much choice, have I,' he muttered exasperatedly. 'Why can't you be like Ffion Jenkins or Megan Edwards and come out on a proper date? They don't keep a bloke at arms length like you do!' His face went a deep shade of red. 'They're happy to kiss and cuddle and even go a lot further than that at times.'

'So how do you know all this?' she asked sharply. 'Have you been taking them out then?'

'Of course I haven't!' he retorted. 'You're the only one I want to go out with, as you very well know.'

'So you've been following them and spying on them, have you?'

'No, I have not! I was talking to Ffion's brother, Rees, and he told me.'

'Rees Jenkins!' Katie's lips curled. 'That little rat,' she said derisively. 'I'm surprised to hear that you have anything to do with him!'

Aled kicked at the pavement with the toe of his shoe and avoided her eyes. 'He lives in the next street to me, doesn't he, and I've known him all my life.'

Katie knew she was being unfair and quickly tried to make amends. 'So what time are we meeting?' she asked.

He shrugged his thin shoulders. 'Whatever time suits you. I'm not sure what time the big picture starts.'

'We want to be there in time to see Pathe News and the trailers, don't we?' Katie challenged.

'That's up to you,' he said balefully. Then he added more quietly, 'I'll meet you on your way home from work tomorrow night and let you know what time the big picture starts when I've checked it out.'

By Saturday night, Aled had forgotten their slight disagreement. He was at the Gaumont waiting when Katie arrived, and he was smartly turned out in grey slacks and a brown tweed jacket, a brown and white check shirt and a bright yellow tie.

Katie was glad she'd taken the trouble to dress up as well. She was wearing her favourite pale green artificial silk dress under her brown swagger coat. Her new high-heeled brown court shoes added on inches, so that her head was on a level with his shoulders.

Aled took her arm possessively, and not only insisted on paying for her ticket, but also bought her a box of her favourite chocolates.

To her dismay, he managed to find them double seats right at the back of the stalls, so there was no way she could stop him sitting as close to her as he possibly could.

He waited until halfway through the big picture, when she was completely absorbed in what was happening on the screen, before he slipped his arm around her shoulder. When she slipped off her swagger coat so that she could shrug his arm away he took advantage of her moving to let his hand slide down the back of the seat and encircle her waist.

It ruined the rest of the evening as far as Katie was concerned. She knew the seats he had chosen were popular with courting couples because they could kiss and cuddle, but she thought she'd made it quite clear that she didn't feel like that about him.

What was more, she wanted to watch the picture and, once he had his arm around her, only half her mind was on the screen because she was uneasy about where his hands were roaming.

Now that she had removed her coat he was able to slip his hand up under the blouse of her silky voile two-piece and the sensation of his bony fingers on her bare skin sent shudders through her.

Whenever she tried to pull away he held her even more tightly. When she sat very still he seemed to think she was happy about their closeness, and his fingers began exploring much more intimately than she liked or was prepared to permit. It seemed to Katie that she couldn't win and she was relieved when, finally, the lights went up and he had to desist.

On the way home she hardly spoke to him. She was so annoyed with him for the persistent way he'd tried to take liberties.

As soon as they reached Loudon Square she stopped on the corner and said, 'Goodnight', then walked off quickly before he could try to kiss her. She sensed he was still standing there watching her as she ran up the metal staircase at the back of the house. When she reached the top and risked looking back she felt quite guilty, because he was still standing where she'd left him, his gaze fixed on her.

Chapter Twenty-Six

Katie didn't sleep well on Saturday night and she felt tired and out of sorts all day on Sunday. She felt guilty about the abrupt way she'd walked off and left Aled standing on the corner after their night out.

Aled had always been a staunch friend and she knew he deserved better treatment than that, but it was his own fault because he wouldn't accept that she didn't feel the same way about him as he did about her.

To make amends she resolved she would ask him to go out with her on Wednesday night. It would be her treat. If she met him straight from work they'd catch the first showing at the Gaumont, so it needn't mean a late night.

She knew by the enthusiasm he'd shown when the trailer had come up on the screen on Saturday night, that he wanted to see the western that would be on. It wasn't really the sort of film she enjoyed, but for once she'd go along and see it with him and not say a word against it.

Aled looked so pleased when she told him that Katie felt even more uncomfortable about her behaviour the previous Saturday night.

Fortunately, she was so busy at work that she didn't have time to think about it during the day. In fact, she didn't even have time to stop and talk to Roderick Thomas when he came in just before one o'clock.

When she brought in his order, and placed it on the table in front of him, he reached out and caught her by the wrist as she was about to hurry away.

'One minute, Katie,' he smiled. 'I know you're rushed off your feet, but I was wondering if you could look after Barri and Rhia for an hour on Wednesday evening?'

'Yes, of course,' she smiled warmly, her colour rising.

'Could you come straight from work? I'll arrange for Mrs Clarke to stay on until you arrive. Can you be there by six o'clock?'

She nodded. 'I'm sure I can manage that. Sorry I can't stop to talk!' She raised her eyebrows and glanced around the busy room.

'I can see you're busy! I'll talk to you tomorrow then, and we can confirm the details.'

'Oh!' Suddenly, Katie remembered her arrangement to go out with Aled.

Roderick frowned. 'Something wrong?'

'Well, I had planned to go to the pictures with a friend. Don't worry, I can easily put it off.'

'There's no need to do that, is there? I'll be back home again before half seven.'

Katie smiled with relief. 'That will be fine, then!'

'Good! Mrs Clarke will have prepared a meal ready, so I'll tell the children they can wait and have theirs with you, shall I?'

'Right. I'll make sure they're both bathed and ready for bed by the time you get home.'

'Don't worry about that. I'm sure they'd much sooner you played a game of some kind with them, and I can put them to bed when I get home.'

Katie smiled. 'I'll remember that! I'll go along with whatever Barri and Rhia want to do, though.'

He gave her one of his wide warm smiles. 'I can see why both of them are so fond of you! I'll leave it in your hands.'

'I'll be very late tonight, Mam,' she told her mother as she left the house on Wednesday morning.

'Going out with Aled, are you? You tell him I think he looks very smart in his postman's uniform.'

'Yes, I'm going to the Gaumont with Aled, but not until later. When I finish at the café I'm going straight to Cathedral Close to look after Roderick Thomas's two children for an hour.'

Rachael's face tightened. 'Mad, you are, cariad! That Roderick Thomas is putting on you. What's in it for you that you go out of your way to help him, then?'

'I like Barri and Rhia, and they like me,' Katie said sharply.

266

'Once you marry Aled and settle down you can have kiddies of your own,' Rachael told her.

'Mam!' Katie looked annoyed. 'Changed your tune, haven't you, and you're jumping the gun a bit as well! I don't want to get married for years and years and when I do I doubt if it will be to Aled Phillips, even if he is a postman!'

'You could do worse, a lot worse. He's a respectable boyo . . .'

'Respectable!' The scorn in Katie's voice startled Rachael. 'He might be respectable,' she went on, 'but what does that count for if he's living in Tiger Bay?'

'He'd make you a wonderful husband,' Rachael said lamely.

'What's the matter with you, Mam? We talked about this not long ago and you agreed with me that it was daft to marry the first bloke who asked you. Why are you suddenly in such a hurry to see me married off, anyway? Are you fed up with having me around the place?'

Rachael reached out and grabbed hold of Katie's arm. 'No, my lovely, of course I'm not! Never think that. It's just that I'd like to know you were going to be properly taken care of before I go.'

'Go? What are you talking about?' Startled, Katie stared at her mother in bewilderment. Ever since her dad had come out of prison she'd wished her mam would pluck up the courage to tell him that she was leaving him, but she'd never thought for one moment that she ever would. Anyway, she'd thought that her mam would want them to go together, not go on her own.

'You're not really thinking of leaving, Mam, are you?' she asked cautiously. 'I don't want to be stuck here on my own, you know!'

Rachael gave a harsh dry laugh. 'I've not got much choice, cariad. The doctor says if I'm very lucky then I've got three months at the most.'

'What are you talking about, Mam? What doctor?'

'The one I went to see at the hospital a few weeks ago. I've got heart trouble, Katie.'

'Heart trouble!' Katie stared at Rachael in horror. 'Oh, Mam! Oh no, please don't say that.'

Spontaneously, they were in each other's arms, both of them crying and trying to comfort the other.

Katie raised a tear-stained face and looked imploringly at her mother. 'How bad is it, Mam? What did the doctor say they could do about it?'

'It's pretty bad, my lovely,' Rachael told her gravely. 'There seems to be nothing they can do. That's why I gave up fighting your dad and agreed to go and work for Betti Davies.'

'Mam! That was the last thing you should have done.' She shivered at the very thought of what the work entailed, and what her mother was putting herself through. 'You should be resting, having special treatment. You need to be in hospital.'

Rachael smiled wanly. 'It's far too late for all that. I've such a short time left that it doesn't matter now what happens to me. I thought giving in and working for her was a way of getting some money together for you.'

Rachael held up her hand as Katie was about to interrupt her. 'I thought it would make things easier for you to get right away from here, cariad, when the time comes.' Her mouth twisted. 'I reckoned without your dad's conniving. He's made sure that the money I earn goes into his and Betti's pocket. I've not seen a penny piece of my so-called wages.'

'Oh, Mam!' Tears slowly trickled down Katie's cheeks as she hugged her mother. Rachael felt so frail that Katie was afraid she would crush her. It was as if there was nothing but skin covering her thin bones. Her face, too, was so thin that her cheeks were sunken, showing up her cheekbones in sharp relief. Her skin was moist and sallow and there were dark rings under her sad hollow eyes.

As the full horror of what her mam had just told her sank deeper into Katie's mind, the implications it carried filled her with despair. Her heart thudded against her ribcage and she felt overwhelmed by sadness.

Even so, she couldn't bring herself to accept that what the doctor had told her mam was irrevocable. Surely there was some sort of treatment for her illness, or even some hope of a cure.

269

It was easy to understand her mother's fears, and she tried not to think about what life would be like once she was left alone with her dad. He'd try to pressurise her into working for Betti Davies and without her mam there to help her stand up to him she'd have no alternative but to do as he asked, or get right away from the place.

'Come on, my lovely, you'd better hurry or you'll be late for work, and you don't want to lose your job!'

'Are you sure the doctor was right when he said . . .'

'That I had heart trouble?' She nodded her head. 'Oh yes, he knew what he was talking about, cariad. It was what I expected him to say. I've been feeling ill for months and I've been getting weaker by the day.'

'Then you should be in bed, Mam, resting. There must be places you could go to where they could make you better,' Katie persisted.

Rachael shook her head. 'No, cariad, it's too late for any of that. Now don't worry about it. I've been meaning to tell you for a while now, because I want to give you plenty of time to think carefully about what you want to do when it finally happens.'

'Mam! Must you talk like this?'

Rachael smiled sadly. 'You mustn't stay here, my lovely. Not in this house,' she said earnestly. 'Your dad and Betti Davies will talk you into working for them and it's a horrible life, I can tell you.'

'And you think marrying Aled Phillips would be better then?'

Rachael shook her head uneasily. 'It would be better than what I've been doing,' she stated bitterly.

'I don't love Aled, Mam!'

'You like him well enough.'

'Only as a friend.'

'There's no one else in your life though, now is there, cariad?'

Katie didn't answer. In her mind's eye was a handsome dark-haired man with navy-blue eyes and a smile that made her heart beat faster. A man whose deep voice was like music in her ears.

She was sure Roderick Thomas liked her. There was a warmth and empathy between them that was very special and it seemed to grow a little deeper each day. If only she could become his housekeeper and then perhaps in time . . .

She sighed and forced herself back to reality. This was no time for daydreaming.

Even if he did feel the same way about her as she did about him, her Mam would hardly approve of her choice. She'd consider him far less suitable than Aled because, not only was he well-to-do and with a responsible job, but he had a different lifestyle to them. What was more, he was probably twice her age and he already had two children.

Chapter Twenty-Seven

Katie felt utterly devastated by her mother's revelations about her deteriorating health. What her mam had told her kept going round and round in her head, all the time she was working.

Every time she thought about it, the more she reproached herself for not realising that there was something dreadfully wrong with her mother. She should have known that there had to be some underlying reason why her mam looked so frail and gaunt, and why she had lost so much weight.

It had been all too easy to assume it was problems between her mam and dad that were making her mother look so worn out. That, and the worry over losing her cleaning job because she was in no fit state to do it. Yet the doctor had diagnosed that her mother had something wrong with her heart, for which there was very little hope of a cure. This, she supposed, would account for the loss of weight and the fact that recently her mother always seemed to feel so tired and weary.

The thought of losing her mother filled Katie with a deep fear, because she was the only real buffer between herself and her dad and Betti

Davies. The thought of giving in to their demands horrified her. She could see why her mam was so anxious for her to marry Aled Phillips and settle down. It was not the sort of future she had in mind, though.

Aled was a good friend. He was an excellent postman now his training was completed and he'd serve the GPO faithfully for the next thirty years. Then he would retire with a pension and be given a clock or a plaque to commemorate his long service.

She could imagine what life would be like if she married him! She would probably end up with two or three children and they'd all be crammed together in a tiny terraced house in Canton or Splott, or even in Ely, the new corporation estate that was being built on the outskirts of Cardiff.

They wouldn't be hard up, but they would never have any money to spare. His mam would probably end up living with them when she couldn't afford her own place. And when the children were old enough to go to school then she'd have to go out charring, or working in some corner shop, to pay for their clothes and extras.

After the sort of life she'd already known she supposed that it would be a step up, and that should be enough to please her, but it wasn't. She wanted a better future than that. She wanted to live in a nice area where women didn't drop in to borrow a cup of sugar or sit on their doorsteps watching their kiddies play in the gutter, or lean over the backyard wall gossiping.

When she finished work at the café and made her way to Cathedral Close, she looked enviously at the solidly built house that Roderick Thomas and his children lived in. This was the sort of home she wanted.

Barri and Rhia were at the window watching for her to arrive. They rushed to the front door with whoops of delight, hugging and kissing her. Mrs Clarke, the daily housekeeper, was right behind them, already dressed in her outdoor clothes and anxious to leave.

'Everything for your meal is in the oven. Now don't go messing about with those two children and letting it dry up, will you, cariad?'

'No, we'll eat it right away,' Katie promised. 'As soon as these little monsters will let me get inside the door.'

'I'm off then!' Mrs Clarke ruffled Barri's hair, patted Rhia on the top of her head and scurried off.

The minute they had finished eating and Katie had taken the dishes into the kitchen, the two children were ready to play games. Barri wanted Snakes and Ladders, or Ludo; Rhia wanted Snap or Happy Families.

'We'll play two games of each then, how about that?' Katie suggested.

The time passed so quickly that they were all taken by surprise when Roderick let himself in and came into the sitting room to see what they were all doing.

'I'm sorry I'm a bit late,' he told Katie, 'the meeting went on longer than I expected. I hope it hasn't made you too late for the pictures, or kept your friend waiting.'

Katie looked at the clock and gasped. It was almost a quarter to eight. Aled would have been standing outside the Gaumont since half past seven, possibly longer because he always turned up early.

'I like to see you coming down the street and knowing that everyone is looking at you and thinking what a pretty girl you are. The best bit, though, is seeing the look on their faces when you walk up to me and take my arm,' he'd grinned the last time she had scolded him about always being early for their meetings.

Well, he wouldn't be smiling tonight, she thought ruefully. It would be eight o'clock by the time she reached the Gaumont, that was if she was lucky enough to get a tram right away.

Dashing into the hall she snatched up her swagger coat from the hallstand, and hurriedly kissed Rhia and Barri goodbye.

'I'll see you in the café tomorrow, Mr Thomas,' she called as she rushed out of the house, putting her arms into her coat as she went.

Although he was relieved to see her, Aled was anything but pleased by the fact that she was so late.

'We're going to miss the big picture,' he

grumbled, as she paid for their tickets and they made their way into the darkened cinema.

All the double seats at the back were already taken so they had to edge their way past people's knees as the usherette waved her torch to indicate the two empty seats that were almost in the centre of one of the middle rows.

Katie felt exhausted. She was relieved to find the big picture hadn't started and Aled soon became immersed in the Disney cartoon that was on the screen.

By the time they left the Gaumont, Aled's mood seemed to be back to normal and she hoped he'd forgotten that she had kept him waiting for half an hour.

They'd almost reached Loudon Square before he raised the matter.

'Where were you then, what kept you that made you so late? Was it trouble at home again?' he asked.

'No, I was looking after Rhia and Barri.'

He frowned. 'You mean Roderick Thomas's kids?'

'Yes. He had to go to a meeting. He said he'd be back before half seven so I thought I would be at the Gaumont in plenty of time to meet you, as we'd arranged.'

'So what happened?'

'He was late and I had trouble getting a tram. Still, it worked out fine, didn't it? We were there in plenty of time for the big picture and we saw the Pathe News.'

'We missed half the Disney cartoon, though!'
She laughed. 'They're for kids, anyway.'

'No they're not! Anyway, if you have to pay for the whole show then that's what I want to see, not a part of it.'

'It was my treat! I paid and I'm not grumbling,' Katie told him a trifle sharply.

'Well, you wouldn't be, would you!'

Katie felt her temper rising. 'What's that supposed to mean?'

'Roderick Thomas and his kids come first, don't they,' he sneered. 'I'm fed up with hearing about them. You're always talking about those kids or telling me something he's said to you when he comes into the café.'

'And you are always telling me about your silly job now that you are a trainee postman.'

'Yes, well it is important. Once I've finished my probation I'll get a good rise and then we can be married.' He stopped and pulled her around to face him. 'We are going to be married, aren't we, Katie?'

'Married!' She pulled away. Her mam's words drummed in her head, but she didn't intend to be influenced by them. She liked Aled, but she didn't want to be married to him.

'Come on Katie, tell me? Put me out of my misery.' His voice became strained. 'I've been working hard for this promotion and I've been doing it for you. I want you to be proud of me. I'll be earning enough for us to have a life together. I'll look after you, cariad, I'll be good to you, I promise.'

Katie knew this was true. He'd do the very best he could, but his best wasn't good enough. She could never be happy with Aled when she wanted so much more from life than he could offer. If only she could find the words to explain all this to him. Make him see that, for his sake, she couldn't say 'yes' to his proposal.

Not wanting to hurt Aled's feelings, Katie told him that she had other things on her mind.

'Oh, I know that,' he said bitterly. 'Thinking about that Roderick Thomas and his kids, aren't you?'

Katie shook her head and told him about her mother's illness.

Aled was shocked. 'Oh, Katie, I had no idea! She hasn't looked too good lately, but I had no idea it was anything so serious. Of course you can't think about my proposal when you have something like that on your mind,' he said consolingly.

Then, as his strong streak of common sense overrode his concern, he added, 'Remember, I am always here for you. I'll take you away from Loudon Square and make a home for you the minute you need one.'

She nodded her thanks, biting her lip to hold back her tears. She knew that, although he didn't say it in so many words, he had the same concerns about her future if she was left on her own with her dad as her mam had.

They parted friends, which was what she had hoped would happen, but she felt guilty about using her mother's illness to placate him.

Their discussion about the future stayed uppermost in her mind over the next few days. She was almost tempted to tell her mother that Aled wanted to marry her now that he was a fully fledged postman, just to stop her fretting so much about what would happen after she died.

Her mam looked so frail that even Lewis noticed, and he decided she'd better stop coming downstairs in the evening.

'Betti said that the punters are complaining about the way you look,' he told her. 'If they find out you've got a heart condition then that will put them right off,' he added caustically. 'In fact,' he added craftily, 'Betti thinks it would be a good idea if young Katie took your place.'

'Never! We've already had this out and you promised never to mention the subject again,' she reminded him, between bouts of coughing.

Lewis shrugged. 'People often change their mind!'

'I'll never change my mind on that score and neither will Katie, and well you know it, Lewis Roberts,' Rachael told him, her eyes flashing, her voice rasping she was so upset.

'Katie might like the idea,' Lewis pushed. 'It would be much better for her than working her fingers to the bone in a greasy café. She wouldn't be on her feet all day, either,' he guffawed.

'That's enough!' Anger brought two spots of burning colour to Rachael's sunken cheeks. 'I've already told you that the answer is no,' she said fiercely.

'You can't stop her if she wants to work for Betti,' Lewis taunted.

'Over my dead body!'

Lewis looked at her contemptuously. 'She won't have to wait very long then, will she!'

His callousness brought tears to Rachael's eyes and she turned away rather than let him see how much his heartless remark upset her.

When she came home and saw that her mother had been crying, Katie was once again tempted to tell her about Aled's proposal. Even though she had no intention of saying 'yes' to him, it might comfort her mother to think that she would.

The moment passed. Her dad walked out of the room and they could hear him making his way downstairs to visit Betti. Her mother was trembling, exhausted by their bickering. She sank down on the sofa and closed her eyes wearily.

'What's been going on?' Kate asked anxiously. 'What has he been saying to upset you?'

'It's nothing, cariad. Just a spat between the two of us because I'm not feeling well enough to go downstairs.'

'I should hope you're not going down there

ever again,' Katie told her heatedly. 'You shouldn't have given in to his bullying in the first place.'

'Yes, you're right, of course. Remember you mustn't ever take any notice of anything he says,' she told Katie. 'No matter how much he threatens, you must never give in and go to work for Betti. Promise me, cariad.'

Katie smiled indulgently. 'Don't worry, I would never do that. Now, shall I make a cup of tea, Mam?'

'Yes, that would be lovely,' Rachael sighed. 'You're a good daughter, Katie. You deserve something so much better than to be living in a brothel in Tiger Bay with an opium-smoking pimp for a father.'

'Mam, what are you saying,' Katie exclaimed aghast. She reached out and took her mother's thin hands, and held them tenderly between her own.

It might be the truth, it might be what she herself thought, but to hear it coming from her mother's lips shocked her.

'You must try and get out of this place, Katie. Do it before I die if you can, and then I'll know you are safe,' Rachael insisted.

'Stop talking like that, Mam. I wouldn't dream of leaving you here on your own. And don't keep going on about dying. You aren't going to die, not if I can help it.'

'That's the trouble, cariad, there is nothing you or anyone else can do to stop it. My time is almost up and, apart from the fact that it means leaving you to fend for yourself, I'm not sorry. I feel so tired, so utterly worn out, that all I want to do is curl up and sleep. Yes,' she sighed, 'I want to sleep forever. No more struggling to make ends meet, or coping with your dad, or with any of the harsh realities of life. Only the blissful comfort of a deep untroubled sleep.'

Chapter Twenty-Eight

Katie noticed a distinct improvement in her mother's health the moment Rachael stopped work. Her breathing became easier, her skin looked less yellow and her eyes lost their feverish look.

A week later, however, when Roderick Thomas asked her if she could help him by staying with his two children every night for a week because he had to go away for an important conference, Katie demurred.

She very much wanted to help him, but she decided that her mother wasn't well enough to be left on her own.

When she explained the situation to him, he agreed that it would not be the right thing to do.

'You could bring her to the house with you. There are two spare rooms, you know. Perhaps the change would do her good!'

Katie's eyes rounded in astonishment. 'That would be wonderful, that is if you are sure you don't mind.'

'I think it is the perfect solution. Mrs Clarke will collect the children from school in the afternoon and bring them home. I had intended to ask her to stay with them until you arrived. If you are sure it wouldn't be too much of a strain for your mother to be there on her own with them for a short while, then Mrs Clarke can finish at her usual time.'

'I think my Mam would enjoy their company and love having the chance to get to know them,' Katie smiled.

'Excellent! You talk to your mother to make sure that she is happy with this arrangement, and let me know tomorrow.'

Rachael was rather taken aback by the idea.

'Both of us stay there in his house? He doesn't know me from Adam, cariad. Are you sure it's what he's agreed to?'

'Quite sure. In fact, since he has to leave very early on Monday morning he suggested we might like to go on Sunday afternoon and have tea with them. That way you can meet each other and get to know the children as well.'

'Well, it certainly sounds like a nice idea, especially if his home is all you reckon it to be,' Rachael smiled. 'Living like a toff will be a real treat for me. I'm looking forward to it and no mistake!'

'They spent the rest of the week getting themselves ready and deciding what clothes they would need to take with them. Katie told her mother all about the house and how it was furnished, and about the children. She was careful to say as little as possible about Roderick Thomas, in case she said too much and gave away her own feelings for him.

'This is almost like going away on holiday, cariad,' Rachael exclaimed excitedly on Sunday afternoon, when they set out for Cathedral Close.

'How did dad take it when you told him what was happening?'

'Not too well. I didn't tell him what the address was because I didn't want him coming there and causing trouble. If he comes to see you at the café then make sure you don't tell him where the house is, either!'

'Oh, Mam! He'll find out one way or another if he really wants to.'

Rachael shook her head. 'I don't think he'll bother. He'll spend all his time with Betti or with the drinking, smoking, gambling crowd he mixes with in Coalman's Court.' She pulled a face. 'When he's been down there smoking opium he absolutely stinks of the stuff when he comes home. That sickly smell is not something you can cover up.'

Katie shivered. 'I'll never forget when Aled took me there once. It was an awful scruffy room in a filthy little house. Dad was there, on a bed upstairs, smoking a long bamboo pipe. An old Chinese woman let us in and a horrible looking Chinaman, who didn't seem to speak a word of English, came into the room and filled up the bowl of this pipe thing.' Katie shuddered. 'It was so horrible seeing him like that.'

'Aled should never have taken you there! I thought he had more sense than that.'

'Don't blame Aled. He didn't really want to, but I insisted.'

'How did Aled know your dad visited such places?'

'He'd seen him visiting there when he'd been out delivering telegrams. Aled used to get around a lot on that bike of his. He used to go to most places in Tiger Bay.'

Rachael smiled. 'He's a nice young boyo, and he does think the world of you, cariad.'

Katie quickly changed the subject. She knew her mam's feelings about Aled and about her marrying him, but she didn't want to talk about it. At the moment she was so happy about them staying at Cathedral Close, and she didn't want that marred in any way.

Roderick and Rachael were a little reserved with each other at first. He was polite and courteous as he showed her around the house. Katie stayed with Barri and Rhia who were rather shy with Rachael. By the time Roderick was ready to leave, however, they were all firm friends.

'You've no idea, Katie, what a relief it is for me to know that the children are going to be in such capable hands while I'm away,' he told her. 'They've talked of nothing else since I told them.'

The week at Cathedral Close passed blissfully. Rachael seemed so much more relaxed without the tension of coping with Lewis and his moods, or listening to Betti Davies's ribald ranting.

Like Katie, she revelled in the luxury afforded by the well-appointed house. The light airy rooms, a proper bathroom, a spacious kitchen and an extremely comfortable sitting room.

During the day, Rachael tidied around and made tea for Mrs Clarke, who still came in each day as usual. The two women were about the same age and they became quite friendly.

It was from what Mrs Clarke told Rachael when they were having one of their chats, that Katie learned that Roderick's wife had died in childbirth.

'I would have thought Mr Thomas would have told you that himself,' her mother said in surprise.

'It's hardly the sort of thing you discuss in a café while you're having your midday meal,' Katie said dismissively.

'I know that, but I thought he might have said something when you've been here looking after the children.'

'He probably wouldn't want to discuss it in front of them in case it upset them,' Katie pointed out.

'Well, now at least you know the truth about what happened,' her mother said philosophically.

'Tragic, really,' she went on. 'She wasn't all that old, see. Terrible leaving two young children behind, so very sad. And such a great burden for him to have to bear. It's a wonder that a good looking man like him hasn't married again pretty sharpish, so as to give his youngsters a new mother.'

'Stop trying to plan his life for him, Mam,' Katie said tartly. 'Anyway, perhaps he hasn't met anyone who he thinks could fill her shoes. I've thought once or twice that it would be a lovely job for you, Mam, to move in as his housekeeper.'

'He's already got one. Mrs Clarke comes in every day and she looks after all his washing and mending and cooking, as well as cleaning his house. What more could anyone do?'

'Be here every day when the children come home from school?'

'Well, he has a perfect arrangement with Mrs Clarke. She stays on and looks after them until he gets home, doesn't she?'

'I know that, but it must be a bit unsettling for Barri and Rhia to be pushed from pillar to post like that all the time.'

'They seem happy enough. They certainly like being with you, don't they! I suppose it's because you are young enough to join in their games with them. And you're happy to spend time talking to them or reading them stories. Their own mam would have had other things to do around the place and wouldn't be able to give them her whole attention,' she pointed out.

Every night while they were staying in Cathedral Close, as soon as she went to bed Katie thought about what her mam had said. It puzzled her a great deal as to why Roderick Thomas hadn't married again, but, even so, she was quite surprised that her mam had brought the subject up.

She wondered if her mam was waiting for her to admit that she had feelings for him, but she refused to be drawn. Speaking openly about all the things she dreamed and fantasised about would probably ruin them for her, and it most certainly wouldn't bring them any closer to coming true.

Anyway, she told herself, Roderick Thomas was such a lot older than her. If he was looking for a wife he would probably want someone sophisticated, a woman of experience who could fit into the social life of Cathedral Close, not some naïve little waitress who came from Tiger Bay.

Until she moved out of Loudon Square, and out of Tiger Bay itself, there was no chance for her to ever make her way into a respectable world.

Again, the thought came to her that if only her mam could become Roderick Thomas's housekeeper, and they could both live there and never set eyes on her dad ever again, then her life would be transformed.

For the first few days they were in Cathedral Close she had half expected her dad to find out where they were and turn up on the doorstep.

She had warned her mam not to answer the door if he did.

On the Wednesday night when there was a loud knock on the front door, just as she was coming downstairs after reading a bedtime story to Barri and Rhia, her heart thudded.

For a moment she thought of ignoring the knocking. Telling herself what she would do if he did turn up was one thing, actually having to face him was something else again.

Then, realising that if the knocking went on for very much longer it would rouse the two children, who still weren't properly asleep, she changed her mind.

When she opened the front door and found it wasn't her dad who stood there, but Aled Phillips, her relief turned to annoyance.

'Aled, what are you doing here? What do you want?' she asked in surprise.

'We had a date, remember! We always go out on Wednesdays. Forgotten all about it, have you?'

Katie bristled at his aggressive tone.

'I've been busy and I've had other, more important, responsibilities,' she told him loftily.

'Yes, like looking after Mr Thomas's kids,' he snapped. 'That matters more than our long standing arrangements, does it?'

'We don't always go out together on a Wednesday evening and we hadn't made any definite plans for tonight!'

'You mightn't have done, but I had. I intended taking you somewhere special.'

'Oh yes? And where was that?'

'Since it's too late now, it doesn't matter,' he responded sulkily.

'No,' Katie said coolly, 'I don't suppose it does. So why did you bother to come all this way, just to tell me that?'

As he stared at her morosely with his mouth agape and a hangdog look in his eyes, it made his face look even longer than it usually did.

'Let me come in and I'll tell you all about what I had in mind, and perhaps we can do it tomorrow night.'

Katie hesitated. 'It's not my house so I can hardly ask you in, now, can I?'

His surliness was replaced with anger.

'Why ever not? I want to talk to you, not steal the family silver.'

'I can't invite you in because it's not my house,' Katie repeated firmly.

'So you're going to shut the door in my face, are you?' he snapped.

'Not unless you make me! Why are you being so awkward, Aled?'

'I'm not being in the least awkward. I want to come in and talk to you, Katie, that's all,' he said stubbornly.

'Since I am in someone else's house, Aled, I don't think it would be right to invite one of my friends in without asking permission from Mr Thomas first of all, do you?'

Aled made no reply. Thrusting his hands deep into his trouser pockets and hunching his shoulders, he turned away.

Katie almost relented. She was sure that Roderick wouldn't mind her inviting him in. She simply didn't want Aled to think he had any hold on her.

She'd told him so many times that they could never be more than friends and it was about time he accepted this. She was on the point of calling him back when he turned around and said angrily over his shoulder as he strode away.

'Be like that! Some friend you are Katie Roberts. I won't forget this in a hurry.'

Chapter Twenty-Nine

Katie found the surroundings in Loudon Square grim after their week's stay in Cathedral Close. Rachael looked so much better and seemed to be in such good spirits that she found it hard to believe her days were numbered, and felt convinced that her mother had misunderstood the doctor's diagnosis.

It came as a terrible shock when the following week in the middle of a summer's afternoon, Aled came rushing into the Bridge Street Café to tell her that her mother had been rushed into hospital.

'She collapsed on the floor and that Betti Davies had to send for an ambulance,' he told her dramatically. 'I happened to be in Loudon Square at the time and when I saw it was your mam being loaded into the ambulance I stopped to find out what was wrong. When I saw your mam's face was all grey and her lips were blue, I told them I was a friend of yours. One of the girls who works there told me what had happened. They'd heard her calling for help and they knew your dad was out so they went upstairs to see what was wrong. By the time they got there they found she'd collapsed on the floor and was having trouble breathing.'

'And where was my dad when all this happened?'

'I've no idea. He wasn't in the house or the ambulance when it left. That was why I thought I'd better come and let you know.'

When Katie arrived at the hospital, it was to be told that her mother's condition was critical.

Lewis arrived shortly afterwards and Katie was shocked by the state he was in. From his disorientated condition and glazed eyes, she suspected he had recently been smoking opium.

She felt so furious that she wished it was him lying there, the breath of life oozing from him, not her mother. Her mam was a much better person than he was, and she deserved to live.

Her mam's life had been so difficult, Katie thought, remembering the days they'd spent in Louisa Street while her father had been in prison. After her father had been released, when life should have become easier for her mam, it had in fact become harder.

The picture she had built up of a strong wonderful father figure had turned out to be a weak, bitter man who'd made their lives even more difficult.

As they sat by the bedside, Katie was sickened by his hypocritical behaviour as he kept taking hold of her mother's hand and murmuring endearments.

Shortly after midnight Lewis decided that as

there was nothing they could do, and since Rachael was in a coma and didn't even know they were there, he was going home.

'No point you staying here, girl, either, so you may as well come with me,' he said brusquely.

Katie shook her head. 'No, I'm going to stay here with my mam. You can do whatever you like.'

He hesitated, frowning uncertainly. 'Perhaps I'll just go outside for half an hour. I need a smoke to take away the smell of the hospital. Choking me, it is.'

'Make sure it's only tobacco you smoke while you're out there!'

He turned on her angrily. 'What is that supposed to mean?'

She stared back at him contemptuously. 'You know quite well what I mean. I'll never be able to forget seeing you lying on that bed in that scruffy room in Coalman's Court, so doped up you didn't even know I was there!'

He stared at her silently, his face dark with anger. Then without another word he turned and walked out of the ward.

Doctors and nurses came and went throughout the night, ministering to her mother's needs, but none of it seemed to rouse Rachael from the deep coma she had drifted into.

Dawn was breaking and the sky outside had begun to brighten when Katie saw her mother's eyelids flicker and her eyes slowly open. When she realised where she was, she gave a deep sigh.

'It's all right, Mam, I'm here with you,' Katie said softly.

Rachael struggled to raise her head and focus on Katie's face. Within seconds her head dropped back onto the pillow as though she was utterly exhausted.

Katie spoke to her again, but Rachael seemed to have drifted back into a coma. Katie remained where she was, holding her mother's hand, wondering if she had imagined it, praying that her mother would soon regain consciousness again.

An hour later, Rachael made another supreme effort to open her eyes and speak. Her voice was so faint that Katie had to bend low over the bed to hear her words.

'Take care, my darling girl,' she murmured in a hoarse whisper. 'Promise me you won't ever do what your dad and that Betti Davies want you to do.'

A tear trickled slowly down Katie's cheek as she squeezed her mother's hand to reassure her. 'No, Mam, of course I won't! You know I'd never do that.'

Her mother drew in a rasping breath as she struggled to speak again. 'You must get away from Loudon Square,' she warned. 'Right away. Do you understand?'

'I will, Mam, I promise you. Now don't worry about me and my future. You save your strength to get better and then we'll both get away from there.'

'That Aled is a nice steady boyo, and he's in love with you, cariad. He'll look after you, if only you'll let him,' her mother wheezed.

'Ssh! Stop trying to talk, Mam, you're wasting your strength.'

'Get out of Loudon . . .'

Her mother never finished the sentence. There was a gurgling noise deep in her throat as though she was choking, and then all was quiet.

Panic stricken, Katie called out for a nurse.

When she came she summoned a doctor and between them they tried to revive Rachael Roberts, but without success.

By the time Lewis Roberts returned to his wife's bedside it was all over.

'Five minutes and then I must ask you both to leave,' the Sister told Katie and Lewis, as she whisked the curtains shut and then walked away.

Lewis clutched at Rachael's hand, tears streaming down his cheeks as he bent forward and rested his head on the pillow.

'I did love her, you know!'

Katie stood up and gently stroked back the hair that was lying across her mother's face. 'You had a funny way of showing it,' she muttered, as she bent and kissed Rachael tenderly on the brow.

Her eyes filled with tears, but as well as sadness she had a feeling of relief. Her mother looked so peaceful. The network of lines had disappeared from around her eyes and there was uplift to the corners of her mouth, almost as if she was smiling.

The Sister returned and pulled the bed sheet up over Rachael's face, indicating that it was time for Lewis and Katie to leave.

Half an hour later they left the hospital, after finding that there was nothing more they could do until the next day.

'Come back after ten o'clock and you can collect the death certificate, and then you can go ahead with making the funeral arrangements,' they were told.

Lewis clutched at Katie's arm. 'I need a drink,' he gasped hoarsely.

She pulled away from him, sickened by his words. 'Then go on your own,' she snapped. 'I'm not going into a pub with you.'

'Duw anwyl! You're worse than your bloody mother was,' he snarled.

'Leave my mam out of this,' Katie told him heatedly. 'You may have made her life hell, but you're not going to ruin mine as well.'

They avoided each other over the next few days, after Katie made it clear that she was the one who was going to make the funeral arrangements since it was the last thing she would be able to do for her mother.

Each evening, the minute she came home from work, Lewis went downstairs to Betti's quarters. Katie still felt afraid, though, and each night before she went to bed she used the chest of drawers to barricade her bedroom door.

Her greatest solace was her midday chat with Roderick Thomas. Having suffered bereavement himself not so very long ago, he was able to offer the sort of support she needed. Whereas other people skirted around the subject, afraid to mention her mother or her recent death, Roderick encouraged Katie to talk about her.

Twice she accepted his invitation to go back to his house when she finished work. The children's exuberance at seeing her momentarily obscured her grief and unhappiness.

'You can stay here overnight anytime you wish,' Roderick told her. 'There's plenty of space. In fact,' he laughed, 'Barri and Rhia call the room you use "Katie's room", did you know that?'

His words were tremendously comforting because they made her feel wanted. He was always so kind and caring that she wondered if he felt the same way about her as she did about him.

It was something that troubled her deeply. Every night before she went to sleep she would lie there in the dark analysing her feelings, and trying to see why her feelings for Roderick Thomas were so very different from the ones she had for Aled Phillips.

If only she could swap over her feelings for the two men, she thought sadly.

Common sense told her that Aled was the

one she should be in love with, because he was her own age. She knew he had never looked at any other girls; she was his first and only sweetheart.

He not only loved her, but he was always there when she needed him. So why was it that she didn't love him in return, she asked herself.

From her first day at school, and all the time she was growing up in Louisa Street, he had been her champion. He'd always protected her from the other kids when they tried to bully her. Even now, when they were both grown up, he was always eager to help her in any way he could.

Roderick Thomas, on the other hand, was so much more mature and, in her eyes, so very much better looking. In fact, she thought wryly, there was no comparison at all between the two men. With his thick black hair, navy-blue eyes under dark brows, and smooth clean shaven face, he was the most handsome man she had ever known.

Try as he might, Aled would never look smart or well dressed. His hair always looked as though he needed a visit to the barbers and his long, lugubrious face was doleful, even when he was smiling.

She felt a different person when she was in Roderick's company. He never tried to pressurise her into doing things his way, but treated her as a responsible adult who knew her own mind.

For all that, there were constant doubts in her mind. She knew that, whatever happened, Barri and Rhia would always come first in Roderick Thomas's list of priorities.

When she was feeling particularly despondent, Katie would even wonder in which role she mattered to him most. Was it as a friendly face to greet him when he went into the Bridge Street Café for lunch, or someone he knew he could rely on whenever he needed somebody to take care of his children?

The day of Rachael Roberts's funeral was dull, and there was a light drizzle falling as though the skies themselves were in mourning.

The grass around the graveside in Cardiff cemetery was wet and muddy and sent a chill right through Katie as they stood looking down into the deep hole where Lewis's parents had been buried, and watched as Rachael's coffin was lowered down into it.

Katie felt incensed when she found that Betti Davies was standing there beside them at the graveside. She felt it was an outrage to her mother's memory that her dad had invited along the woman her mother disliked most in the world.

She felt so upset that she barely took in what the priest was saying as he carried out the interment ceremony.

When it ended and she turned to walk away, a movement nearby caught her attention and she was startled to see Aled Phillips coming towards her.

'What are you doing here?' she frowned.

'I thought you might like some company.' He nodded his head in the direction of Lewis and Betti Davies. 'Better to be with me than tagging along with those two, cariad.'

Katie bit her lip, trying to hold back her tears. After the way she had been treating Aled lately his kindness touched her deeply. She wished she could go along with his idea that they should marry and set up home together, but much as she liked him she knew in her heart that she didn't love him and never would.

Chapter Thirty

Katie found there were problems to deal with, the moment she returned home to Loudon Square after the funeral.

Aled walked with her as far as the bottom of the metal staircase, but she refused to let him come any further.

'What's the reason this time?' he asked sourly. 'This is your home, isn't it, so you should be able to ask your friends in.'

'Some other time,' she told him evasively. 'My dad is pretty cut up about losing Mam and will want to be alone, so I don't think he'd be very pleased if I invited anyone in at the moment.'

'It might be as good a time as any for me to have a chat with him, so that I can tell him we are going to be married,' Aled told her boldly.

His eyes held hers as he watched her reaction keenly. Then he squared his thin, sloping shoulders defiantly when she shook her head.

'What does that mean? No, it's not a good time for me to tell him, or no, you don't intend to marry me?'

'Aled, it's not something I want to talk about at this minute,' she said wearily. 'Can't you understand how upset I am feeling? We've just come from the cemetery, it's only a couple of hours since we buried my mam, and my head is going round like a spinning top.'

Clumsily, he pulled her into his arms and tried to hug her. 'I'm sorry! I know you think I'm trying to rush you, but it's just that I feel so concerned about you living in Betti Davies's house when I know all about what goes on here. I want to take you away from all that before it's too late.'

'What goes on downstairs in Betti Davies's part of this house has nothing at all to do with me,' she told him angrily, as she pushed him away from her.

'Not yet it doesn't! If you go on living here then sooner or later it will have plenty to do with you. You'll be one of them!'

'What is that supposed to mean?'

'Duw anwyl! You know perfectly well what it means, so stop playing the innocent with me! Now that your mother isn't around to stand up for you, that father of yours will make you work for Betti Davies. You know they both want you to work for them. And if you do,' he added threateningly, 'then you can count me out. I want nothing more to do with you if you ever get yourself involved in that way. Understand?'

'Thank you for having such faith in me, Aled. So you think I'd sell my body just because those two asked me to do so,' Katie said bitterly.

'Well? Come on, do you?' she persisted, when he made no reply.

Aled ran his bony fingers through his lank brown hair in exasperation. 'Oh Katie, you know I don't think that. Stop making it so difficult for me. I'm worried about you, especially about you being on your own. They might force you! You never know what your father might do when he's under the influence of drink or has been smoking opium.'

Katie smiled wanly. She knew there was some truth in what Aled was saying, but her mind was in such turmoil that she couldn't think straight at the moment. All she wanted to do was to barricade herself into her bedroom so that she could be on her own and give way to the tears that she had been bottling up all day.

She knew she had to make plans for the future and work out if she could afford a room somewhere else, some place where she could be on her own.

Marrying Aled Phillips was certainly not one of the options she wanted to take. She wished he would listen to what she kept telling him, accept her decision as final and leave her alone.

In the weeks that followed, however, every time her dad and Betti started pressurising her to put in an appearance downstairs, it went through her mind time and time again. Sometimes, it seemed as if it was the only solution to her problems.

'Come on down, Katie, even if only for half an

hour, and get to know some of the girls,' Lewis kept urging her. 'Several of them are about your age so you'd enjoy meeting them.'

'I don't wish to know anyone who works for Betti Davies,' she told him hotly. 'Next thing you'll be asking me, your own daughter, to work as a tart!'

'You could do a lot worse. All of Betti's girls earn good money. They pick up a damn sight more in one night than you get in a week working in that café.'

'At least mine is clean money!'

He laughed disparagingly. 'Clean money? What on earth is that supposed to mean? Money is money, cariad, no matter how you earn it. It's how much of it you get that matters.'

'Yes, and the more they earn, the more money ends up in your pocket as well as in Betti Davies's,' she said contemptuously.

He smiled wryly. 'That makes good sense to me and to them. They know I'm right here to look after their interests if they run into any trouble. Not that they do very often. Betti selects her clients as carefully as she chooses her girls. You'd be safe enough working for her,' he assured her.

'Never in this world,' she told him sharply.

'So what are you planning on doing then, finding a millionaire to marry you, so that you can swan around in comfort for the rest of your days?'

'I'm happy enough working in the café and

earning my wages honestly,' she told him stubbornly.

'Oh yes? Then why do you keep that dolt Aled Phillips hanging on? Is it in case you can't find anyone better to marry?' He laughed derisively. 'I can't see you having a very grand lifestyle if you end up married to a postman, mind!'

When Lewis found that neither threats, persuasion or ridicule had any effect on Katie, he turned to Betti for advice and help.

'Leave matters with me,' she told him confidently. 'You are quite sure, though, that you want her to come and work for us?'

'Of course I do! I thought we were agreed on that?'

She looked at him shrewdly, her heavily made-up eyes raised questioningly. 'Well, Lewis, not all fathers would approve of their daughter being on the game, you know.'

'Are you trying to get out of taking her on?' he blustered.

'Most certainly not! Your Katie is a very pretty girl and I can think of one or two wealthy clients who will pay handsomely for her services.'

Lewis rubbed his hands together and grinned broadly. 'Then the sooner you do something about getting her on the payroll, the better.'

However, Betti got no further than Lewis with her pep talks or with her persuasive hints about the wonderful lifestyle Katie would be able to enjoy, if she spent a couple of hours with an attractive man a few nights each week.

Katie listened to her politely and calmly then scornfully dismissed all her suggestions.

Betti felt so piqued by her manner that she resorted to threats.

'If you don't want to work for me, that's fine,' she blustered, 'but it means you can't go on living here and taking up space that I could be using for my own purposes.'

'You told my mam that these three rooms were only ever used for storing things in, before we came here to live,' Katie reminded her.

'Maybe that was so in the past, but now I have other ideas about how they could be used. In fact, I am thinking of turning them into a cosy little love-nest for your dad and me.'

'I don't believe you! He wouldn't shack up with an old tart like you,' Katie exclaimed vindictively.

Betti's eyes narrowed dangerously. 'Oh no? You ask Lewis yourself then, if you don't believe me!' she retorted, smiling triumphantly as she saw Katie colour up in anger.

'I tell you what, Katie,' Betti's voice softened, 'I know you must still be feeling a bit upset about your mam dying and everything, so I'll give you a little longer, see, to think things over, cariad. It's almost Christmas and in the spirit of goodwill we'll leave your decision until after then. I want an answer by the New Year, mind! 1935 can be a new start for all of us . . .'

Betti let her words trail off, but Katie knew by the gleam in her sharp green eyes that it was not going to be the end of the matter, by any means.

She tried not to worry about it, but Betti's subtle threat was at the back of her mind all the time she was at work. It gnawed away at her peace of mind like some rabid rodent.

Roderick Thomas noticed her distracted manner and the frown that seemed to have permanently welded itself between her grey eyes, but attributed it to her recent loss.

It worried him, but he wasn't sure of the right way to express his sympathy. He was afraid she might feel he was overstepping the mark if he tried to persuade her to confide in him. The only way he could think of to help her was to invite her to his house. He made the excuse that Barri and Rhia were asking after her.

Seeing her face light up with pleasure delighted him. It also disconcerted him to think that it was his children rather than him that Katie was interested in.

Ever since he had first come to know her she'd had a special place in his heart. In many ways she reminded him of his late wife, Helen. Not in looks and stature, Helen had been short and dark haired and with a full rounded figure, but in her manner. She had the same sweet nature and he hoped his own daughter would grow up to be as kind and considerate.

If only Katie was a few years older he would

have been tempted to try and take their friendship to a deeper level. When Helen had died he had vowed he would never marry again, his heartache at losing her had been so great. Now, with hindsight, he saw that as a spur of the moment decision, because he'd been so heartbroken at the time.

Not only was he lonely, but Barri and Rhia needed a mother. Mrs Clarke did a wonderful job as a part-time housekeeper, but she had her own life and family to worry about.

So far he had been very lucky in that neither of his children had suffered any serious illness since their mother had died. Only twice in the past three years had it been necessary for him to take time off work in order to be at home with them.

Finding a wife who was interested in taking on two young children, would not be easy, he knew. One possible answer was someone who was in a similar situation to himself. A woman who had been widowed and who also had young children, and therefore needed support and companionship.

That, however, was a pragmatic solution and one he had no wish to contemplate. He was far too much of a romantic to accept such a situation. If he remarried he wanted it to be to someone he loved and who loved him in return.

Whatever happened, he decided, whatever his ultimate decision might be, the happiness of Barri and Rhia was paramount.

It was since he had met Katie that he realised how much his own happiness also came into the equation. He thought about her a great deal and there was no doubt in his own mind that his feelings for her seemed to increase daily.

Whenever she visited his home it seemed so natural, as if she belonged there. He wanted her to stay, not for a few hours, not for a couple of days, but forever.

He tried to steel himself against his growing feelings for her. Katie Roberts was not for him, he told himself repeatedly. He was so much older than her that it really wasn't sensible for him to even contemplate such a liaison.

In May, Katie would be seventeen; she was on the threshold of life. She deserved a young man of her own age, someone who would mature alongside her and share all the joys and surprises life might bring.

Why should a young and lovely girl like Katie saddle herself with another woman's children? Even though she might think the world of them, and they of her, actually acting as their surrogate mother was an incredibly big step to take.

Added to that, there was the delicate matter of Katie's feelings for him, and really he had no way of ascertaining what they were.

There was no doubt about it that she always seemed to be pleased to see him and that their friendship had developed to a point where she felt happy to discuss almost any topic with him.

Whenever it was something that affected her

personally, then Katie always seemed to welcome his opinion and more often than not she followed his advice, he reflected.

Maybe she simply turned to him because she regarded him as a father figure, he thought despondently.

Chapter Thirty-One

New Year's Day 1935, the date that Betti Davies had given Katie as the time by which she must make up her mind whether she was going to conform to her wishes and work for her, or vacate the rooms at the top of Betti's house, came and went without incident.

When no further reference was made to the matter, by either her dad or Betti, Katie relaxed and assumed they accepted that she had no intention of doing what they asked.

She had other things on her mind, anyway. Mario had told her that he might have to cut her wages. The café was not as busy as when she had started working there. It was due to the Depression and its effect on the ladies who came in after a shopping spree. Many of them had started going to the Lyons Corner House that had opened in Queen Street because it was cheaper there.

She rarely saw her father. Most of the time she didn't know if he was out of the house, visiting the opium den in Coalman's Court, wandering around the remoter parts of Tiger Bay, or whether he was simply keeping out of her way by staying downstairs with Betti Davies.

As a precaution, however, she stayed out as much as possible. Whenever Roderick Thomas asked her if she could look after the children in the evening she jumped at the chance to use the bedroom that Barri and Rhia had dubbed 'Katie's room'.

On the comparatively few occasions that she went out with Aled, it was usually to the pictures. When they came home she would ask him to wait at the bottom of the iron staircase until she had unlocked the door.

'Why not let me come up and unlock it for you and have a look around inside to make sure it is safe?'

'What would you do if my dad was there?'

Aled shrugged his thin shoulders. 'Tell him I was seeing you safely home, of course.'

Katie looked doubtful. 'He'd probably be very angry about it.'

'I could deal with that!'

'Yes, but what about after you'd left? He'd be sure to have a go at me, and what could I do knowing I was in the wrong.'

Aled ran a hand through his lank hair. 'I don't understand you, Katie, how would you be in the wrong?' he asked in a puzzled voice.

'Letting you come into our home!'

Aled shook his head in despair. 'We've been through all this before. I really can't see what you're doing wrong, inviting a chap to come in

314

when he's brought you home after you've been out together all evening,' he muttered angrily.

Katie refused to discuss it. At the moment life was going so smoothly that she felt it was wiser to leave things as they were and not cause any ripples.

After several weeks of virtual isolation, with no questions from her dad and no interference from Betti Davies, Katie felt she had been worrying far more than was necessary.

She came and went as she pleased, and ate most of her meals at the café. Her dad didn't ask her to hand over her wages as he had done in the past so she opened a Post Office Savings account and paid the bulk of what she earned into that. She also added the money Roderick Thomas paid her whenever she looked after his children.

She gloated over the total as it slowly increased. She was still determined to strike out for herself. This was her nest egg. By the end of the year, at this rate, there would be twenty pounds in it, and then she could start looking for a room of her own.

It would be well away from Loudon Square. Then, and only then, would she feel completely safe. She wouldn't tell anyone where it was, not even Aled.

Her plans were going so well and Katie felt so happy and relaxed that she no longer went out of her way to avoid her father.

When, for the first time in weeks, she found

him in their living room when she arrived home from work one evening, she thought he had come to ask her why she hadn't been handing over her wages.

Instead, to her great surprise, he wanted to know if she needed any money.

She was tempted to take it and add it to her nest egg, but common sense warned her it might be a trap.

'No, I don't need any,' she told him warily. 'I can manage on what I earn.'

'You're quite sure about that?'

'Absolutely!'

'Well, cariad, if you are quite certain,' he said, as he put the money back into his trouser pocket. 'I heard that the café wasn't doing too well these days, so if you do need any help you have only to ask me, remember.'

For a moment she felt as if she was a little girl again and Lewis the lovely handsome dad that she adored, and who carried her on his broad shoulders, and she felt tears prickling her eyelids.

If only he could always have been thoughtful like this, the three of them could have had such a happy life. Like her mam had always said, it was taking to drink and opium that had been his downfall, she thought sadly.

She was relieved that her dad made no reference again to the idea of her working for Betti Davies. She was convinced that it proved that they had both accepted that she had no intention of becoming involved with them, in any way. She was so confident about this that she even stopped barricading her bedroom door at nights.

When she told Aled, he looked dubious.

'Do you think it's safe to do that?' he asked worriedly.

Katie smiled happily. 'Yes, I'm quite sure. My dad's a changed man. I think he must have given up the drink and the opium.'

'He might have packed in drinking, but I doubt if he's given up smoking opium. Once you're hooked, that's it. You can't just stop because you decide you want to.'

'You can do anything if you're strong willed enough,' Katie boasted. 'Look how I've managed to stop my dad and Betti Davies pestering me to work for her.'

'I hope you're right, but don't build your hopes too high,' Aled cautioned. 'I still think you should move out and find somewhere else to live. Some place he doesn't know about.'

'I will. Give me time. I want to save up more money first so that I can afford a really nice room.'

Aled shook his head. 'Why do you have to be so independent, Katie? Why won't you marry me? We could afford a place in Cathays or even out Roath way, whichever one you think would be best.'

'I'm too young to marry and settle down,' she told him stubbornly.

'Well move out of Loudon Square then, or out of that house at least, before it's too late.'

A few nights later Katie had reason to wish she'd listened to Aled.

She'd been in bed for about ten minutes and was propped up against her pillows reading a magazine before settling to sleep, when the door opened.

As she looked up she saw a man coming into the room. For one brief moment, before a frisson of alarm went through her, she thought that it was her dad.

Then she realised it wasn't him at all, but a younger man of similar build, and right behind him was Betti Davies.

Startled, Katie pulled the covers up to her chin and glared at them balefully.

'Get out of here!' she gasped, her voice breaking as she realised the danger she was in.

Betti gave a low chuckle. 'You see! I told you she'd be shy,' she murmured to the man.

He laughed sardonically. 'That's exactly how I like them. Young and sweet and so innocent that they're frightened.'

Katie felt terrified as she looked from his angular leering face to Betti's self-satisfied smirk.

She took a deep breath, summoning up her natural resilience to try and boost what little courage she had left.

'Get out of my room, both of you, before I

start screaming,' she threatened. 'If my dad catches you in here ...'

'Your dad?' He looked at Betti in a puzzled manner.

'She means Lewis,' Betti explained. 'Take no notice of anything she says, he knows we've come up here and he won't interfere.'

'Well!' He came closer to the bed, leering down at Katie, his mouth twisted in an ugly grin as he studied her. 'This is going to be even more fun than I had expected,' he gloated.

'Do you want me to go?' Betti asked.

'Yes, yes. Leave this little beauty to me. I'll soon tame her.'

'Well, call out if you need me,' Betti told him, as she moved towards the door.

'Take no notice if you hear this one yelling out though,' he grinned. 'It might be pleasure or it might be pain, but you can simply ignore it.'

As the door closed behind Betti Davies a fresh wave of panic swept over Katie. She could feel her entire body trembling. She knew she had to get out of the room, out of the house even, and she had to do it fast.

Desperately, she tried to control the panic that was making her heart pound. She knew that it would do no good at all to scream. It was unlikely that anyone outside would hear her and if they did they would probably walk on, deciding it was wiser to mind their own business than investigate or interfere in any way.

She didn't know if her dad was in the house,

and even if he was she wasn't sure whether Betti was telling the truth or not when she claimed that he knew what was going on.

She refused to look at the intruder. The important thing was to concentrate on getting away, but she was so scared that she couldn't think how she was going to do that.

She sensed that the man was watching her closely and suspected he was waiting for her to say or do something. She tried to keep perfectly still, holding the bedcovers tightly underneath her chin, as she waited for his next move.

She'd thought he might make a grab at her, but to her surprise he moved over to stand by the window. As if he had all the time in the world, he drew out a packet of cigarettes and calmly proceeded to light one.

'I'm not in any hurry, we've got all night and since I've already paid Betti in advance she won't be coming back to check whether or not I'm still here,' he told her in a thick drawling voice.

As she watched the smoke rising languorously from his cigarette, Katie tried desperately to think how she could escape. He was too powerful to fight and probably too clever to trick. From behind the steady stream of cigarette smoke, she knew he was still watching her every movement.

What would he do when the cigarette was finished, she wondered? Would he stay by the window or would that be the time for action?

She scanned the room. Her coat was hanging on a peg behind the door; her shoes were at the side of the bed. If she could manage to grab both of those and make her escape down the iron staircase outside, she might possibly be able to get away.

She knew every twist and turn and every alleyway around Loudon Square, so she felt confident that if she could manage to get outside the house she could escape from him.

Before she could make a decision about her next move, he stubbed out the cigarette and moved towards the bed. As he grabbed at the bedcovers and yanked them off her, Katie grappled with him desperately. Then she threw herself at him, aiming her head towards his face.

He ducked slightly to avoid the impact, but her head caught him full on the nose. The blow was so great that it brought tears to Katie's eyes and she felt a throbbing pain inside her head.

The effect on her would-be assailant was even more devastating. He let out an agonised groan as blood gushed from his nose.

Katie took full advantage of the fact. She could see that he was stunned so, shoving him to one side, she scrambled out of bed, slipped her feet into her shoes, grabbed her coat and headed for the door.

Once she was outside and scrabbling down the iron staircase, she kept telling herself that she would soon be safe.

It was bitterly cold, pitch dark, and there was a fine rain falling, but none of that seemed to matter. The knowledge that she had managed to get away obliterated all other discomforts from Katie's mind.

Struggling to get her arms into her coat and run at the same time, she scurried away from Loudon Square as fast as she could. She had no idea where she was going, but instinct guided her towards The Hayes. From there, she headed blindly along St Mary Street towards Cathedral Road, and the next thing she knew she was outside Roderick Thomas's house in Cathedral Close.

Her head was aching and she had a stitch in her side, but that no longer seemed to matter. She'd reached a haven of safety.

Her feeling of relief as she hammered on the front door, saw lights go on inside the house and then heard Roderick padding across the hall, was overwhelming.

When Roderick Thomas opened the door and saw her standing there, soaking wet and wearing only a coat over her nightdress, her hair dangling around her face, he was completely taken aback.

'Katie? Whatever has happened to you?' he exclaimed. 'You're soaked to the skin!' He reached out and gently took her arm and pulled her inside. 'Duw anwyl! What's happened to you?' he repeated apprehensively. 'Look at the state you are in!' Concern made him brusque

but his touch was tender. 'You'd better come in
and tell me all about it.'

Chapter Thirty-Two

As they stood in the hallway, Roderick held her close in his arms, murmuring softly as he did his best to comfort her, and Katie wondered if she was dreaming.

As she felt the heat from his body warming her, and the gentleness of his hands as he tenderly stroked her streaming wet hair back from her face, she felt that the dreadful trauma had all been worthwhile simply to experience this wonderful intimate closeness between the two of them.

With his arm still supporting her, he guided her through to the kitchen where, because the fire had been banked up ready for morning, it was warm. Very gently, he helped her into one of the wooden armchairs.

'Rest there for a moment. I'm going upstairs to run you a hot bath, otherwise you'll end up with a chill,' he added firmly as she tried to protest.

When he returned a few minutes later, he was carrying a red and blue check dressing gown over one arm. 'I've put out some towels and you can put this on when you've had your bath,' he told her. 'Come on, I'll help you up the stairs.'

Katie was shaking so much, not only from cold but from delayed shock, that without his help she would never have managed to climb the stairs.

'Take as long as you like, have a good long soak,' he told her. 'Don't lock the door in case you feel faint. The children are both sound asleep so you won't be disturbed. By the time you come down I'll have a hot drink waiting for you.'

Shivering violently she struggled out of her soaking wet coat and pulled off her nightdress, and dropped them in a heap on the floor.

Her teeth were chattering as she stepped over the side of the bath and slid down into the steaming water. As the warmth of the water engulfed her she felt a wave of spasms running right through her entire body, every nerve-end seemed to be tingling and painful. Then her muscles relaxed and a delicious sense of comfort and well-being oozed over her.

She lay back, closed her eyes and let herself float in the fragrant water, moving fractionally every few seconds so that the warmth could lap over her body afresh.

She could have happily stayed there forever. When the water cooled she forced herself to get out and dry herself. As she did so, she caught sight of her reflection in the bathroom mirror and gasped in horror at the state her face was in.

There was a lump over her right eye the size of an egg as well as a gash where they had collided when she'd bashed her head against her assailant. A bruise was already beginning to appear underneath the eye. Within a few hours it would be quite black.

There were bruises on her upper arms as well where he had seized hold of her as they'd grappled before she'd butted him away, and these felt very tender.

She wrapped the check wool dressing gown around her, finding comfort in its fleecy softness. It was obviously one of Roderick's and it swamped her. She turned back the cuffs and tied the cord as tightly around her waist as possible. Then she bunched it up so as not to trip over it as she went downstairs.

Roderick regarded her anxiously. 'How are you feeling, now?'

'Much better!'

'Really?' He took her face gently between his two hands and examined her cut and swollen eye. 'That's going to be completely closed by the morning,' he said worriedly. I wish I had a piece of raw steak to go on it, but I'm afraid you are out of luck! I can put a plaster on the cut if you like?'

'No, leave it. It's quite clean now after my bath and it will soon heal.'

'Very well, if you're quite sure. I'll take another look at it in the morning and decide then if you should see a doctor, or go to the hospital so that they can put a stitch in it.'

'It's only a small cut,' she murmured.

'All right!' He smiled. 'Come and sit in the armchair by the fire. Your drink is ready and I've added a measure of whisky. That will help you sleep and ensure you don't catch a chill after being out in all that rain.'

'Are you having one as well?' she asked, looking up at him as he handed the drink to her.

'Of course! And I want you to tell me exactly what happened.'

Katie shook her head and looked away. 'I'd rather not talk about it,' she said reticently.

He frowned. 'Surely you can understand my concern when you turn up on my doorstep well after midnight, and get me out of bed at such an unearthly hour?'

She looked up quickly, her eyes wide with fear. 'I didn't know where else I could be safe.'

'It's all right,' he leaned forward and patted her knee. 'I'm pleased you came to me. I do think you ought to tell me what happened, though.'

Katie sipped at her drink and pulled a face as the flavour of the whisky hit her.

She took another sip. 'Yes,' she smiled tremulously, 'you're quite right. With this lump on my forehead it probably looks as if I've been fighting!' She smiled to herself. She supposed that in some ways that was exactly what she had been doing. She'd been fighting for her reputation, if not her life!

'Come on then, tell me what happened,' he persisted.

'I was attacked.'

'I suspected that! Who attacked you?'

She shook her head. 'I've no idea who he was, I'd never seen him before in my life. Betti brought him up to my room. I was alone. I was lying in bed reading a magazine when they burst in.'

'Betti?'

'Betti Davies, the woman who owns the house where we live in Loudon Square.'

She saw his face darken as the realisation of exactly where she lived penetrated his mind.

'You mean THE Betti Davies? You live in HER house?'

Katie nodded uncomfortably.

'She runs a brothel!'

Katie nodded miserably. 'We have three rooms right at the very top of the house,' she told him quickly. 'It's quite separate and I never use the main door. There's an iron staircase up the back and I always use that.'

'But you do have access to the rest of the house?'

'Yes, I suppose you could say we do. I never go down there – never! My dad works for her,' she added unhappily, looking down at her cup so as to avoid Roderick's eyes.

Roderick frowned. 'What is he, a handyman around the place or something?'

'No! He works for her as a pimp! He also acts as a bodyguard to the girls.'

'Duw anwyl! Do you know what you are saying, Katie?'

She lifted her head and stared at him defiantly. She'd never before admitted the truth to anyone outside her family by saying that dreadful word to describe what her father did, not even to Aled. When Aled had first told her what her dad did for a living she had strongly refuted it, she recalled.

She knew she was taking a great risk in telling Roderick Thomas so much about her background, but suddenly she was tired of all the deception and wanted him to know the truth.

If it affected the way he felt about her coming to his house and looking after his children, then it was better that he heard it from her rather than from someone else.

'And where was your father when Betti Davies brought a man up to your room? Was he out?'

She shrugged. 'I think so. My dad wants me to work for Betti, but I refuse to do so,' she said in a small unhappy voice. 'It was all right when my mam was alive because she refused to let them pester me about it.' Tears came to her eyes and her voice choked as she added, 'Now she's dead it's just me against them, but I won't give in. Never!'

'Oh my poor child!' He was on his knees beside her chair, his arm around her shoulders. 'This is terrible. Of course you mustn't give in to them. This is criminal! It has to be reported to the police.'

'No, no, you mustn't do that!' she implored, pulling away from him. 'My dad's not long been out of prison and if you say anything at all to the police they'll put him back inside.'

'By the sound of it, that's exactly where he should be!' Roderick declared indignantly.

'He is my dad,' Katie said wanly.

'I understand how you feel, but he's behaved in an outrageous way!'

Roderick's mouth tightened as he stood up and moved back to his own chair. 'His own daughter! The man is unnatural.'

'I wouldn't want to think that I had been responsible for sending him back to prison,' Katie repeated stubbornly.

'So what exactly happened when Betti brought this man to your room?' he asked in a flat voice.

Katie shivered. 'At first this chap simply stood by the window and smoked a cigarette. He wasn't all that old, probably about twenty-five, but he was quite well built. I was terrified. I pulled the bedcovers up to my chin and sat there all hunched up, praying that he'd go away.'

'Did you ask him to leave?'

She nodded. 'He only laughed at me, though.

All the time he was sneering and saying what he was going to do to me, I was trying to think of some way of escaping. I knew it was no good calling out because Betti wouldn't come up to help me and I didn't know where my dad was. Anyway, I didn't think he'd do anything,' she added bitterly.

Roderick was gripping the arms of his chair, his face grim. 'Go on!'

'Then ... then,' her voice shook and she covered her face. 'He tried to get into my bed.'

'So you fought him off! Is that how you got your face hurt?'

Katie nodded. 'I grappled with him and our heads met like two rocks cracking together. I think mine must have been harder than his because his nose was streaming with blood and he seemed to be stunned and was holding his head in his hands.' She grinned weakly. 'That's probably how I came to get the lump over my eye and the cut on my forehead.'

'And that was when you made your escape?'

Katie nodded. 'I grabbed at my coat, stuck my feet into my shoes and ran for the door. As I was clambering down the iron staircase I was afraid he might be coming after me. Once I was on the ground I knew I was safe and would be able to get away because I know every alleyway around Loudon Square. I didn't plan to come here, my feet just brought me.'

'Well, I'm glad they did!' Roderick smiled. 'It must have been a terrible ordeal for you, Katie. I still think you should go to the police,' he added grimly

'No!' She shook her head emphatically. 'It would be bound to land my dad in trouble. Promise me you won't tell them?'

'Not if you really don't want me to do so,' he agreed reluctantly.

He stood up and took her empty cup out of her hand and placed it on the table. 'I think you should get to bed now, Katie, before the effect of the whisky wears off. Your room is up there waiting for you and I'll see you in the morning.'

'Thank you! Thank you for helping me! I'm sorry to have caused so much trouble. I don't know what I would have done if you'd turned me away.'

Katie knew her words were inadequate, but she was at a loss about how to express her gratitude. She would have liked to kiss Roderick Thomas good night, but she was afraid he might interpret her action wrongly, even if it was merely a peck on his cheek.

'Goodnight, Katie. See you in the morning, then,' he murmured, as he turned away and started to bank down the fire again.

Chapter Thirty-Three

Roderick Thomas wakened Katie quite early the following morning with a cup of tea, and to enquire how she was feeling.

She looked at him in a rather dazed manner. 'I feel fine! It's almost as if everything that happened last night was all a bad dream,' she said awkwardly.

'It certainly seemed more like a nightmare when you turned up on the doorstep in such a terrible state,' he said gravely.

Katie shivered as she remembered her fears of the night before. It hadn't been a nightmare, it had been real enough and she'd been lucky to escape without getting hurt far more seriously than she had.

Katie managed a shaky smile as she took the cup of tea. 'I really do feel all right now,' she assured him. 'I think that whisky you put in my hot milk knocked me out.'

'That, and the fact you'd walked all the way here from Loudon Square and you were probably worn out!'

'Well, I'm feeling all right now,' she repeated, 'so I'd better get up or I will be late for work.'

'What about your clothes?'

Katie looked at him puzzled. 'I'll have to wear what I came here in. I don't suppose it will matter for just one day if I haven't a clean dress.'

'When you arrived here you were wearing your coat over your nightdress,' he reminded her. 'Also, I don't think Mario would be very pleased if you turned up for work dressed like that!'

'Oh!' She covered her mouth with her hand. 'I'd forgotten about that.' Her face clouded. 'That means I'll have to go back to Loudon Square to collect my clothes.'

'You shouldn't really go back there at all, Katie,' Roderick Thomas said worriedly. 'Look what's happened to your face! In fact, I'm not at all sure that Mario will want you at work looking the way you do. Anyway, you can't go there dressed in a nightgown and coat!'

'But I'll have to. My clothes and all my belongings are there.'

'I don't think it is safe for you to go anywhere near that place, either this morning or at any other time,' he persisted.

'So what am I going to do?'

Roderick looked thoughtful. 'I'll tell you what, you give Barri and Rhia their breakfast and get them ready for school while I go to Loudon Square and collect your belongings.'

'You can't do that!' Katie gasped.

'I can, and I certainly intend to do so. I don't want my neighbours seeing you leaving here

334

sporting a black eye and dressed in only your nightdress,' he scowled.

'It will make you late for work.'

'Only if I stay here talking to you instead of getting on with it. I'll take a taxi-cab. Is there very much to collect?'

'Not really. Only the clothes that are in my cupboard and the things on the shelf. Oh, and my handbag. Everything else in the room belongs to Betti Davies.'

'Right. Is there anything there for me to pack them in, or should I take something with me?'

Katie bit her lip. 'No, there's nothing there, I'm afraid.'

'Then I'll take a couple of suitcases with me.'

Katie still looked worried. 'I'm not sure you should be doing this,' she protested.

'It's the safest way to sort things out,' he said abruptly.

'How will you get in? I didn't pick up my door key when I came rushing out!'

'Even if you had I wouldn't be prepared to use it. I'll knock on the door, and . . .'

'I'm not sure if Betti Davies will let you in, especially when you tell her you've come to fetch my clothes. She's bound to object,' she warned him.

'Oh, she'll cooperate when she hears that I know exactly what happened last night and that I intend to inform the police.'

'The police?' Katie looked frightened. 'Oh, no,

335

please don't involve them. You promised me that you wouldn't go to the police. I'm not worried about Betti Davies, but it would get my dad into serious trouble again.'

He frowned. 'I know what I said last night, but you really should report what happened to you, Katie.'

She shook her head fiercely. 'No!' she repeated stubbornly. 'I really can't do that. He is my dad, after all, don't you see!'

'Well, think about it until I come back.'

The children were amazed to find Katie in the house when she went into their rooms to waken them, and curious about her cut forehead and black eye.

'Are you going to tell us all about it, Katie?' they chorused as she shepherded them into the bathroom to wash their hands and faces before they started to get dressed.

Katie smiled down at the two eager little faces. 'Only if you get dressed very, very quickly,' she promised, desperately trying to think of what to tell them. 'I'm going downstairs to get your breakfast ready and I'll tell you all about what happened while you are eating it.'

Barri and Rhia were all ready for school when Mrs Clarke arrived. She looked taken aback at seeing Katie in the kitchen wearing one of Roderick Thomas's dressing gowns and sporting a black eye.

'I didn't know Mr Thomas was going out last night. He never said a word to me. So where is he now? And what has happened to your face?'

'I'll explain everything to you later, Mrs Clarke,' Katie whispered, nodding her head in the direction of the two children.

Mrs Clarke's lips tightened disapprovingly. 'Yes, very well. I'd better take these two off to school, then.'

Katie cleared away the children's breakfast dishes and then went into the sitting room to watch out of the window for Roderick to return.

He was taking much longer than she had expected and she wondered if it was because Betti Davies or her dad were being awkward, and causing trouble because he wanted to collect her things.

She had hoped he would be back before Mrs Clarke arrived so that she didn't have to make an excuse about why her eye was swollen, and why she was there at that time of the morning, wearing his dressing gown. Now she wondered just how much she ought to tell her if she got back before Roderick did.

The moment the taxi-cab pulled up outside the house she had the door open, although she kept herself hidden behind it so that no one could see her.

She stayed concealed behind the door as he dumped two suitcases in the hall and then went to pay the driver.

When he came back in, he carried the suit-cases upstairs to her room and lifted them up onto the bed so that she could empty them.

She breathed a sigh of relief as she opened them. It looked as though everything she possessed was safely there. 'They let you have my things, then?'

'Yes, after a heated discussion. Your father was there and at first he was insistent that you should go back. When I told him that I knew everything about what had happened last night he denied being involved in any way. He claims he was out all evening.'

Katie shook her head. 'I really don't know. He may be telling the truth. He was there when I got home from work, but he went downstairs to Betti's place and I didn't see him again before I went to bed.'

'It must have been about eleven o'clock when the incident took place, would he still be out that late?'

'Possibly.' She flushed. 'He goes to an opium place down the other end of Tiger Bay, behind the pub called the Coalman's Arms.'

Roderick looked shocked. 'How long has that been going on?'

'I don't know. It was Aled who told me about it. He says he thinks my dad's an addict.'

'Well, he certainly didn't seem too happy when I told him the details about what had happened to you, and described the state you

338

were in when you arrived on my doorstep,' Roderick went on.

'Perhaps he didn't know,' Katie said thoughtfully. 'It was the sort of thing Betti would do,' she added bitterly.

'I hope you are right,' Roderick said grimly. 'I wouldn't like to think that any man would want his daughter to be involved in that sort of life.'

Katie opened her mouth to speak, to tell him that her dad was just as eager as Betti for her to work for them, but then thought better of it.

'Anyway, the point is you are not to go anywhere near there again,' he said firmly. 'Is that understood? From now on, you stay here. This room is yours for as long as you need it.'

'But . . .'

'No arguing, Katie! I want you to live with us from now on. It will help me,' he added by way of persuasion, 'because it means you will be here in the evenings if I ever have to go out.'

'Thank you!' Katie managed a weak smile as she accepted the arrangement. 'By the way,' she said awkwardly, 'Mrs Clarke seemed surprised to see me here.'

Roderick frowned. 'Why? You've often stayed the night before!'

'Yes, I know, but I think it was because I had a black eye and was wearing your dressing gown!'

'Oh, I see!' His frown deepened. 'I'll deal with it. She'll understand when I explain how you got drenched last night and that the reason I went out so early this morning was to collect some dry clothes for you.'

Surely, Katie told herself, as she dressed ready for work, this was what she had always dreamed about. To live here in this lovely house in Cathedral Close with Roderick Thomas and Barri and Rhia.

So if her dream was at last coming true, why did she feel so despondent and so reluctant to accept it, she asked herself.

She knew the answer, even though she didn't want to admit it to herself.

She wanted to live there, but not as a live-in baby-sitter! She didn't want to be there as someone Roderick Thomas was offering shelter to because he felt sorry for her. She wanted to be there because he wanted her to share his home, because he cared for her as much as she did for him.

She wasn't even sure if she could live under the same roof as him and not let him know how she felt about him. Even if she never put it into words then surely he would guess. How could she keep the love she felt for him out of her voice and her eyes when they were spending so much time together?

Every fibre of her being seemed to be alive and vibrant when he was close to her. She wanted to touch him, to run her fingers through his dark hair, to stroke his clean-shaven face, to feel his firm lips on hers.

When she'd arrived and he'd hugged her,

feeling the heat and strength of his body as he'd held her close had been both a comfort and a torment.

She never experienced any warm feelings when Aled took her in his arms. When he kissed her, his skinny body and thin wet lips repelled her rather than aroused her. That was the reason why she always preferred to arrive late when they went to the pictures, in the hope that the double seats at the back would all be taken.

Having to spend the evening sitting so close to him that she could feel his bony knees pressing into her leg, and have his scrawny arms resting across her shoulders, was tortuous, and always ruined the outing for her.

This would be a different kind of torment. Now she would be sitting at the opposite side of the table to Roderick at mealtimes, or in an armchair at the opposite side of the fireplace in the evenings, and all the time she wanted to be sharing the sofa with him.

It wouldn't be so difficult when the children were there because she could divert her attention to them, but when she and Roderick were in the room alone then it would be exquisite torture.

Yet the alternative was even worse! Roderick was right, she reminded herself. It wasn't safe for her to go back to Loudon Square. If she did, both Betti and her father would think she had capitulated and was ready to fall in with their demands.

The memory of the man who had invaded her room the previous night came vividly to her mind, and she knew she never wanted to face another ordeal like that.

As she slipped the door key Roderick had given her into her handbag and pulled the front door shut behind her, she squared her shoulders and made her decision. Cathedral Close was her home from now on, and if it had to be merely that she was living there to look after his children then she'd have to make the best of it.

At least she'd be living under the same roof as Roderick Thomas!

Chapter Thirty-Four

Barri and Rhia Thomas were ecstatic when they learned that from now on Katie would be living with them all the time.

'Does that mean you'll tell us a story every night before we go to sleep?' Rhia asked with a wide smile, her dark blue eyes shining with anticipation.

'Yes, if you want me to.'

Rhia clapped her hands in delight.

'And will you take us to Roath Park on Saturdays and Sundays?' Barri asked hopefully.

Before she could agree, Roderick intervened. 'Now you two, you can't monopolise all of Katie's time, you know. She probably has friends of her own and she will want to see them occasionally.'

'I'll take you to Roath Park whenever your dad is too busy to do so,' Katie told them quickly.

Katie found the routine at Cathedral Close soothing. She knew exactly where she stood, and what to expect, and the very orderliness helped to restore her confidence.

For the first few days she was on edge, half-expecting her dad to walk into the Bridge Street

Café at any moment and demand that she went back to Loudon Square. When nothing of the sort happened, she began to breathe easier.

Roderick had explained to Mario and Gina as much as he felt necessary about her 'accident' and why she had a black eye. They were both shocked and sympathetic and Gina insisted on applying some of her make-up to disguise Katie's bruised eye.

'We don't want customers thinking we've been ill-treating you,' she smiled.

Roderick also mentioned to them quite casually that Katie was staying at his place so that she was on hand to look after his children, because he was expecting to be away from home quite a bit in the near future.

He'd given the same explanation to Mrs Clarke.

At first Katie found that Mrs Clarke treated her in a slightly suspicious manner.

'If you're moving in here permanently then I don't suppose I shall be needed for much longer,' she said rather huffily, the first Sunday morning Katie was at Cathedral Close and she found her in the kitchen washing up the breakfast dishes when she arrived.

Katie looked at her in surprise. 'Would you rather I left this for you to do, then?' she asked apologetically. 'I was only trying to help since my being here must mean more work for you.'

'I thought that perhaps you were going to

344

take over the running of the house,' Mrs Clarke said, giving her a wary look.

'No, not at all,' Katie laughed. 'I've got enough on my plate working at the café all day.'

'So you're not thinking of giving up your job, then?' Mrs Clarke sniffed.

'Of course not! All I'm going to do is be here to keep an eye on Barri and Rhia when Mr Thomas has to go away on business. Nothing's changed! I couldn't run this place half as well as you do. Mr Thomas is always saying what a treasure you are and that he couldn't manage without you.'

Katie's fulsome flattery appeared to appease Mrs Clarke. From then on they became allies, and Mrs Clarke went out of her way to make sure that Katie was comfortable in every way she could.

The only person who wasn't happy with the new arrangement was Aled.

'I never see anything of you these days,' he grumbled.

'Of course you do! We still go to the pictures together.'

'Yes, once in a blue moon. The last couple of Saturday nights you've said you couldn't come because you had to look after those two kids.'

'So? I did.'

'Why can't I come around and stay with you when you can't come out? I like kids. I wouldn't mind playing games with them until it was time

345

for them to go to bed, and then we would have the rest of the evening to ourselves.'

'I've told you before,' Katie said impatiently, 'I can't ask you to come around there because it's not my house.'

'Well, surely Mr Thomas knows you have friends of your own, and wouldn't mind if you invited me in for an evening?'

'He mightn't mind, but I would,' Katie told him defensively. 'I'm only a lodger there and I wouldn't dream of asking him.'

'Then you can't think very much of me,' Aled said angrily.

Katie looked at him bewildered. 'What is that supposed to mean?'

'If you told him that we were engaged and that we will be getting married very soon, he'd understand that we wanted to be together.'

'But you know quite well that we are not engaged, and I've told you before, I'm not going to marry you,' Katie told him heatedly.

'We could be engaged, though!' Aled scrabbled in his pocket and brought out a small box. 'I bought this for you and I've been carrying it around for weeks and weeks, waiting for the right time to give it to you,' he said rather bashfully.

Katie stiffened. 'What is it?' she asked hesitantly, secretly praying it wasn't what she feared, but knowing from the size and shape of the box that it must be.

He handed her the box. 'Open it! See for yourself what it is.'

Reluctantly, she lifted the lid of the small black box that had a jeweller's name engraved on it and then stared in dismay at the thin gold ring with a small diamond set in it that was inside.

'Aled, I can't take this,' she told him, shaking her head firmly.

The look of eager anticipation on his face faded, and was replaced by a scowl. 'Why not? What's wrong with it? Isn't the diamond quite big enough for you now that you've gone all posh because you're living in Cathedral Close?'

'Aled, please. You know I'm not like that,' Katie said angrily. 'The reason I can't accept it is because, as I keep telling you, I don't want to marry you.'

His face was beetroot red as he snatched the little black box from her hand and thrust it back into his pocket.

'I've told you this time and time again,' she reminded him.

'No, you'd sooner live in sin with an old man like Roderick Thomas who's already got a ready-made family, wouldn't you,' he said bitterly.

'I'm living there to help look after Barri and Rhia, nothing else,' Katie retorted primly.

Aled completely ignored her explanation. 'You might just as well have stayed in Loudon Square and worked for Betti Davies. At least you'd have been an honest whore instead of some old man's mistress!' he muttered.

Tears filled Katie's eyes. She didn't want to quarrel with Aled. He was her oldest friend, her truest friend, and she thought the world of him, but as she had tried so often to explain to him she wasn't in love with him. She didn't want to marry him under any circumstances and she had no intention of being forced or bullied into doing so.

Her decision to accept Roderick Thomas's offer that she should move into Cathedral Close had been the right one for her, and she was perfectly content with things as they stood.

There was only one problem which she still had to overcome and that was her recurrent nightmares, when she relived over and over the last night she had spent at Loudon Square.

She couldn't bring herself to tell anyone about her nightmares, but they haunted her. Even when she was awake, the frightening details kept coming back into her mind.

Apart from that, she had never felt more settled or content. She had her own room, she enjoyed the company of the children and the easy friendship between herself and Roderick Thomas. Whatever anyone else might think or say, she was happy, and she knew she had made the right decision.

Katie went on thinking that right up until the night that Rhia was taken ill.

She had no idea how long she had been in

bed and asleep, but she was in the deepest throes of her recurring nightmare when she sensed someone was in the room and woke with a start.

Vaguely, she could make out the shape of a man standing in the doorway of her bedroom and heard him call her name.

Immediately she sat bolt upright in bed, clutching the bedcovers up tight to her chin, and gave a wild scream.

'Katie! There's no need to be alarmed, I just wanted your help with Rhia.'

Dimly, she realised that it was Roderick Thomas standing in the doorway.

'Sorry!' She swallowed hard and tried to control her trembling and the terror that was raging inside her. 'You startled me.'

'Well, I didn't mean to do so. I wondered if you'd come and take a look at Rhia. She's in terrible pain and she seems to be burning up with a fever of some sort. I think I had better fetch the doctor.'

Without waiting for her to answer he turned and walked away. Katie scrambled out of bed, put on a dressing gown and followed him along the passage to Rhia's room.

As soon as she entered Rhia's bedroom and saw the state the little girl was in, all her own worries and concerns faded into obscurity. She felt as anxious as Roderick as she heard Rhia's pitiful whimpering and watched her writhing in

349

pain. She placed her hand on the child's brow and realised that she had a raging temperature.

'I don't think a doctor can do very much to help her,' Katie told him worriedly. 'I think Rhia needs to be in hospital.'

'Will you stay with her while I call an ambulance, then?'

It seemed an eternity before an ambulance arrived and Rhia was gently moved onto a stretcher and carried downstairs.

'Will you stay here with Barri and explain everything to him when he wakes up?' Roderick Thomas asked, as he pulled on his coat. 'I'll be back as soon as I can to let you know what's happening.'

'Of course I will. You must go with Rhia. Don't worry about us, everything here will be fine.'

'Will you let Mrs Clarke know what's happened when she arrives in the morning?' he asked anxiously, as he followed the two men carrying the stretcher.

'Yes, of course! Make sure Rhia gets the best attention possible and stay at the hospital with her for as long as you are needed.'

Chapter Thirty-Five

Katie went back to bed after Roderick left, but she was unable to sleep. The sound of Rhia's pain-wracked little cries kept echoing in her head.

Finally, around six o'clock when she heard the paperboy and other delivery men in the street outside, she got up and dressed. She went downstairs determined to find something to do that would take her mind off what might be happening at the hospital.

She made herself a cup of tea and sat down to read the paper, but found she was unable to concentrate on what was happening in the rest of the world when her own immediate world was in such turmoil.

'Where's Rhia?' Barri asked, when he came downstairs for his breakfast.

He looked very upset when Katie explained that Rhia had been taken ill in the night and that she had been taken to hospital.

'Is she going to be all right? She isn't going to die like Mummy did when she went into hospital, is she?' he asked worriedly.

'Of course not! Rhia's going to get better and

she'll be back home again in next to no time,' Katie assured him.

Barri looked perplexed. 'She's not having a baby, is she?'

'No, cariad, of course she's not,' Katie told him gently. 'Little girls don't have babies.'

'What's the matter with her then?' he asked suspiciously.

'Well, I'm not too sure, but we'll know as soon as your dad comes home.'

'Has she broken her leg, or has she got a pain somewhere?' Barri persisted.

'She's got a pain. It's a very bad pain in her tummy.'

'That's what my mummy had. They said it was a baby. They took her into hospital and she died,' Barri said morosely.

Katie shook her head. 'It's a very different sort of pain to the one your mum had, Barri. I think it may be appendicitis,' she explained.

'And is that very bad?' he asked seriously, his dark blue eyes still anxious.

'You have to go into hospital and have an operation, but she'll be all right, I promise you.'

'So can I go to the hospital and see Rhia?'

'Yes, you'll be able to do that after she's had the operation and a little rest.'

'So when will she be coming home again?'

'I'm not sure. She will probably have to stay in hospital for a while.'

'For how long,' he persisted.

'Well, a week at least. Maybe a little longer.

And when she does come home we will have to take great care of her. She won't be able to play any rough and tumble games for a while.'

Barri didn't seem to be very reassured by her answers and it took a lot of persuasion from Katie to get him to eat any breakfast.

'Can't I stay here until Daddy comes home from the hospital,' he begged when Katie told him to get his coat on, so that he was ready when Mrs Clarke came to take him to school.

'No, I think it would be better if you went to school,' Katie told him. 'That was what your dad said he wanted you to do.'

'I want to stay here until I know that Rhia is going to get better,' he argued.

Katie shook her head. 'Your dad wants you to take a note and give it to Rhia's teacher so that she knows why Rhia is away from school. You can do that, can't you?'

'Yes, I suppose so,' Barri said dubiously. 'Where is the note, then?'

'I'll write it now,' Katie told him.

When Mrs Clarke arrived, Barri became increasingly upset as he listened to Katie telling her about what had happened.

'Taken ill in the middle of the night, was she, poor little mite,' Mrs Clarke said ruefully. 'I thought she hadn't been looking too bright for the last couple of days. She's been a bit picky with her food lately, hasn't she, and that's not a bit like young Rhia. Both of them have such good appetites, haven't you, Barri?' she added garrulously.

Barri scowled, but made no reply.

'So do you know what's wrong with her, then?' Mrs Clarke asked.

'Well, I think it might be appendicitis,' Katie told her.

'Oh, do you?' Mrs Clarke nodded. 'Well, we'll know for certain when Mr Thomas comes back from the hospital, I suppose.'

'Katie says she won't die like Mummy did,' said Barri.

'No, of course she won't, cariad,' Mrs Clarke said quickly. 'No fear of that! She'll be back home again in a few days and running around as though nothing has happened.'

Barri was still reluctant to go to school, but Katie reminded him again that it was very important that he went, because she was relying on him to deliver the note she'd written to Rhia's teacher.

'Couldn't you take it and then I could stay home and wait for Daddy?' he suggested.

Katie's heart ached for the little boy as she saw the concern in his deep blue eyes that were fixed on her face so trustingly. 'I've got to go to work now, Barri,' she told him gently. 'Perhaps we can both go and see Rhia tonight.'

His distress haunted her as she made her way to the Bridge Street Café. They were such sweet children and she was so fond of them that she hated the idea of Rhia being ill and Barri so upset.

'You look as though you have been up all night,' Mario joked, when halfway through the morning she started yawning.

'I was!'

When she told him and Gina about what had happened, Mario was insistent that she went to the hospital right away to find out what was happening.

'I can't do that!' she protested. 'It's almost midday and we'll be rushed off our feet in about half an hour.'

Mario gave one of his big shrugs. 'Gina, she will cope for one day. Anyway,' he gave one of his jovial belly laughs, 'your most important customer will not be here at his special table, so why all the worry. The rest,' he waved his hands wide, 'the rest, they will have to wait, no?'

'Well, if you are quite sure,' she beamed. 'I'm probably not much good here today with my mind somewhere else.'

'Off to the hospital with you, then,' he ordered. 'Tell Mr Thomas I send my best wishes for the little one, and so too does Gina.'

Katie's heart was in her mouth when she arrived at the hospital and was directed to the small side ward where Rhia was.

'It was appendicitis and they've operated,' Roderick told her quietly as he stood alongside her by the bed, looking down at Rhia. She was still under sedation and lay there with her eyes closed looking like a wax doll. She seemed so tiny and frail that Katie's heart ached. She wanted to find words to comfort Roderick Thomas but she felt tongue-tied as she saw the strain on his face and the dark shadows under his eyes.

'Do you want to go home and have something to eat, and a wash to freshen yourself up?' she asked.

Roderick ran a hand over the dark stubble on his face and chin. 'I suppose I should,' he agreed.

'Go on then. I'll stay here until you get back, in case Rhia wakes up. Why don't you have a couple of hours' sleep as well while you are at home,' she suggested.

'Well . . .' he paused doubtfully.

'By that time Barri will be home from school and you could bring him back here with you,' Katie told him. 'He was very upset when I told him about Rhia so I think it might help to put his mind at rest if he could come and see her.'

'While she is looking like this!'

'Yes, even looking like this,' Katie said firmly. 'At the moment he is worried out of his mind that she is going to die.'

Roderick ran his fingers through his hair. 'That's what is worrying me, too. She's so tiny to have undergone an operation. If I should lose her, I don't think I could bear it.'

'Nothing like that is going to happen to her,

so stop worrying,' Katie told him confidently. 'She's had the operation, and once she's spent a few days here in hospital she will be fine again. In a week or ten days' time she will be back at home and running around and playing with Barri as right as rain.'

He turned away. 'I'll go and freshen up and I'll bring Barri back with me later on.'

Katie sat by the bedside after he had gone, holding Rhia's hand and willing the little girl to get better. She looked so fragile. Her eyes were closed, her breathing shallow, and every vestige of colour was drained from her little cheeks. Katie could understand why Roderick had such qualms about her and she shared his concern.

It seemed to be one of the longest afternoons Katie had ever known. Several times she thought Rhia had stopped breathing, then the child would give a deep sigh and her breathing pattern would return to normal.

When Roderick returned with Barri he had not only shaved and changed his shirt, but he'd even put on a different suit.

Barri stood by the side of Rhia's bed, staring fixedly at her and nervously chewing his lip. He looked as if he was about to burst into tears at any moment.

Katie was so relieved when Rhia opened her eyes and smiled weakly up at them that she couldn't speak, only reach out and squeeze Barri's hand.

'May we wait here until she's fully out of the anaesthetic?' Roderick Thomas asked.

'You can, but I don't advise it,' the Sister said briskly. 'Why not go for a walk, or go and get something to eat and come back in a couple of hours.'

'As long as that?'

'By then she will probably be sitting up,' she smiled.

They didn't feel like eating and it was too late to go to the Museum, so Katie suggested they should visit Roath Park.

'You like it there, Barri, and there will probably be some ducks you can feed.'

'We haven't got any bread for them,' Barri pointed out despondently.

'Then why don't we buy a bag of buns or some cake and when we get to the park we can have a picnic,' Katie suggested brightly.

'Good idea,' Roderick agreed. 'We can eat what we want first and then feed the rest to the ducks.'

Barri looked doubtful. 'Perhaps we should wait until we can take Rhia. She loves going to the park to feed the ducks.'

'We'll go again as soon as she is feeling better,' Katie promised. 'If we go today then you'll have something interesting to tell her when we go back to see her in hospital.'

Feeding the ducks helped to make the time pass, but all three of them were on edge and desperate to get back to the hospital.

When they returned they were allowed to see Rhia, but were told that she still needed rest. She had come through the operation successfully. There were no complications and she was doing well, but it was really too soon for her to have any visitors.

'When you come back tomorrow you'll probably find she is sitting up in bed,' the Sister told Barri. 'Children of that age recover from surgery remarkably quickly,' she added, looking at Katie.

Barri was very quiet when they reached home and refused to have any supper.

After he was in bed Katie sat with him, talking to him and trying to help him overcome his fears about Rhia. He finally fell asleep, while she was still reassuring him that his sister would be so much better the next day that he'd wonder why he had ever been so worried about her.

As she tiptoed out of Barri's bedroom, Katie found Roderick was sitting on the stairs, his dark head resting against the newel post.

'Have you been sitting there all the time I've been talking to Barri?' she said in surprise.

He nodded and smiled gratefully at her. 'I was listening to what you were telling him.' Taking her hand, he squeezed it gently as he whispered, 'you were wonderful with him. I could never have consoled him like that. Come on downstairs and we'll have a drink. I think we've both earned one.'

'It has certainly been a long day,' she agreed, trying to smother a yawn.

'You had hardly any sleep last night so you must be completely tired out. Would you sooner go straight to your room and get some sleep?'

Katie shook her head. 'Not until I've had that drink,' she grinned.

For all her tiredness she felt happy. There was a different atmosphere between them, as if Rhia's illness had brought them closer, and she wanted to hold on to that feeling for as long as she could. They were both so much more relaxed with each other that she felt they could talk about anything, and she sensed he was feeling the same way.

As soon as they were settled in comfortable chairs in the sitting room, Roderick told her how indebted he was for all her help with Barri and Rhia.

'They both love you a great deal, you've become very much part of their lives and I am so grateful to you for all that you have done for them.'

She shook her head smiling. 'I'm the one who should be grateful. You've done far more for me than I could ever do for you. As for the children, well, anything I do for them is because I want to do it, because I care about them, so much. They feel like family to me. I only wish it could stay this way forever.'

He sat up straighter in his chair, a worried

look on his intelligent face. 'You've no other plan in mind at the moment, though?' he asked anxiously.

Katie shook her head. 'No, of course not. I'm very happy, but I can't expect you to let me stay here forever, now, can I?'

Roderick picked up his glass and drained it in one gulp. 'I wish you would,' he muttered.

'Stay here forever?' She was about to laugh, but stopped herself from doing so when she saw the look in his dark blue eyes. As she realised how serious he was, her heart beat faster.

'Katie,' he hesitated, then went on in a rush, 'I don't know how to put this, and perhaps this isn't even the best moment to be doing so, but it has been on my mind for quite some time. After the trauma of today and last night, and what with everything that has happened recently, I feel I have to say it.'

Katie stared at him wide-eyed. 'Say what?' she asked anxiously. Her feeling of hope was replaced by dread, in case he said he no longer wanted her to look after Barri and Rhia.

He shook his head, as if unable to go on. Then he leaned forward, taking both her hands and holding them between his own. His dark blue eyes studied her face intently. She felt hypnotised. It was as if he was trying to read her innermost thoughts.

'Katie, I know I am probably twice your age, but I care about you a great deal.' His voice

became husky with emotion as he added softly,
'not only as a friend, but because I'm very much
in love with you.'

Chapter Thirty-Six

Although she was tired to the point of exhaustion, it took Katie a long time to get to sleep. She tossed and turned, her brain whirling with the last words Roderick had said to her before she had shot upstairs as though the devil himself was after her.

Several times during the night she was on the point of going along to his room and telling him she hadn't meant to behave like that. Each time she felt so overcome by embarrassment, so disconcerted by her childish reaction that she pulled the bed clothes even higher around her ears, as if to shut out his words.

What must he think of her! She wondered if he would ever speak to her again. She'd have to leave Cathedral Close, there was no doubt about that. She wouldn't be able to face him after last night.

How could she have run out of the room like that the minute he had told her he loved her, she asked herself over and over again. They were the very words she had always longed to hear him say. Words she had never expected to ever pass his lips.

What must he be feeling? Mortified probably,

she told herself. Hating her for embarrassing him in such a manner.

Tears rolled down her cheeks as she remembered the expression on his face and the tenderness in his voice as he'd said those precious words; 'I am very much in love with you'.

She'd felt mesmerised. She was sure she must be imagining he was telling her he loved her. This was what she had hoped for, what she had dreamed might one day happen.

She'd wanted to rush into his arms and smother his handsome face with kisses. She yearned to run her fingers through his thick dark hair and tell him over and over again how much she loved him.

Instead she had run out of the room without a single word! She had bolted up to her bedroom and slammed the door. That in itself was tantamount to saying she didn't love him, so how was she ever going to convince him that she did?

Her heart pounded against her ribs so hard that she could hardly breathe. She could hear it drumming in her ears. She began to count in time to its beat to try and block out all other thoughts from her mind, hoping that drowsiness would then claim her.

How long she had been asleep she had no idea, but she found herself back in the throes of the monstrous nightmare that had been haunting her sleep for the past weeks.

This time it wasn't a single stranger that Betti

Davies brought into her room, but two men. One was tall and gangly with lank brown hair. The other man was older, broader with a strong handsome face, thick dark hair and penetrating dark blue eyes.

The younger of the two rushed towards the bed. His wide loose lips were wet and shiny as he leaned over her and drooled her name.

She could hear herself screaming as she struggled to avoid him. As she shrieked again and again, the older man stepped forward and grabbed him by the shoulders and pulled him away from her.

She woke sobbing and drenched with sweat to find Roderick Thomas sitting on the side of her bed, his arm around her in an attempt to stop her shaking.

'That old nightmare back haunting you again, is it,' he murmured, stroking the damp tendrils of hair back from her face as he tried to console her. 'You're safe now, cariad. Try and go back to sleep.'

As he gently released her she clung onto him. 'Please don't leave me,' she begged, her grey eyes pleading. 'I want to try and explain about last night.'

He stiffened and averted his eyes.

'I'm sorry for what happened, Katie . . .'

'No, you mustn't be!' she exclaimed, and this time it was her voice which was husky with emotion.

'Let me finish,' he said grimly, 'then you can

365

laugh, feel insulted, or walk out of my life forever, but at least you will know the way I feel about you. I'm not sure if you have any feelings at all for me, but I did mean every word I said last night, Katie. I do love you deeply, so much so that I am ready to accede to anything you might suggest, as long as we can be together.'

Katie stared at him wide-eyed as she struggled for words.

'I'm not going to pressurise you into anything,' he hastened to assure her before she could speak. 'I will respect your wishes, and you are welcome to go on living here for as long as you want to, no matter what your answer is.'

'Please. Let me say something . . .'

'Katie, I know about Aled, of course, but I am not sure how deep your feelings are for him. He is your own age and it was his name you called out in your nightmare tonight . . .'

'Aled is a friend,' Katie interrupted quickly. 'A very dear and loyal friend . . . but nothing more.'

'Are you sure about that, Katie? I don't want you saying it to save hurting my feelings.'

Katie shook her head. 'That's the truth. He's been my friend since I first started school and he's always looked out for me, but there is nothing serious between us. At least not on my part,' she added, her colour rising.

Roderick nodded diffidently. 'Even so, Katie, if you want things to stay exactly as they are between us for the present, until you are quite sure that you know your own mind, I quite understand,' he told her tentatively.

Katie shook her head. 'There is no need,' she told him shyly, her eyes shining with love as they locked with his.

'You are very young, Katie, so if you do say you will marry me, but feel you want to be my wife in name only,' Roderick rushed on, 'I will respect your wishes.'

He saw her chin go up and her mouth tighten.

'In time, when you are ready, we can put things on a proper footing.' He stopped and looked at her exasperatedly. 'Katie, please tell me you understand what I am trying to say.'

Katie gulped, still struggling for words. Her head was spinning. It wasn't an illusion, he was saying all the wonderful things she'd dreamed of hearing from his lips. She tried again to speak, but the words wouldn't come.

He drew back, alarm etched on his face. 'I've upset you, frightened you! I didn't mean to rush things.'

Leaning forward she grasped his hands, pulling him towards her. 'I do love you, Roderick, truly I do,' she told him earnestly.

'You mean you are willing to marry me?'

She nodded, still too choked with emotion to speak, tears of happiness filling her eyes.

He stared at her in amazement. 'Do you really mean that?'

She nodded. 'I have been in love with you

ever since we first talked to each other in the café,' she said softly.

'And you'll marry me?'

'Of course I will marry you! I simply can't believe you've asked me.' She gave him a radiant smile. 'I've dreamed about this happening for so long. There's nothing I want more in the world than to be part of your life. And a part of Barri's and Rhia's,' she added softly.

'Oh, Katie!' He pulled her into his arms, holding her so close that she felt as if her very bones were melting into his. His touch sent ripples down her spine.

She wanted to stay in Roderick's arms forever. Her dreams had been only shadowy figments of imagination compared with the overpowering emotions which now surged through her.

She caressed his face, first with the tips of her fingers and then with her lips, burning with innocent desire as they clung to each other.

As his lips found hers and took possession of her mouth she closed her eyes, and gave herself up to the ecstasy of the moment.

Her warm, sweet breath mingled with his and her excitement mounted as he crushed her willing, pliant body against his own.

He returned her kisses eagerly, hungrily but with gentle passion. His need for her was so great that the constraints of the past weeks were put aside and forgotten by both of them.

Her heart beat faster as desire took hold of

her. He would be her first lover, but lost in the magic of the moment she had no fears, only implicit trust and a feeling of tremendous happiness.